Splendor Bay

LB COBB

To Linda

Enjoy

Lawrence
aka LB Cobb
August 2002
40th year Class 1962

ADVANCEBOOKS
HOUSTON, TX, USA

The people, places, and incidents portrayed in *Splendor Bay* are fictitious. Any resemblance to actual events, locales, or persons, living or dead, is purely coincidental.

ADVANCEBOOKS

AN IMPRINT OF THE

ADVANCE BOOKS COMPANY

HOUSTON, TEXAS, USA

Website: www.advancebooks.com

Email: staff@advancebooks.com

Library of Congress
Control Number 2001118509

ISBN 0-9706224-1-4

Trade Paperback
First Printing December 2001
10 9 8 7 6 5 4 3 2 1

Printed on acid-free paper
Manufactured in the United States of America

To Quincy, for making my life
a happy-ever-after adventure.

No writer is an island, especially this one. The list of accomplices who aided and abetted the publication of *Splendor Bay* is long, and I am thankful for each of them. My husband, Quincy Cobb, who has encouraged my other absurd obsessions over the years, cheered me on in this one as well. My sisters, Janet Biery and Geneva White, and my mystery-reading friends—Becky Williams, Hannah Powell, Andrea Perkins, Liz Etnier, Cathy Howard, Cindi Miller, Martha Wilson, Irene Herd, Ann Knapp, Kathy Carroll, and Elizabeth Pitillo—read early drafts of *Splendor Bay* and ferreted out defects. Dorrie O'Brien edited the "almost final" manuscript. Talented writers Roger Paulding, Mary-Rose Conti, Linda Posey, and Thelma Zirkelbach vetted the final manuscript. And Kimberly Cameron, my literary agent, always provided the encouraging word.

Splendor Bay

ONE

Saturday, May 26, 8:00 AM

There's not much to see around here if you don't count the view of sparkling turquoise water and ivory sand below buff-colored cliffs where mint-candy-colored houses dangle precariously. Some folks say the spectacular bay view is the reason God gave people eyes. Other folks don't say much. So unless you're into tight-lipped people, glorious scenery, candy-colored houses, or our main drawing card, cutesy-touristy restaurants enhanced architecturally by the hulls of old boats attached to their roofs, there's no reason to be here.

The view is what does it for me. On a clear day, and with a clear head, a jog along Splendor Bay beach is reason enough to be living. It's my coming-of-age panorama, the place where my teenage ghost plays the male lead in the *Beach Blanket Bingo* adaptation of *Splendor in the Grass* always running on the drive-in movie screen in my mind's eye. The view and my ghost are the reasons I've never been able to grow up and leave home. Correction. I did leave once, for too many years, but I don't plan on ever doing that again.

Anyway, the day was one of those crisp, crystalline May days that come just before summer's heat, a day with a shimmering cornflower-blue sky and not a whiff of the refineries down the coast, a day for feeling young in my little spot of heaven on planet earth. Even the booze ache behind my eyes had eased up enough for me to contemplate a jog on the beach as my workup to a day of pretending I still had my life ahead of me, still had time to get it right if only I'd give it one more try.

There I was, contemplating my woebegone past and my uncertain future, thinking maybe this would be the day I really would give it one more try, when I glanced down from my perch on the deck of Sally Solana's bayview manor and had an entirely different thought: why the heck is that John Doe near the water's edge choosing to be dead on such a day?

There he was, in a black tuxedo with the diamond-studs in his shirt glistening brighter than the mica in the quartz sand, washed up with the seaweed, spoiling my view, interfering with my contemplation of activities physical, right out there on the good stretch of beach where I should have been running. Looking back, I guess it wasn't a matter of choice, for the stiff or for me. Things happen. Sometimes you have to ride the wave.

I had strolled out to the deck with my first cup of coffee just as the beach patrol discovered the body. That caught my eye. After shrugging their shoulders at each other, they called out Splendor Bay's finest. The men in tan arrived quickly with the siren blaring. That got my full attention. I finished my second fix of caffeine while watching the activities below through Sally's opera binoculars.

Tiny Sanders, the biggest of our local cops, was stomping around, doing just about every dumb thing imaginable to destroy the integrity of the crime scene, everything but kick the body to see if the stiff really was dead. His partner, the newest and youngest member of the three-man Splendor Bay PD, a twenty-one-year-old black kid with the Hispanic name, Gomez, was puking his guts out behind the dune in front of the department's one and only squad car, a vehicle that I now respected. The Police Caprice, with a 5.7 liter V-8, could outrun Baby, my sleek '57 Corvette rag-top with her original 283-cubic-inch, gas-guzzling, many-times-lovingly-rebuilt engine. I had discovered that sobering fact when Gomez gave me a run for my money, just before I failed his breath-analyzer test, just after I burned up what remained of Baby's brake shoes trying to stop before I landed in the middle of the bay.

When the rescue squad's elderly Bronco ambulance/coroner's meat wagon pulled in behind the Caprice, I bet myself that Splendor Bay's premier crime fighters would get one of the vehicles stuck in the sand before they finished the paperwork on the dead dude. And when they pulled out the zip-lock stiff bag, curiosity got the best of me. I doubled my bet with myself and made the fateful decision to leave the safety of my girlfriend's cliff-hugging house for a closer look-see. Actually, "girl" is a mild stretch of the facts in Sally Solana's case. And, I don't suppose you could call her my friend anymore, either.

Just so you know, I don't normally go poking my nose into crime scenes I'm not paid to poke my nose into. But this one was different. I don't normally find death on my doorstep. And, with Sally's opera glasses, I had counted a dozen glittering diamond studs in the John Doe's pleated shirt. Since we don't get many stiffs on this section of beach and the ones we do get don't usually turn up wearing a tux, that had me extra curious.

I wanted to see who he was, something I couldn't do from Sally's deck because his face tilted away from me in his final view of the bay. I was figuring someone might be willing to pay for a photo or two, or a few unofficial facts on a stiff who could afford to die in diamonds. I could definitely use the cash since this month's Scotch trust-fund allowance had already been spent at Fred's Fine Liquors, down the boardwalk from Fred's Fine Seafood Bar and Grill, up the beach from my own humble shack.

You never know, I told myself, John Doe might be somebody interesting enough for a grocery store tabloid. Or some rich relative might want to know where he was and/or who or what had done him in, which was part and parcel of my current line of work—private eyeing—when the weather wasn't suitable for surfing. Besides, I reasoned, if someone who knew something about protecting the evidentiary value of crime scenes, such as me, didn't get down there soon, what few clues there were would be washed away in the next tide.

Having concluded the cops could use my help, I pulled a pair of shorts on over my briefs, slipped on a T-shirt and flip-flops, picked up my camera, and casually descended the steep wooden stairs to the beach. Gomez was through puking when I got close enough for it to matter. He had started back around the vehicles toward the dead dude, ready to be a man about it, when I caught up with him.

"Who is it, Gomez? Anybody who anybody would care is dead?" I asked politely. I believe in being polite, and direct. You never know, sometimes the truth pops out when you confuse people like that. If that doesn't work, you can always go to phase two—intimidation, or bribery.

"What're you doing here, Fragile Dick?" Gomez asked, being impolite as heck as he hitched up his pants just like Barney Fife on the old *Andy Griffith Show.*

Fragile Dick had been my handle since third grade. It was the worst thing any of the little guys could think of to do with a last name like Glasscock; there wasn't much you could do with a first name like Bill. Fortunately, for my self-respect, and for the women in my life, Fragile Dick was a misnomer.

"Just happened to be in the neighborhood, visiting a friend. Guess you could say ex-friend if you want to be meticulous in your terminology. Up there," I said, pointing to the enormous house where Sally-with-the-gorgeous-body-and-exceptional-brain graciously allowed me to spend the night. Not that I was in any condition to leave when our friendship ended, mind you. Sally must have been. Able to leave, that is. Because she wasn't there when I woke up with the strong belief that a little sun on my face would take away the too-much-whiskey pain behind my eyeballs. So far, I had been half-right. If I squinted with the left eye closed, I didn't hurt as much.

I squinted at the kid. "Come, on, Gomez. Who's the stiff? Anybody important?"

"Maybe," Gomez allowed. "Tiny just told the Chief he ought to get his white honky ass out here, real quick. I was heading back over there when you so rudely interrupted me from my duties to the citizens of our fair town."

"Fair is right, Gomez. Do your superiors know you're a bigot? I bet Tiny never said the Chief had a white honky ass. It's probably a red, pimply ass, anyway. You're the only guy in town who doesn't have sun-bleached hair and all you do is lord it over us white guys. Just because you have a tan to die for. What do you use anyway? A minus SPF 45 sunscreen?"

"Why? You want to be beautiful like me, Fragile Dick?"

"Definitely. Why do you think I spend so much time in the sun? I've seen the way girls turn their head when you drive around in the cruiser."

"I'll need some official identification before I let you near my crime scene," Gomez said, a bit chattier now that I had acknowledge his superior swordsmanship. "How do I know they didn't pull your license for good cause since the last time I saw you? And I'd like to inventory the guy's pockets before you get within ten feet of him. Routine procedure. Remember?"

"Come on, Gomez, just one teeny, tiny favor," I whined, "and I'll let you keep the diamond studs."

Gomez didn't answer. At that moment, we heard the squawk of the Police Caprice radio. Tiny Sanders, the other cop, was communicating with the world at large, the Chief in particular.

"Yeah, done that," Tiny shouted over the surf's roar. "Have a tentative ID on the floater. Driver's license says he's Wallace Moreno. Had five hundred in cash in a money clip, so he wasn't robbed. I'd say you'd better get ready to vote for a new governor, Chief. The current one is a little under the weather."

I have to admit, when I heard that my first thought was—There is a God!

My second thought was—Oh, what a beautiful morning! In my mind's eye my teenage ghost did a quick *Swan Lake* up and down the beach.

The slimy bastard was dead. Joy! Joy!

In addition to being the late Governor Moreno of our great state, he was the same self-serving cur who had aided and abetted my beautiful and soon-to-be-ex-wife in the fine, old practice of cuckoldry, or cheating, as in "Your Cheating Heart," if you prefer Hank Williams to William Shakespeare, as most folks do.

My prayers had been answered. For reasons as yet known only to God, instead of enjoying my wife, the governor was now enjoying the state of final repose I had wished upon him.

My third thought was—Darn! I bet they'll think I did it.

I was right. It didn't take long for the cops to give my third thought serious consideration. By then, I had more acute concerns.

TWO

Saturday, May 26, 9:00 AM

I snapped a quick dozen shots of Silent Wallie before three carloads of state police barreled onto the beach, followed a few minutes later by two cars of FBI special agents. What with the uniformed state guys and Brooks-Brothered Feds assisting the locals in kicking sand at Moreno, it was clear my volunteer services were excess to the event. I left the other guys to play murder investigation and climbed the stairs up to Sally's house. No one seemed to notice my leaving.

I showered, shaved, and changed into clothes that I kept at Sally's in case she wanted to dine out where shoes and shirt were required for service. I found a button-down shirt left over from my suit-wearing days, a clean pair of jeans, and a pair of tassel loafers. Socks were too formal for my planned activities. Having gotten myself presentable for snooping around Splendor Bay, I fixed an omelet, took it and a beer out to the deck, and watched the entertainment below through Sally's opera binoculars.

An hour passed while small groups of cops conferred with one another, milled about, conferred with other one-anothers. Lab guys showed up looking for something to collect. The governor and a few sprigs of seaweed were it. Two carloads of state cops loaded up, squealed onto the pavement, ran a red light to make the turn onto Cliff Road, and headed up the ridge in the general direction of Promontory Point.

Then the rescue squad loaded the sun-ripening governor into the meat wagon for his trip to the county morgue in the basement of Brewer's funeral home in downtown Splendor Bay. I felt a momentary pang of regret seeing those diamond studs drive away. They could have paid my tab at Fred's, a couple of months rent, and bought Baby some new brake shoes, with enough change left over for a day at the pony track. However, just knowing Moreno was now waiting his turn for the coroner's carving table tempered my regret immensely.

As soon as the recently departed governor departed the beach, the remaining state cops and the Feds took off in the same direction the first two cars had taken up the cliff. I briefly wondered what sort of cop convention was going on at Promontory Point today, then I turned my attention back to Gomez and Tiny who had been left on the beach, looking as if they had been told by their big brothers that they were too little to play cops and robbers.

The whole show was over in less than two hours. By then, it had turned into a dazzling morning. So resplendent a morning that even with the lingering pain in my head I felt like exercising my inquisitive nature. I rejoined Tiny and Gomez on the beach to see what the official story was before I went snooping in town for gossip.

The new information I picked up was that Moreno wasn't the only dead dude. His limo driver had been found in a burned-out crash just beyond Promontory Point, the reason the big cops had sped away in that direction. The crash site was outside the city limits and SBPD's jurisdiction, the reason Tiny and Gomez had been left behind, or so Tiny said.

Tiny readily confirmed my initial observation—Moreno's cause of death wasn't immediately apparent. No gunshot wounds, no blows to the head, no slashed throat, no stab wounds, just dead and already stiff. That left a host of natural and unnatural causes of death for the coroner to choose from.

Gomez put his money on the safe bet—drowning—since the beach patrol had pumped a little sea foam out of Moreno before calling SBPD. Why he had gone for a swim in a tux wasn't a significant issue in Gomez's mind. Tiny picked the heart-attack-stroke-aneurysm category because of Moreno's age—fifty-eight— betting it occurred while Wallie was getting a little nooky on the beach. I placed my bet on drug-overdose because I preferred to think the worst of Wallie, and I didn't want to think about who the nookee might have been. Besides, this section of beach had its share of transactions which might lead to drug overdoses as thrilling as Viagra.

According to Tiny, the FBI was sending in an expert to assist the county coroner in analyzing Moreno's innards. The lab work would be expedited. Inquiring minds wanted to know. In the meantime, there were the matters of a state funeral and a successor to pick. And possibly a murderer to find.

The list of potential suspects was too large to go down the whodunit road, so we examined our political science knowledge and placed our bets. Tiny and I last had civics in high school, and Gomez had skipped that course, so our knowledge wasn't extensive. But we all agreed it would be the Vice President and then the Speaker of the House if Moreno had been President of the United States. Tiny and I remembered when Reagan was shot and knew for sure it wasn't Alexander Haig. Gomez was too young to remember Reagan or Haig, so he was easily convinced. None of us had any idea what happens in state government when you don't have a vice-governor, although we tried to remember what they called the job in Texas when Bush II resigned to be president.

Gomez put his money on the state controller, since, according to Gomez, looking after the money is the most important job. Tiny picked the head guy of the state senate, whatever that job is called, because making the laws sounded like an important job to a peace officer. And I put my money on the attorney general. I knew her. We agreed a special election was in order.

"Well, it sounds like you have everything under control," I said, intending to climb the stairs back to Sally's place to see if I could summon the courage to test Baby's brakes down Cliff Road, or the larger question, whether I could make it down Cliff Road without winding up in the same condition as Moreno's limo driver. In addition to buying Baby some new shoes, I thought I might poke around to see if anyone had anything to say on the subject of Moreno's passing, starting at Oma's Kitchen, one of the few places where you can get any chitchat from anybody.

"Wait up a minute," Tiny said as he headed over to the cruiser. "I need to call in."

"Yeah, sure," I said and turned to take in the bay view and a deep breath of sea air while Tiny did his calling-in. I fully expected Tiny to suggest a cup of coffee at Oma's so we could play one of our little games of guess the perpetrator, a passable substitute for a game of checkers with Old Man McPeters.

I was reciting the verse from John Keats' *Endymion* to myself—*Wide sea, that one continuous murmur breeds along the pebbled shore of memory*—one of the few verses I know, when Gomez strolled over to visit.

"You can tell me," I said, "What was the governor doing when he got himself killed?"

"I can't tell you anything, Fragile Dick."

Gomez wanted me to beg. "Just a tiny bit of speculation," I whined. "Something I can trade for lunch at Oma's."

"I might as well tell you," he said.

The thing I liked most about Gomez is you didn't have to beat information out of him. Usually, you didn't even have to buy him a drink.

"It's this way, Fragile Dick. We've got nothing."

"I owe you one."

"Nothing but speculation," Gomez expounded in response to my expression of gratitude. "You know his reputation. The governor was out tom-catting last night."

"So I've heard," I said. Sally Solana, my most recent ex-friend and the current state attorney general, was a Moreno staffer, until she had enough on him to convince him to give her a real job. From time to time, Sally shared with me some of the sordid facts she picked up in her work, Moreno's habits included.

"Nobody thought anything about his outing from the Mansion until he didn't show up for his seven a.m. staff meeting. Then they started looking for him."

"Really?"

"There's a car that trails Moreno's limo," Gomez continued, "manned by two sharpshooters state cops. The limo driver's also a state cop, which gives the governor three body guards with him at all times. For some reason, that didn't happen last night. Seems this backup car had mechanical trouble. By the time they switched vehicles, the governor was out of sight. Cramer is grilling the two cops now."

"Which two?" I asked.

"Last names was all I got," Gomez said. "Block and Sartin. Bet their heads are going to—"

"Bill, the Chief wants you to give a statement," Tiny yelled, interrupting Gomez just as he was getting to the good part.

I'd heard something recently about Stan Cramer, head of the state police. But, with my still pounding head, I couldn't remember what it was, something Sally had insisted on sharing while I watched a ball game on TV. I'd filed it away in the gray matter, so I'd be ready for one of her you're-not-listening-to-me pop quizzes. The question was, what category? Work stuff? State secrets stuff? Can you believe cops stuff? It would come to me.

"Bill, you hear me?" Tiny yelled again.

"Why me?" I yelled back. "I didn't see anything until I saw you guys down here destroying evidence. I can give him that statement over the car radio if he wants."

"Don't get smart with me, Bill," Tiny growled. "One of these days, you're going to push me too far."

Tiny Sanders outweighed me by a hundred pounds and he was almost a head taller than my six-three. That didn't scare me. Tiny was too good-natured to scare anyone. He was like having a big teddy bear for a cop. If you could keep him from grinning, his size did a darn good job of scaring the tourists into good driving habits. The rest of us liked him too well to misbehave much.

Tiny was one of only two guys I had gone through school with who never called me Fragile Dick. Fred McPeters, of Fred's Fine Seafood Bar and Grill and Fred's Fine Liquors, was the other. Which, to my way of thinking, proved Tiny loved me like a brother like Fred did. Tiny ought to. I was the one who explained the facts of life when we were eight and got him his first date in high school. If Mary Louise hadn't seen the potential in him back then, Tiny probably never would have married.

Heck, if Mary Louise hadn't seen the potential in him, he never would have had sex. He was just that aggressive.

"Don't shout at me, Tiny. I'm a little under the weather." I rubbed my head where it hurt the worst, between the eyes.

"Damn it, Bill. When are you going to get your act together? You had more going for you than any of us. Look how you've turned out."

"I turned out fine," I said. "I'm a has-been, not a never-was. I'm on sabbatical from life. Early retirement, if you will."

"Sure. I bet Davy is real proud of his daddy these days. Now, wait for me in the cruiser. I need to talk to Gomez."

"I don't mind listening to you talk to Gomez," I said, deflated, rightly chastised by Tiny's remark. I looked away to my favorite view of the bay. Tiny had hit me where it hurt. My son was the only good thing I had produced in my entire life. I hoped Davy would forgive me for taking time off from being an adult.

"I don't have time for your crap today," Tiny said in a tone that almost made me think he didn't love me anymore. That bothered me. I was running out of people who cared.

"Get in the cruiser, Bill," he ordered, throwing me the keys. "Listen to the radio or something."

I got in the front seat, shotgun side, put the key in the ignition and turned it far enough to get the radio playing. Then I pushed buttons until I found the local station that played Peter, Paul and Mary, and other fine musical artists from my youth. I turned the radio off when I heard their plea for money to support the arts. That is, their plea for money to support the odd-ball tastes of people like me, who can't handle new-age rock and roll and need to get over it, and the station workers, a group of long-haired, tongue-lip-ear-eyebrow-nipple pierced graduate students who ran the station out of their camper most sunny weekends. I was afraid that if I gave them any money they'd use it to pierce as yet unrevealed parts of their anatomies. As much as I love "Puff," I didn't want that on my conscience.

With nothing else to do, I lowered the windows to catch the breeze, hoping to overhear Tiny and Gomez, and lowered my seat back as far as I could with the cage in place to pretend I was taking a nap and wasn't interested in their conversation. Surf noises prevented much snooping.

Before I got bored enough to push the button for the siren, the Center City Channel 12 Eyewitness News van arrived. Out jumped their babe reporter, Pam Somebody, and a cameraman with a long, greasy ponytail. That's one thing you can say for being an out-of-the-way seaside town. By the time the TV news folk show up, there's little but the weather to report.

As Pam leaped around the news van gazelle-like, her high heels stuck in the sand. But nothing could keep Wonder Reporter Pam from her story. She slipped out of the shoes and vaulted the rest of the distance in her stocking feet.

"Officer? Officer? What happened here this morning?" Pam shouted. "We've learned that a body, reported to be Governor Moreno, was discovered on the beach. What can you tell our viewers?"

"No comment," Tiny commented loudly, pulling Gomez by the arm to the cruiser and pushing him into the back seat. Tiny went around the car, slid in behind the wheel, and cranked the engine.

Being a helpful person, I pushed the siren button.

Pam was quick. She stuck her head, microphone-holding right arm, and torso into the open window, draping her plasticized boobs across me as she aimed the microphone for Tiny's tonsils.

"Please, Officer, the citizens are entitled to know what the police are doing about this situation," she shouted, making my ears ring. "Are the state police and FBI involved? Who's in charge of the investigation?"

"No comment," Tiny muttered.

I decided to help Tiny. Since Pam was draped across me anyway, I pulled her into my arms and kissed her on her collagen-injected, red-tattooed lips.

She broke away sputtering.

While she was still confused, I pushed her out the window and pushed the button to raise it.

"Now's your chance, Tiny," I said, blowing a kiss at Pam who stood there with an open mouth, apparently in shock that lips had a purpose other than as an outlet for loud sounds.

"You better hope she doesn't file assault charges on you," Tiny said as he put the Chevy in gear and pulled around the Channel 12 van, not once losing traction in the sand.

I reached in my right pocket and moved the twenty over to the left pocket, promising myself I'd pay up on the rest of the bet when I got some cash.

THREE

Saturday, May 26, 11:00 AM

Splendor Bay Police Chief Murphy Sanders was redder-faced than usual. "Damn it, Bill, what did you see?"

We had been talking only a minute when Chief decided to get high-handed on me and I shut up. You would have thought the voters were watching his performance, but I suspected the viewing audience was merely a minor contingency of state police and FBI agents behind the two-way mirror. Heck, the video camera wasn't even on, or the little red light was burned out. Equipment maintenance wasn't a major item in the city budget.

"Have you had your blood-pressure checked lately?" I asked, politely. "A man your age ought to avoid stress."

The least I could do with my part in this passion play was to act like a concerned citizen. Chief Sanders, Tiny's uncle, was pushing seventy-five. He'd been Splendor Bay's police chief most of our lives, his father, grandfather, and great-grandfather before him. Best I could figure, his ancestor must have broken up a gun fight in one of the founding father's saloons, been appointed chief, and like some English lordship, the title had been passed down to the male heirs ever since.

"Cut the crap, Bill," Tiny interjected, resting his big hand on the flap of his holster like he was going to draw on me. Tiny didn't like any sort of controversy but he was big on respecting elders and protecting children. Besides, he had to set an example for Gomez as well as a starring role to play in the SBPD version of *Hill Street Blues*.

I acted contrite. "I've already told you, Tiny. I didn't see anything until I saw you guys down at the beach. I had just come out on the deck to drink my coffee. Saw you guys messing around. Thought I'd see what all the commotion was about."

"Did Sally see anything?" Tiny asked.

"I don't know. She was gone when I woke up. Our state's attorney general has more important things to do than lie in bed past daybreak with the likes of me."

"Know where she is?" the Chief asked, his face not quite as red as before since I was now being a cooperative witness, and I'd reminded him I had connections. I'm not proud of it, but I can name drop with the best of the have-beens or never-weres.

"No," I answered the question asked.

When I was a lawyer, I always told my clients to never volunteer information. As the Miranda warning clearly declares, what you say to the police can, and will, be twisted in ways you never dreamed possible and used to screw you over in a court of law if they can't find anyone else to pin the blame on, or just because you're handy, or just because they don't like your face. The only smart thing to say to an inquiring cop is, "Get me a lawyer." Then shut your mouth.

"Do you know when she left?" the Chief asked, politely.

Cops were taught in police school to ask questions lawyers were taught in lawyer school to tell their clients not to answer. If both the suspect and the cop play the game properly, it can take a long time before the suspect gets trapped in enough uncertainty to raise the ante to probable cause for an arrest.

"No," I answered, disregarding my own internal lawyer advice so we could get this game of twenty-questions over. I then proceeded to elaborate. "We were getting along just swell until she got mad about something and left our bed. I have no idea what she did after that."

"When was this?"

"I don't remember. In the heat of the night. Before dawn."

"What did she get mad about?" Tiny asked.

I shrugged my shoulders over the mystery of it all. "Who knows with women? One minute we were being friendly. Then she got mad and started yelling. Now that I think about it, it was when she asked me if I loved her enough to marry her. Have you ever noticed how women wait until you're too weak to argue to ask such a question?"

"So what happened next?" Tiny asked.

Tiny liked my women-adventure stories, which I fabricated just for him. To my credit, I never talked about the actual details of any intimate relationship I've ever had, because those have been with women I cared about. Of course, I've fabricated the number of adventures and the number of women and given lots of those "you know" hints, which Tiny was too proud to admit he didn't.

"Guess I gave the wrong answer," I answered, in time to keep Tiny from beating it out of me. "So nothing happened. She left the bed. I went back to sleep. Next thing I know, the sun's up, I'm awake. She isn't there. So I made coffee, took it out to the deck, saw you and Gomez on the beach kicking sand at the stiff. And now we're here. Together again."

The Chief glared at Tiny, then at me, and snapped, "Where can we find Sally?"

Good question, I thought, and proceeded to elaborate on my connections. "Seeing as how it's Saturday, I doubt you'll find her in her Center City office. She might be at her Center City townhouse though. But you probably should try her sister's beach house first. That's where Sally usually goes when we have a tiff. Her sister's name is Lizabeth Thorton. She's married to Chester Thorton, Harvard Law, back when it meant something. They have a small cottage, about an acre under roof off Bayside Road, and a house on Grandview Avenue in Center City, and an apartment in New York, a ranch in Texas, and a place in Beverly Hills, and one in Paris, and—"

"That's it for now," Tiny said, concluding the interrogation before I got around to confessing under the pressure of it all. "But, just in case you were thinking of leaving town, don't. We'll be talking to you again."

"Looking forward to it," I said, extending my hand. "And thank you, Tiny, for the ride into town. I'll find my own way home, if you don't mind."

In the hallway outside the interrogation room, instead of turning right toward the front desk and outside doors, I turned left. I reached the room behind the mirror in two steps and opened the door to find the head of the state police, Stan Cramer, six or seven other big-belly state cops, the trim Feds from the beach, and the skinny Gomez huddled together discussing my probing interrogation.

Stan, who could have played the mean-son-of-a-bitch captain of the guards in that all-time-great prison movie, *The Longest Yard*, tipped his hat at me and glared a warning. Then Stan put his hand on his billy stick and stroked it purposefully, in case I mistook his glare for a friendly smile. I took his glare-smile to mean Stan liked his stick. Some cops do.

I winked at Stan. "Was it as good for you as it was for me?"

Tiny reached around me and pulled the door shut. "Damn it, Bill," Tiny said as he pushed me down the hall, "Why the hell do you pull crap like that?"

"Just checking to see who's wearing white hats today."

"Pissing on the wrong man's shoes, you mean."

I shrugged and left the building, swaggering like Elvis in his jeweled white cape, strolling right through a quacking flock of newspeople, pretending to be both deaf and dumb as they yelled at me. I looked back to see Tiny shrug at the hopelessness of trying to redeem a screw-up like me. Then he turned his attention to Channel 12 Pam and her brothers and sisters in crime-reporting.

Across the street, I contemplated the situation. Tiny had been joined by Stan Cramer for a meet-the-press moment. Observing Stan in action, I bet myself he watched *The Longest Yard* on the cable TV free movie channel just like I did, and he was aching to get even for losing that ballgame between the guards and the prisoners. Fortunately, I didn't look like the football-toting prisoner/hero of that movie.

Sally said I reminded her of *Magnum PI,* running around in shorts and driving a red convertible. I saw myself as more of a *Quigley Down Under* kind of guy, wearing chaps and shooting a big gun. Actually, I'm probably more a sitcom *Coach* kind of guy. My misadventures are usually of the chronic weekly variety, and I have a Dauber and a Luther in my life—Tiny and Fred. Well, sort of. Actually Tiny was an *Armed and Dangerous* kind of cop, and Fred, even though he looked like a Dauber, was definitely an *Archie Bunker* at heart. Besides, Sally wasn't a Christine kind of gal. She wasn't anywhere near as tenderhearted as Christine. Sally was a . . . was a . . . Heck, I didn't know who Sally was. Sally was mystery enough for any man.

After another moment of silent reflection, I came to three conclusions: I definitely watched too many reruns and old movies on television; my friends and acquaintances were all archetypes; and I really should spring for the expensive movie channel so I could watch movies from the more recent past decades. Maybe two more conclusions: I probably needed to get my own big stick or one of those big, long *Quigley* gun just in case Stan Cramer ever caught me alone in a dark alley, and I really needed to get on with my Sally hunt before she ran into Cramer in a dark alley. On the other hand, Stan could probably look out for himself.

As I ambled down the street like a Matthew Quigley with a saddle across his shoulder *sans* saddle, it came to me there was always the possibility Tiny was Duke, the maniac killer in *The Wrong Guys*, the best cub-scout-reunion camping movie of all time. If Tiny was Duke, then I'd be Tim, the aging surfer going over the killer waterfall on a log in classic surf-rider pose. In that movie, the elderly den moms had saved the day.

It was definitely time to call on Mom. Come to think of it, Oma was our Cub Scout den mother when Tiny, Fred, and I were kids. How's that for karma?

FOUR

Saturday, May 26, 12:15 PM

I swung into the drugstore to drop off the roll of film with the Wallie-in-death poses on it, scooted on down the sidewalk to the auto parts store and ordered Baby's new shoes, then headed to Oma's Kitchen, my home away from home during the daytime. Fred's Fine Seafood Bar and Grill was my nighttime home away from home. My home at home wasn't much.

The first thing on my list of questions was—where had Sally gone after she left me? Maybe she had stopped for breakfast at the Kitchen. Maybe somebody had seen her somewhere else. And maybe Oma was still serving lunch. Then there were the deeper questions. Had Sally happened upon Moreno when she left our bed? It wasn't just an idle question. One thing Sally had shared with me about her days as a Moreno staffer was that she and Wallie had been chummy for a while. She was just one of many ladies our late governor had been chummy with, including that special lady, my soon-to-be-ex-wife, Eleana.

Did it bother me that Moreno and I had slept in two of the same beds? A little. Especially when I found him sleeping in my favorite bed. Which was before I started sleeping in a bed he no longer used. A good prosecutor looking for a little publicity might see enough in a bother like mine to conjure up motive.

Did the fact that Sally had once told me she hated Moreno enough to kill him bother me? Yeah. Just a little. Because Sally Solana was the kind of girl who did what she set her mind to do. She could do it. I didn't think she had done it. At least not last night. Because it seemed to me I was the object of her anger last night. Unless Moreno happened to be handy when she was enraged about men in general.

The question was—was Moreno as handy as it appeared he might have been? If so, why?

Mom always told me a gentleman saw a lady to her door. For now, I would concentrate on being a gentleman. I needed to make sure Sally had made it to her intended destination, wherever that was, in one piece. But first, it was time for another consultation with Mom. Maybe she had something else she wanted to tell me.

Mom, now called Oma out of respect for her age and flock of grandchildren, was a short, round, German woman of seventy-something years who wore her silver-and-gold hair in braids around her head. She still spoke with an accent after over fifty years in the United States, coming to Splendor Bay as Bruce McPeters' war bride and staying to raise her own five children and a passel of strays on the proceeds of the town's breakfast and lunch appetites.

Oma's Kitchen was the only place where you could get a decent meal before Fred McPeters' Fine Seafood Bar and Grill opened for dinner at four in the afternoon. The McPeters family's two restaurants not only served delicious meals, they were about the only places to pick up gossip in Splendor Bay. Once folks started spooning Oma's gravy across her homemade biscuits or rolls, they forgot about being so tight-lipped. If you caught them after the strudel, they could be downright talkative. And, if they were on their third round of drinks at Fred's, they might even tell the truth.

Fred McPeters, Tiny Sanders, and I were best friends all through school, pals before kindergarten, sworn blood brothers by the second grade, Cub Scout den mates, high school varsity teammates, all that makes childhood friends closer than brothers. Oma took pity on me when my own mother died and did her best to overcome nature with nurture. Whichever kid around her house was most in need of mothering got her frontal lobe attention. The others were watched by the eyes in the back of her head. I got my share of frontal lobe. Being the work in progress I am, I still do.

When I showed up in Splendor Bay looking for a place to lick my wounds, Tiny and Fred took over their old buddy roles and Oma resumed her mothering. Anybody in town who wanted to mess with me had to worry about Oma cutting them off from her strudel, or Fred cutting them off from their booze, or Tiny giving them a speeding ticket. That might not sound like much of a deterrent to city folks, but in small town Splendor Bay, that's about as punitive as you could get.

"*Morgen, Bill! Wie geht's* (Morning, Bill! How's it going)?" Oma called out as I opened the door.

"*Nicht schlecht* (Not bad)," I answered, taking a seat at the counter where she was busy preparing her famous chicken salad for Sunday's lunch menu. Today's lunch service was about over.

Oma opened the bread drawer, took out two slices of sourdough, and spooned a large helping of the fresh chicken salad between them. She placed the sandwich on a plate, grabbed a handful of potato chips out of a canister on the counter behind her, and placed the food in front of me.

"*Bier?*" she asked.

"Sounds good," I said, looking around. The State Farm insurance guy was getting up. He nodded in my direction, dropped a five on the table to cover the lunch special, and left. Oma and the Hispanic busboy seemed to be the only people in the place. Then I heard Bruce McPeters snoring in the far booth, resting up from his waiter job in the sun-warmed window seat.

Oma whispered, "*Hast du gehoert?* (Have you heard?)"

"*Hab' ich was gehoert?* (Heard what?)" The word was out.

"*Über den Governor?* (About the governor?)"

"*Was über ihn?* (What about him?)"

"*Er wurde um die Ecke gebracht.* (He was assassinated.)"

"Huh?"

She repeated without the idiom, "*Er wurde ermordet.* (He was assassinated.)"

"Who the hell would want to assassinate the governor?" I asked, giving up on German since running Oma's idioms through my brain for interpretation made my head hurt worse. "He's put a chicken in every pot."

"They say it's because he was pro-choice. Or the drug dealers, or someone he put in prison. Many people had reason. He was not a nice man, Bill. He was not a nice man at all."

Obviously, Oma hadn't voted for Moreno. She had her own grudge against him, one of those never-forget-or-forgive German grudges, for Moreno's part in Fred McPeters' one brush with the law. Moreno, never one to overlook an opportunity, used the publicity surrounding Fred's trial to turn a mediocre career as a county assistant district attorney into an appointment as the state's attorney general.

From there, Moreno led the charge against major oil companies on the environmental front during the 1980's, generating enough publicity and party support to run for governor a decade later. He won his first term on a pro-choice/anti-gay/anti-drug campaign, an interesting position when you thought about it. In his view, women, but not men, could do whatever they wanted with their bodies, except take certain nonprescription drugs.

Fred, on the other hand, had seen a promising future in the outside world derailed at the station by Moreno's opportunism. Thrown out of college and with nothing better to do in life, he came back to Splendor Bay and learned the restaurant business from his parents. Fred's grudge against Moreno was even stronger than Oma's. After all, he had his dad's Scotch blood as well as Oma's German, which made for the human equivalent of a Rottweiler crossed with a pit bull.

"Oma, nobody assassinates governors because they're pro-choice, or if they do, they use bombs. And his anti-drug program was only words. The drug dealers threw him hundred-thousand-dollar a plate dinners. More likely it was a jealous husband. Who's been telling you all this assassination stuff, anyway?"

"Don't say that," Oma whispered, looking around to make sure neither the non-English-speaking busboy nor the sleeping elderly Bruce McPeters were listening. Old Man McPeters couldn't have heard us if he had been awake, and he wouldn't have remembered the conversation if he had heard us.

"Don't say what?" I teased. "It's okay to slander the dead. At least that's what the law books used to say. Maybe not Elvis or Jerry Garcia. I'm not so sure either of them is dead. But, take it from me, Wallie was no Elvis or Jerry Garcia, and he's for sure dead. I saw the body myself."

"Stop it, Bill," Oma whispered, one hand partially covering her mouth as the other twisted her apron. "Don't tease. And don't say that about the jealous husband."

Oma seemed truly distressed, and her distress bothered me. She had her share of old-lady medical problems, including adult-onset diabetes diagnosed a few years ago. "Okay, I'll behave," I said and dived into the sandwich.

Oma fluttered about, putting the place in order. I chewed and drank, watching her efficient movements as she wiped the food-assembly and serving counters, cleaned and filled salt, sugar, ketchup, and mustard containers, and arranged them around the napkin dispensers.

I hadn't spilled my guts to Tiny or Fred. Them, I told macho lies, that Eleana kicked me out, the implication being I was the swine who had been caught lusting with more body parts than Jimmy Carter's heart. Eleana had been discreet enough to wait several months after filing for divorce to show up at political events with Moreno, so they believed me. I had told Oma the whole truth. She could be trusted with my heart's pain.

The whole truth was that I had played the my-work-is-more-important-than-God-big-prick-lawyer-bread-winner game too long. Eleana found someone else to pay attention to her, and our son lost his parents. Blame me. I did. So did Eleana. I felt better when people blamed me. Heck, I kept the hair shirt and ashes at the ready for any Blame Bill Festival that came along.

When I found out about my wife and Moreno, I walked away from my *successful* life. I gave her the house and everything in the bank. I didn't force Davy to choose which parent he wanted to live with, reasoning that he needed the stability of his room, his home, his friends, and his mother. Whatever else she was, Eleana was a good mother. But the real reason was that I just didn't feel up to the job of being me anymore. Davy didn't need to witness my mid-life crisis. That's a hard thing for a boy to see in his father. I know. I had watched my own father go through his when my mother died.

So I walked away from my big-prick lawyer game, leaving a big-ticket case in the middle of trial. Both the judge and the client complained to the state bar. The state bar suspended my license to practice law. Still not happy, the client sued me for malpractice and quickly won a fat settlement from our firm's malpractice insurance carrier. That didn't bother me as much as it should have. In my sober moments I even enjoyed the poetic justice of it all.

The new judge in my former client's second trial—first verdict overturned for ineffective assistance of counsel, namely me—ordered the former client to pay the money he had received from our insurance carrier as restitution to the people he'd defrauded, then sentenced him to a ten-year term, eight years longer than he'd received in the first trial. Our malpractice insurance carrier gave up some of the premiums our firm had paid over the years, because I admitted the malpractice right off and left them no room to stretch out the defense of the claim until everyone died. Then my law partners, miffed when the firm's insurance rates shot up, booted me out. That got me out of attending any more of those insufferable partners' meetings.

As my bonus for going quietly into that good night of hasbeendom, my ex-partners transferred my share of the firm's net worth into the two trusts I'd set up—the major money for Davy's education and some change to be doled out to me each month for the rest of my life in sufficiently small increments to ensure some degree of moderation in my vices. Score one for Lady Justice, score one for me. If anybody ever sued me again, they'd have to do it for the fun of it. Nobody could touch a penny of the money in those trusts, and I'd given Eleana title to the rest of our formerly joint assets. All of which proves life can be simple when you open your clenched fists and let the grains of bondage fall through. Lawyer, heal thyself.

I came back to Splendor Bay to lick my wounds, rented a small house on the low-rent section of beach, taking up the life I'd left off at eighteen, not bothered any longer by those pesky earning-a-living-and-insuring-your-future concerns. I spent a couple of months in near solitude, running up and down the beach and riding waves, dispossessing the nastiest demons in my soul.

Then I ran into Sally at Fred's Bar. She, fully advised of the sad facts of my disappointing life, decided she could rehabilitate me. Neither of us could think of any good reason why she shouldn't try.

I now filled my days working on getting the vow of poverty stuff right and my nights getting the living-with-Sally thing right. I kept my rented shack, but more often than not, I enjoyed the view from Sally's house and dallied in Sally's life of luxury. It's hard to break old habits, especially in support of a vow of poverty. Besides, her family had been living a life of luxury for centuries, since her Conquistador ancestor stole the Indians' gold, or to be politically correct, the Native Americans' gold, or the Indigenous Peoples' gold.

Whatever. At this stage in my life, I didn't see much wrong in being a kept man. I had been the keeper of womankind for years for all the good it had done me. And it was, after all, the Indians' gold. Every red-blooded European American ought to steal some of it just to keep in practice for when we figure out how to rape and plunder another planet. Besides, the gold had been stolen so long ago nobody was going to make Sally give it back so she might as well share with those late to the theft.

My pride didn't keep me from eating Sally's food or enjoying her air-conditioning or playing pet gigolo at social events, but it stopped me short of asking her for spending money. So I let her get me a job. Sally used her state government connections to get my ancient PI license reinstated, the one I'd acquired when working my way through law school because I was then too proud to take my father's blood money.

I now had a means of earning enough cash to supplement my liquor-trust income until the state bar lifted the suspension on my law license. When the rent was due or Baby needed new shoes, I hustled a little PI work out of one of my lawyer buddies. But mostly, I watched the waves and the sunsets and the stars, and survived through the kindness of Sally and Oma and Fred and Tiny and anyone else I could make feel sorry for me.

Oma finished her cleaning and came back to take my empty plate. She looked me in the eyes and said, "Promise me, Bill."

I knew exactly what promise she wanted. "Don't worry, Oma. I didn't kill him. I never had the guts. If I had, he would have been dead a year ago."

"Don't talk like that," Oma said in her frightened whisper.

"Trust me," I said, then took a sip of beer. "I didn't do it. I was with Sally last night. You wouldn't happen to know where she is, would you?"

"No." She frowned. "You're the second person to ask today."

"Who was the first?"

"Chester Thorton stopped in for breakfast. He said Sally called Lizabeth at their beach house very early to say she was coming over, but she never arrived. He thought she must have stayed with you."

I didn't say anything, chewing on this new piece of information, finishing my beer.

"Bill?" An alarmed look settled on Oma's sweet old lady face. A troubled expression must have been on my own.

"Sally and her Jaguar were gone when I woke up. Don't worry, I'll find her."

At that moment, the phone rang. Oma wiped her hands on her apron and reached into the shelf beneath the cash register to retrieve it. She also kept a 38-caliber Lady Smith in there in case a robbery-minded stranger crossed her path. She might look like a sweet old lady, but Oma knew how to use a gun.

"Davy!" Oma smiled her grandmotherly smile when she learned the identity of her caller. "When are you coming to see me? I'll make you my special strudel."

Oma's face went from pleased to troubled. "Bill," she said as she passed me the receiver. "Davy needs you. It's Eleana."

"Dad," Davy said. "Mom wasn't here when I woke up. I've called everywhere looking for her. She's not answering her cell phone or beeper or the phone at her office. I just heard about the governor on TV. I'm scared, Dad."

My heart skipped a beat. "I'm on my way," I said, praying this wasn't the day I got my three wishes. "Try not to worry. She's probably shopping."

I pushed the off button and handed Oma the phone. "Eleana wasn't at home when Davy woke up this morning."

"You don't think she was out with—"

"I hope not. Can I borrow your car? The brakes on the Corvette are—"

"Sure, sure, the keys are on the hook."

As I headed toward the alley door, Oma called me back. "Here, take this," she said and pulled her Lady Smith from beneath the counter. "Telephone me when you know anything."

I almost refused the gun. Then I had second thoughts. You never know, I said to myself as I took it from Oma. Looking back, it's hard to say what the right choice should have been.

FIVE

Saturday, May 26, 1:00 PM

I almost made it out of Oma's rear parking lot unaccosted. I was familiarizing myself with the buttons on Oma's new Cadillac, having just discovered the switch that allowed the edges of the seat to come up and hug my butt snugly, when Fred McPeters opened the door and slid into the passenger's seat.

"Hi, Bill," Fred said.

"Hi, Fred," I said, looking at a flabby-biceps, bald-headed ex-jock. Fred had a forceful build, a few inches shorter than Tiny, but taller and bigger all around than me. The young, firm-body version of Fred had been our senior class football hero the only year Splendor Bay High won the state championship. He landed a football scholarship to State U and was starting to look like an all-star in college ball when his luck ran out.

All the girls loved the blond, blue-eyed, good-looking, muscle-clad Fred of those days, which led to his undoing when Fred and a cheerleader named Beth Ann Somebody were caught in the act on a ping-pong table in the student lounge late one night. Beth Ann's parents brought statutory rape charges in a misguided effort to assert the virtue of their then still seventeen-year-old freshman daughter.

The charge was eagerly prosecuted by the daring young Assistant DA, Wallie Moreno. The trial made the papers and the start of Wallie's public career. Fred won a probated two-year sentence on a felony conviction and lost his college scholarship. The last anyone ever heard of Beth Ann she had married a Texas oil man who got some secretary of something job in Washington when Bush the First was President. On occasion, I've wondered whether, while Beth Ann ate dinner at the White House and enjoyed a lively discussion on the Federal debt with some old senator, she ever thought of Fred and the ping-pong table.

"Where you going?" Fred asked.

"Haven't decided," I answered.

"Heard there was a murder on Sally's beach."

"Yeah, I heard that, too."

"Heard it was Moreno."

"Yeah, that's what I heard."

"Did you kill him?" Fred asked.

"Somebody beat me to it," I said.

"Those are the breaks," said Fred.

"Yeah, life's a bitch; then you die."

"You ever think of going into the bumper sticker business?" Fred asked. "You'd be a natural."

"Hmm. Clichés for dollars? That's not a bad an idea. You know, I've always wondered why the intellectually elite are against clichés. Seems to me they sum up life's truths in neat little packages everyone can understand, like sound bites on the news. Clichés, truisms, platitudes, proverbs, sound bites, bumper stickers? No additives like adverbs or adjectives needed. Like whole wheat bread. Hmm. You really think there's money in bumper stickers?"

I convinced Fred I didn't know any more than he did and got him out of the car. When I reached Bay Highway, I set about trying to read the buttons on the digital cell phone in Oma's new Cadillac. Her car also had a satellite tracking system to find it if it got lost. I felt comforted knowing that somewhere in GM's vast empire a technician was sitting in front of a big screen eating his or her hoagie and monitoring my progress as well as that of thousands of other Caddy owners to our final destinations, ready to send out a search party as soon as someone reported any of us missing.

I envisioned this screen looking like one of those big wall-size electronic maps in all the old bombs-are-coming and the new aliens-and/or-meteors-are-coming movies, with little blinking lights where Caddies scooted here and there. Since I didn't want a GM technician missing lunch or any search parties coming after me, the prudent thing to do was to let Tiny in on my plans so he wouldn't report me missing.

"Hey, buddy," I said, "I'm informing you that I've left town. Davy called me. He needs my help."

"What's wrong?" Tiny asked, concern in his voice. Tiny was more concerned about my son's welfare than he was his own son's welfare. After all, his son had a father and mine didn't.

"Davy's fine. Eleana's missing. She wasn't at the house when he woke up this morning and she's not answering any of her phones, which isn't like Eleana at all."

"Was she out with Moreno?"

"I hope not."

"You need my help?"

"I may, but for now I'd rather not make a big deal out of it. She could be out committing random acts of shopping. Could you call in her Lincoln's tag number to the Center City PD and have them call you back if they spot her car? You know, cop to cop, friend to friend. If they locate her, you call me. I'll take it from there."

"I thought locating Sally was your agenda."

"That was my original agenda, until Davy called."

"This is a record for you, isn't it?" Tiny said.

"What's that?" I asked.

"Losing two women in one day?"

"They're not lost yet, just misplaced. But, with recent events, I'm not taking any chances."

"You don't think—"

"Not yet," I lied and steered away from the question I didn't want to think about. "Sally just wants me to chase her down and plead for her hand. I wouldn't be concerned at all, except Oma said Chester Thorton was in the Kitchen this morning asking about Sally. Which means she's not at her sister's house. It wouldn't hurt for you to call her Jaguar plates in as well, if you haven't already."

"Stan Cramer did that. Seems he thinks he's in charge of the investigation, wants to talk to our state's attorney general 'to resolve our respective jurisdictional issues,' as he calls it."

"That doesn't surprise me. He's afraid if you guys get into a pissing contest, someone might point out it was his guys who lost Moreno last night. He's covering his backside."

"Yeah, and he's running an offensive as well. He's real hot to pin it on somebody before the press hits on him. Which brings me to the subject of you."

"What about me?" I asked in my aggrieved-innocent voice.

"For some reason, Cramer doesn't like you. He thinks you're too smart-mouthed. Thinks I ought to haul your ass back in here and beat a confession out of you."

"Run interference on Mr. Wonderful for me, pal. After I find Sally, I might have more to say to him. I seem to recall she didn't regard him that highly, from an investigation she had going. It seems strange to me that the night the governor gets killed, Cramer's people have car trouble. Have you had anybody check out the facts on that one? Just in case Splendor Bay PD is actually in charge of the investigation. Sounds like a good job for Gomez. Well, I have to go. Oma's not going to like me running up her car phone bill."

"So that's how you managed to disappear," Tiny remarked.

"Didn't Oma tell you?"

"No, but you'll love the story she told me."

"Tell me later. As soon as I hang up on you, I'm going to my ex-house to pick up Davy and see if I can find his mother. Call Oma and get the number for this phone, will you? You'll be able to reach me on it or at my ex-house. Let me know as soon as anyone spots either of my ladies. Oh, and another thing. I need to amend a gun permit. Oma loaned me hers. Get the info off her permit and make me legal. Please?"

"Bill, don't do anything foolish," Tiny said.

"I don't plan on it," I said. "It was Oma's idea that I take her gun. She's all spooked about Moreno."

"I told her there was nothing to worry about."

"Me, too. I hope we're right. But you have to admit Splendor Bay doesn't have a dead governor wash ashore every day. And I've never lost two women in one day."

"If you need fire power, call me," Tiny said.

"I hear you. Now hang up so I can find Sally and Eleana. Once I do, I'm giving up women and joining a monastery."

"And donate your pecker to the Smithsonian?"

"Nah. It goes to the Tagata shrine in Japan."

"The what?" Tiny asked.

"The Tagata shrine, north of the city of Nagoya, in Japan. Adjacent to the shrine is a museum claiming to be the only one of its kind in the world. It contains the willies of scores of mammals, ranging in size from the dormouse to the sperm whale. Mine would go next to the sperm whale."

"Where do you come up with this shit?"

"*National Geographic* or maybe the nature channel. When you're on sabbatical from life, you have time to read and watch television. And you know what?"

"What?' asked Tiny.

"They seldom ever have pictures of bare-breasted native women in *National Geographic* anymore. For that you still have to read *Playboy.*"

"Yeah, I wouldn't know," Tiny said, embarrassed.

So I continued. "Anyway, on March fifteenth every year, they hold a fertility festival celebrating the male god, Sky Father, coming from above to impregnate the female god, Earth Mother, so Earth Mother will bear fruit and grain, to feed man and womankind."

"You can stop now."

"That's not the best part. A Shinto priest leads the procession, scattering salt to purify the way. He's followed by another priest carrying this huge pecker carved out of wood and painted red, which at the completion of the procession rests for one year at the shrine. Along the way, the local populace drinks sake and enjoys the occasion, sort of like a New Orleans Mardi Gras."

"Sounds like a hell of a party."

"Yeah, next time I get rich, we'll have to go."

"First you'll have to get a job."

"First I have to decide what I want to be when I grow up."

"Don't wait too long," Tiny said.

SIX

Saturday, May 26, 2:20 PM

On the drive over to Center City, I called all of Sally's known numbers—townhouse, office, and cell phone—and got only recorded voices, mine at the townhouse. I was more successful in damsel-saving at my ex-house. I found Eleana alive and well, curled up into fetal position on the leather sofa in my ex-study, bawling her eyes out. Davy was trying to talk his mother into a sip of my-ex-Scotch.

I focused on the tranquil view of Eleana's garden outside. The white rose with the pink center that Eleana had spent several years perfecting and had named *Angela* was in full bloom. I glanced around the room. My ex-lawbooks were still on the shelves. Photos of my smiling face, cheek-to-cheek with one celebrity-crook client or another on my ex-boat, still hung on the wall. One glance could tell you what kind of whore the ex-me had been. Then I looked at Davy. He must have grown another two inches since last month. Now, at sixteen, he was almost my height. Damn, I hated not getting to watch him turn into a man this past year. I tried to tell him that when his like-mine brown eyes met mine, but I chickened out.

"Your mother doesn't drink Scotch. See if you can find some water. I'll get her a glass of wine if that doesn't do the trick."

"Sure, Dad. Thanks."

"I'm glad you called me, son."

Davy nodded. He seemed relieved to see me, and relieved to turn his sobbing mother over to a man more experienced with the tears of women. He pushed the like-Eleana blond hair out of his eyes, looked at her with his like-mine frown, then bounded to the kitchen.

"It's all your fault!" Eleana screamed at me as soon as Davy was out of earshot.

"What's all my fault?" I asked.

"Wallie's dead," she sobbed.

"Yeah, I know. So, how is that my fault?"

"I don't know," she wailed. "I don't know..."

"But we'd both feel better if it was my fault, wouldn't we?"

I sat down on the sofa and patted her rump in what was intended to be a comforting gesture. Eleana still had a girl-sized rump neatly attached by a tiny waist to the rest of her. Well, maybe not as small a waist as I had remembered, but at age forty-two, she only looked a few days older than the girl I had fallen in love with twenty years ago. When I wasn't hating her, I still remembered how much I had loved her.

I offered my condolences. "I know you loved him, and I'm sorry for your grief." You loved me once, too, I thought.

Her sobs turned into muffled sniffing as she buried her face in a pillow. Davy returned with a glass of water and a bottle of herbal-medicine calming pills. She waved the pill bottle away. "No," she said, taking the water. "I don't need them. I'm okay."

I pulled the twenty from my pocket. "Here, Davy. I missed lunch. Could you run out and get some burgers. I'll look after your mother."

Relief flooded his face. "I'll be back in fifteen minutes," he said and headed to the driveway where my ex-Land Rover, now his, was parked beside Oma's Caddy.

"You want to tell me where you've been?" I said when the front door slammed. "You scared Davy by not letting him know where you were."

"Don't start with me, Bill," she said. "Don't start."

"I'm not starting anything," I said, moving to my ex-chair, a leather recliner, for a more tranquil view of the rose garden through the French doors. "I'm asking you, in a reasonable manner, where you were that you couldn't let your son know you were okay?"

"You're starting. And I'm not up to your recriminations."

"I'm not. I was just worried about you. When Davy couldn't find you, I came here, determined to save the damsel in distress."

She glared at me. "They called me about a fire at the Archives. I thought I'd be back before Davy woke up."

"Why did it take so long?"

"We weren't able to get into the building immediately. Smoke spread through the ventilation system, so they had to make sure the fire was completely out. Then the fire marshal had to inspect the building to make sure it was safe—"

"I get the picture. So why couldn't you have called home and let Davy know where you were?"

"I'm in no mood for this, Bill. If you want to depose people, go back to practicing law. I oversee a state office. I had to locate staff to begin a damage inventory. That's not easy to do on a Saturday with the switchboard down. Then I had to make sure someone was in charge before I could leave."

"How bad was the fire?"

"A lot of smoke and sprinkler damage, but only the files in one room burned. . ." Eleana trailed off, then gave me a quizzical frown. "Wallie's campaign records. . . You don't think the fire is connected to his death, do you?"

"Not until now," I said, knowing instantly they were connected. The first thing I had learned practicing law was that whenever you issued a *subpoena duces tecum*, a demand to a party in a lawsuit to produce records in their possession, they almost always responded no-can-do because "all my records were destroyed in a fire." The one exception was a company on the Gulf Coast that responded their records had been stored in a trailer that had blown away in a hurricane. Their records were gone with the wind, as it were.

"Do you know where Moreno was last night?" I asked.

She walked over to the French doors and looked out. "He had a fund-raising dinner at Stan Cramer's house at Promontory Point. Dinner and then poker with contributors."

"Really?" I said.

She turned around. "He asked me to go to dinner and I told him I couldn't. Then I heard the news on the car radio on my way home. They said Wallie was found on the beach at Splendor Bay. That you. . . How, Bill? How did it happen?"

I ignored the implication in her question. "That hasn't been determined. No obvious wounds on his body. He may have drowned. They found his car and driver in a crash off

Promontory Point, several miles from where they found his body. He might have been thrown into the water during the wreck and washed up on the beach. Nobody knows at the moment."

"They said you were questioned. I thought—"

"Thought what?"

"I thought maybe the two of you had a fight and—"

"Eleana, you, above everyone else, should know there's no fight left in me. Besides, I don't blame him for taking advantage of a beautiful, available woman. Moreno, I merely hated. You, I blame for being available, and I blame me for letting you be available. Blaming I have time for. But, I'm afraid the time for fighting for your hand has passed. A year ago I might have killed him. Not now. Feel free to screw whomever you want."

Eleana glared at me with unblinking eyes. Then, with a sigh, she turned to gaze out at her garden. Finally, she turned her ever-changing, blue-gray-green eyes back on me, her angry eyes now the dark green of a rose stem.

"What did you expect? That someday, when Davy was grown and you were finally too old to stand up in a courtroom, I'd be here waiting for you? To do what? Grow more roses? Serve you drinks? You didn't have time to be a part of my life. I made the best life for myself that I could under the circumstances."

"I'm sorry it didn't work out," I said just as Davy came through the door, loudly.

He glanced at us and apparently decided it was safe to venture into the toxic cloud of conflict in the room.

"I felt like a pepperoni pizza instead of burgers," he said. "I had them put anchovies on your part, Dad."

I smiled at my son. Pepperoni pizza had always been our father-son meal, the salty little fishes only on my portion. I looked at Eleana and she nodded, agreeing to a time-out from our marriage-busting encounter. Time for a united parental front, for the sake of the kid.

"Shall we eat in the kitchen?" Eleana asked, coming away from the French doors to give our son a hug, assuring him she was okay, that he was okay. "What do you guys want to drink?"

SEVEN

Saturday, May 26, 3:30 PM

After we ate, Davy wanted to practice his backstroke. I wanted to stay and visit with my son, but Eleana said she wanted to take a nap, a very clear hint that I should leave. Davy turned on the television to wait his requisite thirty minutes after eating, so I said good-bye to my ex-family and climbed back into Oma's Cadillac, ready to dash off and save the next distressed damsel on my list.

The first order of business was to define the search. I called Sally's numbers again—townhouse, office, cell—and this time the bayview house at well since she might have come home by now. The same recorded voices answered, mine at the townhouse and bayview house. Then I called Tiny.

"It's Bill. I thought I'd report in."

"Did you find Eleana?"

"Yeah, she was at the house when I arrived. It seems the State Archives had a fire early this morning. She went to check it out. And you'll never guess what burned?"

"What?"

"The Moreno campaign records."

"That's interesting!" Tiny said, clearly impressed with my new information.

"Isn't it though? And you know something else?"

"What?" Tiny asked.

"Moreno was at Stan Cramer's house at Promontory Point last night, for a fund-raising event and poker game."

"How do you know?" Tiny asked.

"Eleana told me."

"Did you get the guest list?"

"Forgot to ask. How far is Stan's place from the limo crash?"

"Less than a mile," Tiny said.

"Isn't that interesting," I said.

"Maybe. So how did Eleana react to Moreno's death?"

"Shocked, dismayed, in tears. What you'd expect. Well, unless you have anything else, I'll get on with my damsel saving."

"You tell her that you danced a jig when you found out it was Moreno?" Tiny persisted.

"That wasn't a jig. It was *Swan Lake*. So I didn't like him. It had nothing to do with Eleana. As you'll recall, I'm the one who switched beds first," I lied. "Nobody else liked him, either. He wasn't a nice man. Ask Oma. But there's something else you should know about his love life."

"I'm warning you. If you say he messed with Mary Louise, I'll have to kill you."

"No, Mary Louise only has eyes for you, Lord knows why. But several years ago Sally and Moreno were close."

"Let me get this straight. Moreno and Sally. You and Eleana. You and Sally. Moreno and Eleana. Isn't that incest?"

"No, it's just complicated."

"You city folk sure know how to screw up your lives."

"We try hard to be all we can be," I said.

"Don't you though," Tiny said. "By the way, you need to know that Cramer has state cops on stakeout at Sally's place in case she shows up there, or you do."

"How do you know that?"

"He was in here a few minutes ago," Tiny answered. "And, believe it or not, he didn't mention a thing about the Archives fire or the party at his house last night."

"Maybe he had other things on his mind."

"Yeah, maybe," Tiny conceded. "But he was pretty insistent we ought to be talking with you again, since they haven't found anyone else who saw anything on the beach, and he knows about Moreno and Eleana."

"You can't expect Eleana to pine over me forever. I moved on. She moved on. No big deal. Why isn't he talking to the beach patrol guys? They saw him first. Or you and Gomez? You saw him next. And I didn't see anything."

"I don't think any of us are newsworthy enough for a state police investigation. You, on the other hand, make good press. 'Former big-time ex-lawyer is suspect in Governor Moreno's death.' Catchy headline, don't you think? He has the state cops looking for you now, except they don't know where to look. He's confused by the fact your Corvette is still at Sally's place."

"Doesn't take much to stump him, does it?"

"Not much," Tiny said. "He tracked you as far as Oma's. She said you left her place on foot, told him you like to take long, solitary walks in the hills, working on your karma. Same story she told me earlier, for practice."

"You didn't rat on me, did you?"

"Come on. I always wear my white hat."

"Glad to hear it. Now, if I were you, I'd start looking for those FBI special agents who were in your back room this morning, or their boss, to see if they want to assist the Splendor Bay PD in this investigation."

"I think we have it under control," Tiny said, offended.

"I have the utmost respect for your cop expertise, Tiny. But somehow, I don't see you, Gomez, and the Chief as having much of a chance against a state police chief who wants to direct the investigation into the cause of the governor's death. Especially since he hasn't been open and honest with you so far. Maybe having the Feds on your team could even the score a little."

"What makes you think the Feds would play on our team?"

"Why not? It's a natural. I've never seen a FBI cop who didn't think he was better than a state cop, and you know how they both pity you local cops. The Feds would get their charity points. Why don't you go nibble on their ears and whisper sweet nothings like violation of civil rights, obstruction of justice, stuff like that. That will give them a hard on, maybe get them lusting after Cramer, maybe get Cramer off my tail."

"I'll have to think about it," Tiny said.

"Do that," I said. "'Bye."

My next stop was Sally's townhouse, and the next problem was getting into it without getting nabbed by the state cops. Oma's Cadillac had darkly tinted windows, so unless I rolled the windows down and stuck my tongue out at them, likely as not, they would miss a drive-by inspection. But actually getting into the townhouse might take more work.

I thought about it and, still being in the driveway, got out of the car and went back into my ex-house.

Eleana was in the kitchen, sipping a glass of milk like it was a dose of castor oil. Davy was outside, playing a one-man game of pool basketball.

"Did you forget something?" she asked.

"Since when did you drink milk?"

"Bill?"

"The box. You mind if I take the pizza box with me?"

"If you need money, I could—"

"I'm not starving, Eleana, I just want the box. And does Davy have a jacket and a baseball cap I can borrow?"

"Bill?" Comprehension entered her eyes. "I guess I don't want to know, do I? Upstairs in his room. Help yourself."

"Thanks," I said as I stared out the French doors at the broad shouldered young man in the pool. "He's a fine boy, Eleana. I want to thank you for that."

"He reminds me of you," she said softly.

And he reminds me of you, I thought, and turned away so she wouldn't see the dew in my eyes.

EIGHT

Saturday, May 26, 4:00 PM

I did a once-around-the-block at Sally's townhouse, twice, to place all the state cops on the stakeout. A standard-issue bubble-gum with two uniformed officers inside was parked so they could watch the alley that ran behind Sally's row of townhouses. An unmarked white Crown Victoria occupied by two cops, one in uniform and one in a suit, was parked across the street from her townhouse. Obviously, Cramer didn't intend his stakeout to be a secret. And he wasn't too concerned about Sally's safety or there would have been more cops, blocking off the street, stroking their guns and battering rams, ready to go in and rescue her.

I pulled the Caddy over to the curb on a side street so I could keep the front-door car in view and thought about the situation. I had intended to play a pizza delivery boy when I borrowed Davy's cap and jacket and the pizza box. Unfortunately, that plan wasn't going to work. Now just how can I make a plain-view entry into the townhouse, I asked myself. Hmm.

Before I could solve that problem, a black Mercedes sedan drove past me and turned into Sally's driveway. Garage doors opened and swallowed it. A minute or two later a dark-haired woman who looked like Sally came out the front door and walked to the mailbox at the iron gate. The two cops in the unmarked car sprang to life and out of the vehicle. At the gate, they flashed their badges and talked with the woman. She invited them inside. Five minutes later, the front-door cops were back out, in their car, driving away.

I had two choices. I could risk detection by getting out of Oma's car and knocking on the front door to find out what

Lizabeth Thorton had just told the state police to satisfy their interest in Sally, or I could wait in Oma's comfortable car listening to Frank Sinatra on the CD until Lizabeth decided to leave, then see if she would lead me to Sister Sally. Actually, I had three choices. I could pick up Oma's cell phone and give the townhouse a ring-a-ding and maybe Lizabeth would answer and tell me where Sally was. I dialed the townhouse. My voice on the answering machine tape answered.

"Talk to me, Sally," I said.

No one did. So I pushed the seat button to recline, turned the volume up as Frank crooned "I Have But One Heart," and waited for Lizabeth to make her next move. While crooning with Frank, it occurred to me that I had met the suited cop somewhere, but I couldn't remember where.

Ten minutes later, after Frank and I had crooned three more songs, I noticed the curtain at the living room window flutter. Another five minutes and the curtain in the front upstairs bedroom moved. It would seem Lizabeth was checking to make sure the cops were gone.

A couple of minutes later, the garage regurgitated the Mercedes and it headed out in the direction it had come. The bubble-gum copmobile pulled out of the alley and followed. In the next block, the unmarked car pulled out from a side street and got into line. I joined the parade to Lizabeth Thorton's house, a small mansion on Grandview Avenue, where the old-line, longtime, rich people live.

The Solana twins definitely qualified as old-line, longtime rich. For three hundred years after their Conquistador ancestor's arrival, the Solanas gathered and held onto wealth in the form of great tracts of land that grew grapes and sheep. Their great-grandfather replenished the family coffer with money made from railroads that crossed the land. Their grandfather made more money from oil wells on the land. Their father and his half-brother—my almost ex-wife Eleana's father—had rested on the family laurels and done their best to spend everything left them on worthwhile things like polo ponies and Hollywood starlets and world travel. Fortunately, the grandfather had left the principal of his wealth in trust funds for the next generation.

The Solana women, my almost-ex Eleana and her cousins, Lizabeth and Sally, were all exceptional women. Lizabeth and Sally, as beautiful as their movie star mom, and as willful as two Scarlett O'Haras, had more money than any two women could spend in any lifetime. Still, they tried, especially Lizabeth who had very expensive hobbies.

In her youth, Lizabeth studied art, then occupied her time with society affairs and traveling the world with her much older and much less genteel husband, Chester Thorton, a man she had run away with then married to spite her father. During her travels, Lizabeth acquired art, some of it good, all of it expensive. The Solana-Thorton house was filled with the stuff, which was one reason the Solana-Thortons employed a stable of security guards to keep lesser mortals away from their premises.

Lizabeth and Chester were an interesting study in modern marriage. Chester, a cowboy archetype who used his slow-talking Texan demeanor to disguise his Harvard Law brains, managed Lizabeth's money very well, which kept him fairly busy. Twenty years ago theirs had been a sparky May-December match. They met and fell in love at Eleana's and my wedding. Soon thereafter, Chester left a wife nobody liked and Lizabeth left a too-controlling father for a resorts-of-the-world *Lolita* adventure, covered in great detail in the press. However, in time, all good scandals fizzle. She turned eighteen, they married, and lived reasonably happily ever after for quite a few years.

These days, Lizabeth and Chester were more niece and uncle to each other than wife and husband. Each was still fond of the other, but Chester, being mostly too old for desires of the flesh, didn't pay much attention to which bedroom Lizabeth slept in, or so he had once told me one night after our third round of drinks at Fred's. Chester was lying. Men don't get that old. He resented the hell out of Lizabeth's activities, but he knew if he tried to do anything about it, he would be the one left out in the cold. She graced his arm in public and gave him a loose reign in managing her money, but it was her money, and he was, after all, hired help.

Sister Sally, my recent very good friend, the younger by two minutes and more feisty sister, had studied law and taken up politics, an equally expensive hobby, and an equally rebellious act to a father who preferred women to be arm decorations. Her ambition was to use her current job as the state's first female attorney general as a stepping stone to a term or two as governor, then run for the US Senate. Eventually, when she reached an age where she wasn't viewed as a sexual object, she said, which was still a few years off in my own view of the situation, she would run for President.

Sally had been too focused on her career until recently to acquire a husband so, at age thirty-seven, she was still a single lady. She hoped to change that, she had told me the previous night before she left our bed. She thought I would make her a fine wife since I no longer had any interest in having a career, made a great omelet, and could be cleaned up enough to take out to thousand-dollar-a-plate fund-raising dinners. At least that's what she said when she proposed, before she got teed-off and left when I didn't jump at her offer of a lifetime pension as would be spelled out in a prenuptial agreement.

Don't get me wrong, I love Sally's fine analytical, lawyer mind, almost as much as I love her petite, curvaceous physique. A good battle of wits is definitely a turn-on, and the pension she offered didn't sound bad. I just wasn't into long-term commitments anymore.

But, enough about sex and marriage. After waiting fifteen minutes for the cops to do something, which they didn't, I called Tiny again, to see if he could find out why the state cops had left Sally's place contented.

"I have a dilemma," I said when he answered.

"Moral or otherwise?"

"I'm parked down the street from the Thorton's Grandview Avenue manor, and I was just wondering."

"About what?"

"What Lizabeth told the state cops to get them to abandon their stakeout at Sally's." I told Tiny about Lizabeth's visit to Sally's townhouse. If Lizabeth was calling off the woman-hunt, she wasn't that worried about her sister's whereabouts. "I sort of wanted to know before I go knock on Lizabeth's door. To see if I get the same story."

"Give me a few minutes. I'll call you back."

Sinatra sang "My Way" again. I sang along. We crooned two more songs. I was about to experiment with the Cadillac's control panel to see if I could turn off the music without shutting down the engine and AC when Tiny called back.

"The story is the state cops think they talked with Sally, who explained she left you in bed sleeping to take her Jaguar to the shop for repairs, and then she borrowed her sister's car. They bought it, agreed to come to her office on Monday for a formal statement."

"That's interesting."

"Isn't it though? Now Cramer can concentrate all his effort on finding you."

"I thought you said Sally alibied me."

"Lizabeth, pretending to be Sally, alibied you," Tiny said, "but Cramer wants to know what you did after Sally left you sleeping and before Moreno was found."

"We've covered that."

"Yeah, but he's got this theory you were so enraged when Sally left you that you decided to take a run on the beach to get it out of your system, encountered Wallie who just happened to be there for reasons unknown, and scared him to death or drowned him or something. Whatever Wallie died of, Cramer thinks you did it. Didn't I tell you all that exercise shit would get you into trouble?"

"He wants to keep Sally in his sights, too," I said. "He has two cars watching Lizabeth's abode. I guess if I can prove I didn't do it, he'll try to pin it on Sally."

"Maybe he thinks Sally is visiting her sister and he's just looking out for her welfare. After all, he wouldn't want both a dead governor and a dead AG on his hands the same day."

"Maybe," I said as I shifted the Caddy into drive. "See what you can do to keep Cramer confused. I want to talk with Lizabeth before she takes off again."

"Oh, before you hang up, did you ask Eleana about Stan's poker-party guest list?"

"No, but I plan on stopping by later to see if Davy wants to go to a movie or something. I'll ask her then."

"Beep me when you get it. I'm going to visit the coroner, see if he has any opinions on Moreno's cause of death. "

"Have you given any thought to calling the FBI?"

"Yeah," said Tiny.

"And?"

"Not yet. Let's see how far Cramer goes."

"As long as he doesn't go after me," I said. "'Bye."

I left my protected spot and headed for the Thorton's driveway. I saluted the security guard at the gatehouse.

Apparently he recognized me as being an approved visitor on the photo ID chart inside his booth because he opened the gates and waved me through without checking with the master or mistress.

I drove up the long, curving driveway around to the kitchen entrance in back, hoping the cops parked out on the street hadn't been able to get a clear view of my tags.

On my walk through the house from the kitchen following behind the maid (not a bad experience since she's a pretty maid), I remembered where I'd seen the suited state cop in the unmarked Crown Vic. He had been one of the security guards at the Thorton's Texas ranch last fall when Chester and I played great white hunters while Sally and Lizabeth shopped for new clothes in Paris. He probably moonlighted as a guard to supplement his public servant salary, as many cops do.

"Hello, Lizabeth," I said when the maid ushered me into the Thorton's drawing room, which was twice as large as the whole house I rented at the beach.

"Bill?" she said in that lilting voice so similar to Sally's, giving my first name three syllables. "So nice to see you. Why are you in town?"

"Well, I'd intended to see if Sally was in residence at her townhouse and the most interesting thing happened."

"What was that, Bill?"

"This lady, who looks like Sally, even wore her hair pulled back the way Sally does, drove into Sally's garage. Next thing I know she's out front talking with the state police who were there looking for Sally."

"Then Sally must be at home," Lizabeth said.

"I don't think so," I said. "Because not long after some of the cops left, this Sally-looking person left in your Mercedes."

"And you think it was me?"

"Lizabeth, I know it was you. I followed you here. I want to know what you told the cops."

"I see," she said.

"Well?"

She turned away from me to walk over to the window to assess her grounds. "Sally called me this morning. She thought the police might be at her place and asked me to pretend I was her, see if I could get rid of them. She said she'd be back in town on Monday and would deal with them then."

"Lizabeth," I said. "Do me a favor."

"Certainly, Bill."

"Look me in the eyes. Tell me Sally's okay."

Lizabeth turned her dark eyes in my direction and sighed. "She called around eight. She said she was okay and asked me to go to the townhouse and . . . she said she'd explain everything later. On the way back I heard the news on the car radio about Wallie. You don't think?"

"I don't know," I said, thinking maybe I should listen to Oma's car radio to see what was going on in the world.

"What are you going to do, Bill?"

"I'm going to keep looking for her, of course."

"Bill, be careful," Lizabeth said, sounding exactly like Sally. But the sisters were identical twins. Almost. The only difference I had ever been able to detect was a little mole above Lizabeth's lip and a small birthmark on Sally's thigh, in a location only her doctor or a very close friend would notice. Come to think of it, I'd never checked to see if Lizabeth had one there, too. So maybe the only difference was the little mole above Lizabeth's lip.

"Oh," I said as I turned to leave, "just in case you want to keep this game going, a couple of cop cars followed you here. They're parked across the street. You might want to stay put so they'll continue thinking Sally is visiting her sister. And I'd warn the guards about letting any strangers in, with or without a warrant."

"I'll keep that in mind."

"And Lizabeth?"

"Yes?"

"Were you at your beach house last night?"

"No. I've been in town all week."

"She called you here and not at the beach house?"

"Yes, why?

"Nothing," I said, wondering if she was lying to me. Oma told me Chester had said Sally called her sister at the beach house. But there was nothing to be gained by cross-examining Lizabeth now, so I left. As I was showing myself out, I ran into Chester Thorton coming into the house.

Chester extended his hand. "Howdy, Bill. To what do we owe the honor?"

Chester had an English country squire look about him, which was disconcerting since he sounded just like John Wayne playing cowboy. Chester had been a real charmer twenty years ago, when he and Lizabeth played the staring roles in their home movie version of *Lolita*. In fact, I've known him most of my life, and I'm charmed by him, too. Chester is one of my favorite human beings on earth, a man's man, whatever that used to be—a hunter, a fisherman, a TV-football viewer—and a woman's man as well, one of those guys who always held the door for his lady, walked on the outside of the sidewalk, remembered birthdays with flowers and diamond trinkets, and kissed his wife in public places for no reason at all except he loved her. Chester really, truly loved Lizabeth, all the time. Best I could tell, she loved him when she felt like it.

"What are you doing here?" I asked.

Chester glanced around. "I live here. I should be asking you that question."

"No, I mean, Oma said you came by her place for breakfast this morning. I just assumed you were out at the beach today."

"Oh, I was. Got some fishing in earlier. But I had business in town. So, what are you doing here?"

"Visiting your wife," I said.

"Really?" Chester raised his ample eyebrows.

"I thought she might tell me where to find Sally."

"Did she?" Chester asked, stroking his mostly salt, neatly trimmed salt-and-pepper beard.

"Not yet." I said.

"I presume you've heard about Moreno?"

"What about him?"

"He met his Maker," Chester said.

"Couldn't have happened to a nicer guy," I remarked.

"So I hear," Chester said engaging my brown eyes with his own sky-blues. "Anything you need to talk to me about?"

"Not unless you know where Sally is," I said, irritated that Chester might think I needed to talk with a lawyer.

It really bothered me that the people who knew me best considered me capable of murder. Oma, Fred, Eleana, and Chester had all considered that possibility straight off. Their number one theory, in fact. Maybe they suspected I was as crazy as I acted. And maybe I was. At least Tiny hadn't asked me if I'd killed Moreno.

Chester shrugged a "no," and I continued to the door. That was probably a mistake on my part.

NINE

Saturday, May 26, 5:30 PM

I was at the Thorton's driveway gates when I remembered I'd forgotten to ask Chester about the guards on our hunting trip last fall. My irritation at his implication that I needed legal help had cleared all questions from my mind. I hadn't asked about the details of his inquiry into Sally's whereabouts, either. I was reasonably sure that he hadn't found her or he would have told me, which was all I really needed to know. I'd worry about whose story about who had phoned whom was the correct version later. Right now, I needed to get on with finding Sally.

When I swung out of the driveway and headed toward town, the bubble-gum car followed. I meandered around the leisurely laid-out neighborhood streets, then through a couple of shopping centers at the edge of the residential area. I drove like Oma—in the left lane, below the speed limit, frequent abrupt stops at green lights. I lost the cops, or they'd had enough of my senior-citizen driving style, before I got to downtown. Nearing my destination, I picked up the car phone to call Oma.

"Bill? Where are you?"

"Center City."

"You're not in trouble, are you?"

"No, Oma, I'm not in trouble."

"Is Eleana okay?"

"She's fine. She went to her office and forgot to tell Davy."

"Did you find Sally?"

"Not yet," I said, "but I'm working on it."

"That mean Mr. Cramer came here looking for you."

"I know," I said. "Tiny told me."

"Those awful TV newspeople came, too. Asking so many questions. And so noisy! Like geese."

"You didn't talk to them, did you?"

"No, no. They asked in English. I only understand German. They stopped asking."

"That's one way to handle them, I guess."

"Be careful, Bill."

"Don't worry. I'm always careful."

I spent the next couple of hours checking out the places where Sally and I had been together in the city—the hotel where we had once spent a very warm cold winter night, the restaurants and bars where she bought me dinners and drinks.

The whole time I was desperately seeking Sally, I mulled over the differences in Chester's and Lizabeth's stories about their phone conversations with Sally. Chester had told Oma that Sally called her sister "very early" at the Thorton's beach house, which I'd interpreted as when she left our bed before dawn. Lizabeth had said Sally called her at their Center City house around eight. Both could be true, or both could be lies, or one could be an interpretation of the other.

I put that question on the list of things to ask Sally about when I found her. Then I went into my favorite hole-in-the-wall where Sally and I went for burgers and beer after the society affairs she attended to smooch her campaign contributors. Sally smooched a lot, so I'd gotten to know the bartender quite well. You can't go wrong with a bartender named Moe.

"Howyadoin', Bill?" Moe asked, acting glad to see a paying customer. Sally always paid my tab promptly at the first of the month, including a nice tip for Moe.

"Fine," I said.

"Usual?"

"Usual." I grabbed a stool at the bar where I could watch the comings and goings in the mirror behind the liquor selection. There didn't seem to be much coming or going at six-thirty p.m., too late for the five-martini-lunch crowd, not the right day for the just-one-for-the-road-after-work crowd, and too early for the before-and-after-soirée-movers-and-shakers crowd. Just Moe and me, and the cook and two waitresses at a booth in the back corner eating their early suppers before the soirée crowd started dropping by for their before-party drinks.

"Whatdaya hear?" Moe asked as he served my two fingers of Scotch *sans* soda.

"Not much," I said.

"There's been a lot of talk about Moreno goin' around."

"Really? Hadn't heard."

"Yeah," Moe said, "it's a mystery... how he died. The popular vote of the lunch trade says it was a drug hit."

"Nah," I said, "too simple."

"The minority vote has it his campaign contributors didn't think he was giving them much bang for their bucks," Moe said. "Those guys what spend the big money expect to make money. Know what I mean?"

"Yeah, I know," I said. "If I gave anything to get somebody elected, I'd expect more than a handshake."

"Me, too," said Moe.

"Isn't that the essence of most campaign speeches. 'Vote for me. I'm pretty and I'm smart. I'll tax all the other people and give it to you.' Politicians don't deliver, you get rid of 'em."

"Right," said Moe. "'Course, if I were one of those gays dying with AIDS anyway, why not take Wallie with me?"

"There you have it," I said.

"Then's there's the splinter-faction," Moe said.

"What's that?" I asked.

"He was messin' around with the wrong man's wife," Moe said, looking me in the eyes. "For a man his age, he was real peppy, know what I mean?"

"That's an interesting thought. You haven't seen Sally today have you? We were supposed to meet at her place and she's not there. I thought maybe she went into work, might have stopped in for a bite to eat."

"Haven't seen her. Light traffic in here today, always is on Saturdays. I get a few of them eager-beaver government types at lunch. Not many. Not that many eager-beaver government types to begin with. Fire at the Archives must have sent 'em home early. You tried her office?"

"The switchboard's down. And if she doesn't want to be disturbed, she won't answer her cell phone."

"Ain't that the way with women?" Moe said.

"Yeah, it sure is," I said.

"That reminds me," Moe said, "Ol' Chester Thorton was in here earlier. You might should talk to him."

"Why?" I asked.

"He was looking for Sally, too."

"Oh." I drained my glass. "Sally and Lizabeth probably took off shopping and left both Chester and me in the lurch."

"Yeah, ain't that the way with women?" Moe said.

I supposed it was possible Lizabeth had sent Chester on the rounds to find her sister, but it seemed strange she hadn't mentioned it when she knew I was in search mode. And Chester hadn't mentioned it either when I ran into him. I put talking to Chester and Lizabeth again, separately, on my mental list.

Then I drove to my ex-house, a few blocks away from Lizabeth's mansion, in the slightly lower-rent section of the same high-rent district, to see if Davy wanted to take in a movie. And to talk Eleana into letting me borrow one of her cars, just in case the state cops had figured out Oma wasn't the one driving her Cadillac today. I'd feel better knowing I wouldn't get pulled over because my tags had been flagged for future reference in the cop computer.

It was a good thing I stopped off at my ex-house. Eleana and Davy needed me.

TEN

Saturday, May 26, 7:30 PM

Davy answered the door and seemed pleased to see me again. "You want to go to a movie?" I asked.

"I'd better not," he said. "Mom's sleeping. I'd better hang around, in case she needs me."

"Oh," I said to the man of the house, "you think she would mind if we visited awhile?"

"I have steaks thawing. Thought I'd surprise Mom and make dinner. Want to help?"

"Love to," I said and followed him to the kitchen. I mixed a pitcher of sangria and one of lemonade while Davy started the grill. We sipped our drinks, sangria for me, lemonade for him, talking about nothing more important than which baseball teams had the best prospects while watching black charcoal bricks turn white. I had just walked back inside to get the meat when Eleana came downstairs and caught me in her kitchen.

"You again?"

I looked around in mock curiosity to see who she might be speaking to and smiled. "I guess it must be."

The girl that I married smiled back at me. We were both embarrassed by the moment and looked away.

She declared a truce. "I'll make the salad. Garlic bread?"

"Yeah."

"Put a couple of potatoes in the microwave for you and Davy. The salad will be all I need. Bill?"

"Yes."

"I'm glad you came back." Her eyes, at the moment a liquid turquoise, met mine.

I nodded. My throat hurt. From swallowing my pride.

***

The sun, nestled in orange and gray strips of sky, settled below the trees while we ate. Courting insects in the stand of trees at the edge of the backyard sang backup to Davy as he filled us in on his life—which teachers were screwing with his mind, which guys were driving what wheels, where various classmates were going to college, a girl who was the smartest, prettiest girl he'd ever met but didn't know he existed, yet.

It felt good listening to my son talk as he planned his happy-ever-after life, while I pretended I was still part of his life. I wished the evening would last forever. But wishes are all too often like unicorns that gallop away in the night sky chasing after memories filled with regret.

Too soon, the food was gone and Davy was talked out. I knew I should leave, but Eleana wasn't hinting, and the sangria had robbed me of my willpower. I held my tenuous place in the family circle. Finally, Eleana looked at her watch and I put my glass down.

"You can sleep in the pool house," she said.

I looked at her, questioning that I'd heard her right.

"I mean, you don't need another drunk-driving charge."

"Thanks," I said curtly, not sure I was up to facing the bed in the pool house tonight, or that I appreciated her insinuation. One failed breath test and a joy ride on an isolated stretch of beach road do not an alcoholic make, at least not in my self-serving mind.

I knew alcoholic. My father had taught me everything there was to know on the subject. I wasn't one, not yet. I drank on purpose, to kill the pain in my soul, not because I couldn't stop.

"You want to play a game of pool ball, Dad?" Davy asked as he gave Eleana a thank-you smile for asking me to stay.

I glanced at her.

She nodded and smiled.

"I guess I need to borrow some trunks."

"There's an extra pair of mine in the pool house," Davy volunteered.

"Go tend to your medication first," Eleana said to Davy, looking at her watch again.

I checked mine as well. Ten-fifteen already. He should have given himself an injection at ten.

Davy sighed and gave Eleana that look, the one that made me wish I could take the shot for him. Then he took off for the house and I headed for the pool house. I found trunks and changed without turning on the inside light. I didn't want to see the room.

When I came back from changing, Eleana was clearing the patio table and Davy was waiting for me. She waved at us as we headed for the deep end of the pool for our ritual dive and race.

I reached the shallow end and looked up, panting. She called out, "Your son won."

Davy gave me a high-five, dove again, and pulled me under. Then the serious game of pool ball began, my pride at issue.

It's no contest between a forty-six-year-old man and a sixteen-year-old boy. Youth and vigor win every time in anything but a battle of wits. There, age and conniving and mistrust have the edge. I pulled my worn body out of the pool and into the heated spa, hoping to avoid muscle cramps in the morning.

Eleana had finished in the kitchen and changed into a swimsuit while we were playing ball. She slipped into the pool to swim laps with Davy. A few minutes later Davy said good night, giving us one of his "you two play nice" looks.

"Would you do me a favor?" I asked him.

"Sure, Dad. What?"

"The keys are in my pants pocket. Would you pull Oma's car into the garage for me?"

"Sure."

"And Oma's gun is in the glove compartment. Get it out and put it in the drawer by the range in the kitchen."

Eleana glared at me from the pool, but said nothing. We'd had that argument before. She didn't like guns, and she definitely didn't want Davy handling one.

I heard the car start, the garage door open and shut, then the kitchen door slam. Davy dropped the gun in the drawer, brought my keys back and retreated into the house, supposedly to study for an exam. Still unsure of my continuing welcome, I stayed put and watched Eleana's graceful moves through the water. She swam like a young Esther Williams.

My almost ex-wife was beautiful, youthful, every middle-aged man's dream. But, as I watched her swim, I realized she was even more gorgeous than the vision I carried in my mind's eye. She seemed fuller of figure than a few months before. Not that she'd gained weight. She just had more of the right stuff in the right places. She must have been using some of her single-lady time working out at the gym, I mused.

After a few more laps, she slipped out of the pool and into the spa across from me, careful that none of our body parts touched. For a long time neither of us said anything, my eyes on the stars, her eyes closed.

She sighed, then said politely, "Thank you for coming."

"I should go," I interpreted.

"No," she said quickly. "You don't have to go."

"Eleana, I—"

"There's no reason for you to drive back tonight."

"Oh," I said.

"I mean… your being here makes me feel better. It keeps me from thinking about things I would rather not think about."

"I'm sorry, Eleana. I really am. I know he meant something to you, and I'm sorry you've been hurt."

Eleana looked into my eyes. She must have decided I was telling the truth. "Well," she said as she stood up to climb out of the spa, "the bed in there is made. If you need anything, you have a key to the house."

I watched her walk into the kitchen and lock the French doors. She punched in the alarm code beside the doors, waved at me before turning off the downstairs lights, and disappeared up the back stairs to our ex-bedroom.

I got out of the spa and stared at my former house. I missed Davy. I hurt for Eleana. And tonight, as I listened to a siren in the distance, I missed moonlight on the bay, waves crashing on the beach. I didn't miss this house or the life I'd lived to earn it. I didn't miss doing battle with anyone for anyone else's life, liberty, or pursuit of unjust gains. With any luck, I told myself, this whole mess will go away. With any luck, my life sentence to the quagmire of the criminal justice system had been commuted to time served by that great governor in the sky.

What had seemed so easy when my father did it had always been hard for me. The lawyer's professional-code duty to protect the secrets of the guilty who pay the fee placed above the duty to seek justice had always been the grit of sand in my oyster shell. Like the oyster, I had covered that bit of dirt with secretions from my insides, trying to make it look like a gem stone. But I always knew it was dirt inside my imitation of a pearl. Maybe my father had as well. Perhaps that had been one of the reasons he drank. The smallest one. My smallest reason, too.

My suspension would be over in two days. The new license was probably already in the mail, and I was filled with dread, filled with the loss of my freedom. I doubted I could ever play lawyer again, at least not the way I had, or for any reason I had before. But with the license in hand. I'd be out of excuses, unless I clung to the illusion of incapacity by reason of a soggy brain. And it was an illusion. I didn't act like a drunk because of the alcohol. The alcohol was my cover for acting like a drunk.

The answer was clear. My goals were simple now. I wanted Davy at the beach with me, for whatever time was left of his youth. For the coming summer, if he would agree, and weekends in the fall. Which meant I couldn't continue this façade of a drunk. Davy deserved more.

For now, I would think about practicing law again in the fall, maybe keep an apartment in Center City so I could see more of Davy during the week, practice in some speciality other than criminal defense, maybe a little boutique practice in probate law so all I had to deal with were dead clients and a little paperwork. That would pay the bills for my downsized lifestyle and give me the time to look for the pieces of my soul that had been lost in too many skirmishes with Lady Justice, battles where Lawyer Bill Glasscock had worn the black hat and won.

I stood in the door of the pool house and looked back at the home where my son slept, at the home I had left behind. I would talk with Eleana. Maybe she would agree to share Davy without a battle. Maybe all the battles were over, if I would let them be.

With that consoling thought in mind, I closed the door on my ex-life, changed wet swim trunks for dry briefs, and climbed into the bed where I had found Wallie Moreno making love to my wife. Again I rejoiced in the fact that the bastard was dead.

Falling into a fitful sleep, I saw Eleana's sensual face in the passion of their lovemaking, then her face of fear when she saw me in the doorway watching her betrayal. In my dream, I heard her cries of passion. And I heard the gun, the one I would have fired had it been in my hand when I found them together.

Only I hadn't fired a gun. Then her scream of terror brought me fully awake as I realized that the sound of gunfire had come from the house.

Through the French doors, I saw Davy and a man in a black jogging suit struggling over a gun.

I ran across the yard, crashed through the glass doors, and knocked the gun from grasping hands, breaking Davy free of the intruder.

I grabbed the man's gun as I picked myself up off the floor.

The man backed away. He was almost out the door when a gun fired. His startled eyes met mine.

Then he looked down at his crimson chest and fell silently to the floor amid the shattered glass of the French doors.

I looked at the gun in my hand, bewildered.

Davy dropped Oma's gun.

Eleana ran to him, pulling our son into her arms. "It's okay, Davy. It's okay," she said, rocking him in her arms. "It's okay, baby. It's okay."

I felt for a pulse.

The man was dead.

ELEVEN

Saturday, May 26, 11:00 PM

I checked the house to make sure no one else was there. Then I moved my family upstairs to the master suite and went back to the kitchen. I wiped my prints from the dead man's gun and placed it in his right hand, hoping I'd remembered correctly which one he'd used to hold the gun when struggling with Davy. I left Oma's gun on the floor where Davy had dropped it.

Returning to the bedroom, I called 911. "Lock the door after me. I'm going to the pool house to get dressed."

"Please, don't leave us," Eleana pleaded. "You still have clothes here." Her eyes darted to my ex-closet.

I dashed to the closet, surprised to see all my stuff still there. Tailored suits lined up on a side wall, shirts and ties and sports attire facing them. On the end wall, glistening shoes were neatly racked next to drawers containing socks and underwear. I'd never asked for my stuff, expecting she would have donated it to a charity immediately. My clothes were too big for Wallie to fill.

"How's he doing?" I asked as I came back to the bedroom, tucking a starched white shirt into suit slacks, looking first to Eleana, then to our son. Davy was shivering, even with a comforter and Eleana's arms around him.

I examined his eyes. Dilated. Shock. Davy had just taken his insulin injection, so my fear was that his blood sugar had plunged. A diabetic's blood sugar can drop in times of stress, leading to shock, then a coma, then death if it drops too low. The sugar in juice could bring the level back into balance.

"You need juice?"

Davy shook his head and stared at me from the distant place killing another human being had taken him.

"Listen, Davy," I said, holding his face in my hands, looking into his eyes, willing him to hear me. "The police will be here soon. They'll ask lots of questions. They may even take you downtown. But you don't have to say anything to them, not now, not ever. And I don't want you talking to them without me in the room. You understand?"

Davy nodded.

"I'll handle everything. Do you understand?"

Davy burst into tears. "Daddy? Did I kill him?"

I sat down on the bed on the other side of my son and pulled Davy and Eleana into my arms. He hadn't called me Daddy since he was ten. And he probably hadn't cried since then, either. I met Eleana's eyes. The fear I saw was a mirror of my own, fear for our child that immediately united us.

Anger replaced my fear, a killing anger at the man for invading our home and doing this to our son. But I needed to put the anger aside, concentrate on helping my son, work through the story we would tell the police.

"Davy acted in self defense, and in defense of another, to save your life," I said to Eleana, "a justifiable homicide in every sense of the word."

"Yes, he was defending us," Eleana repeated. "Davy had no choice. That's what happened."

"That's exactly what happened," I said, and clearly so now that the dead man held a gun. Yes, that would be our story.

But I knew from bitter experience that wouldn't be the end of it. Justified or not, Davy would never get over killing another human being. And, justified or not, there would always be some son-of-a-bitch cop or prosecutor who wanted to make a name for him- or herself, and going after my son would get press coverage. But Davy wouldn't be just another notch on a power-trip belt, I vowed. Not if I could help it.

"It's okay, son. You only did what you had to do to protect your mother. Do you understand me? Whatever happened, he brought it on himself."

"I don't think he was a burglar," Eleana said.

"What?" Then it dawned on me what she was saying. "Do you know who he is?"

She nodded. "He's one of Wallie's guards, in the backup car that follows the limo. His name is Andrew Block."

"Who's his partner?"

"Mike, Mike Sartin."

I pretended a calm I didn't feel. Block and Sartin were the cops who had car trouble while Wallie died. And Sartin was still out there. Eleana and Davy might still be in danger.

"Tell me what happened."

"I came downstairs for a glass of milk, thinking it would help me sleep. He grabbed me from behind. I jerked away and screamed. Davy appeared and they struggled. When the gun went off, I thought he'd shot Davy. Then you came crashing through the door and brought him down. You know the rest."

I nodded.

"Bill, if you hadn't been here, he'd have killed us."

At that moment, the sirens turned into the driveway. No time for questions. And no more time to worry about Sartin. The battle for Lady Justice's hand had begun.

"What I told Davy goes for you. Don't say anything to anybody if I'm not with you, and don't answer any questions if I don't say it's okay. Don't say anything except, 'Talk to my lawyer.' I'll give them a statement."

Eleana nodded, her eyes wide with apprehension.

"The house will be swarming with cops and they'll want to take samples of everything. They'll probably trash the place. Cooperate. We'll clean up later. Now, I'm going down to open the front door for them. You lock this door and don't let anyone in until I tell you it's okay. Get on the phone, call Tiny, tell him to get here with the FBI just as soon as he can. Understand?"

Eleana spoke in a trembling voice. "Make it go away, Bill. Make it go away."

"I'll try. Believe me, I'll try."

TWELVE

Sunday, May 27, 1:00 AM

Two hours later an Assistant ME had pronounced Andrew Block dead as of eleven o'clock p.m., my estimate of the time of the shooting. The meat wagon had carted the body off to the morgue. The bullet in the kitchen ceiling and the two guns had been bagged as evidence. The Center City CSU criminalists had taken swabs of Davy's and Eleana's and my hands and faces and confiscated Davy's pajamas for gun powder residue tests. The cops had wrecked various parts of the house for reasons unknown. I personally think cops like to trash houses.

We cooperated fully in the evidence gathering, but when the cop-in-charge realized I had no intention of letting him question my wife and son, the bickering began. The hostilities escalated when I threatened to sue him, individually as well as the city and county, for any harm that came to Davy as the result of improper medical attention. After a little face-saving huffing and puffing, the cop agreed to settle for my statement. Cops don't like being sued any better than anyone else.

The cop-in-charge asked me bad-cop questions and I smart-mouthed him back. Wanda Bodansky, a very pregnant Center County Assistant DA who had shown up an hour into the event, stood back and kept score. A slight smile played on her sleep-deprived face as she crossed her arms over her full pregnancy in an odd mixture of "yes" and "no" body language, which I took as, "I don't care who wins; I just want to go back to bed."

When the cop threatened to arrest Davy, I barked louder. "Any fool, even you, can see this is a plain and simple break and enter, as clear a case of self-defense as it comes. I doubt any grand jury would think otherwise. If you were half the cop you think you are, you'd be out finding this guy's partner before he kills somebody else."

On that note, Tiny arrived with reinforcements. "Ease up, Bill," Tiny said, announcing his presence with a hand around my arm like he was trying to restrain me from violence, but his body language saying to the city cop, "You mess with my friend here, you mess with me."

The barking cop stared up at Tiny, then took a step back. Then the other local cops parted like the Red Sea for Moses as FBI suits moved into the room. An older Fed came to a stop center stage, between me and the bad-cop city cop, and glanced around. "Who's in charge?"

"I am," the city cop answered with a mental hoisting of his pants barely more discrete than Gomez's physical Barney-Fife.

The Fed glared at him, then said softly and firmly so that there was no mistaking the territorial challenge, "No, I am. Name is George Wertheim. What might your name be, Officer?"

"Carson," he spat, like a kitten challenging a Doberman. "Hank Carson, Detective, Center City Homicide. This is a local matter. Back off and let me do my job."

Wertheim moved into finger-poking-chest distance. "The shooting victim is a state cop, one of Moreno's guard squad who screwed-up and let him get killed. That makes it my job."

Carson backed up a step. "But this break-in-related shooting happened within the city limits of Center City. That's my turf."

Wertheim moved in nose-to-nose. "The FBI is very concerned that there's obstruction of justice brewing here. The very presence of a member of the state police in a private home in circumstances indicating he was involved in the commission of a felony certainly makes it a Federal concern. You and the entire Center City police force and Center County DA's office will cooperate fully with my agents or you will leave here this instant. You understand?"

Carson and Wertheim eyed each other. Tiny, Bodanzky, and I watched. Bodanzky yawned. I gave Tiny my "twenty-bucks on Wertheim" look.

Tiny gave me his "what kind of fool do you think I am?" raised eyebrows.

We both could see how this was going down. Big fish eat little fish.

"Okay," Carson conceded. "Let's go outside."

Bodanzky hoisted the strap of her briefcase to her shoulder and headed for the door. She knew as well as I did this wasn't going any further than the station house regardless of who wanted to get their name on TV, and obviously she had more important things to do. Like sleep.

While the local cops and Feds cooperated, I huddled with Tiny. "What's going on?"

"I took your advice. Wertheim started the search for this guy's partner, Sartin, the minute he heard the ID. Those two were in the car that didn't follow Moreno last night. Wertheim has this idea they might be involved in his death."

"You think?"

"Eleana ever tell you anything about the poker party?"

"We haven't had time to chat. This Block person broke in and attacked Eleana when she came down to the kitchen for a glass of milk. Davy heard her scream and came to her defense."

"And you did what?"

"I heard gunfire and came to help Davy. In the ruckus, Block got shot. A simple justified killing of a burglar."

Tiny raised both eyebrows.

"Honest," I babbled on. "Eleana was scared half out of her mind. Davy was in shock after it happened, and I was busy calling 911. No time for a family conference."

I glanced over at the drying blood where Block's body had been. "A man breaks into a house, he ought to get shot."

Tiny pursed his lips and stared at me like a card shark eyeing a crooked dealer. He and I both knew the facts might look odd, but they couldn't prove Davy didn't fire Oma's gun in self-defense. Block's gun had been fired. It was in his hand. And mine was the only version of the story, unless I'd screwed up and left my prints on his gun or put it in the wrong hand.

Tiny glanced down at my bare feet and grinned. "You staying here tonight? I mean, after I get everybody out of your house?"

I shrugged. As long as he was buying my story, he could think what he wanted. "I'm not sure they're safe here."

"Pack 'em up," Tiny said. "I'll take care of things here."

"Thanks, big guy."

"Think nothing of it. If I didn't spend half my time saving your ass, I might not feel needed." Tiny eyed my feet again. "You might want to find a pair of shoes before you step on a piece of glass. If you can remember which bed they're under."

I smiled my Super Stud smile. Then I remembered my other mission. "Has anyone located Sally?"

"Why? You got another date tonight?"

"Have you found her?"

"Gomez went door to door along Cliff Road. No one's seen her. The state cops let up on their search when Lizabeth sold them that bill of goods, so I was hoping you might have found her. But it looks like you've been busy."

"I checked our old hangouts this afternoon. If she's in Center City, she's doing a good job of being invisible."

Just then, Eleana appeared at the top of the stairs.

"Well, I guess you need to take care of your family," Tiny said. "The other is something we can talk about later."

THIRTEEN

Sunday, May 27, 3:30 AM

We arrived at my beach shack in the wee hours of Sunday morning. Davy stumbled onto the daybed in the small room that served as my office and was asleep before I closed the door. That left Eleana and me to decide who got the bed in the bedroom and who got the sofa. Being a gentleman, I offered the lady my bed. Being a lady, Eleana took it.

I had just spread a blanket on the sofa when she came back to the living room in her gown, a low cut, clingy, white silk number that made me remember again what I had lost.

She didn't say anything until she was sure she had my full attention. I met her eyes, now a dark bluish green in the low-watt lamp light.

"Please, this once, Bill. Hold me so I can fall asleep."

"That wouldn't be a good idea."

She smiled. "When did you ever let that stop you?"

I followed her with my eyes as she disappeared into the bedroom leaving the door open.

Then my body followed her to my bed.

I awoke at dawn with Eleana in my arms, feeling my world was whole again. Then I remembered why she was in my bed.

I was her security blanket to keep the Wallie demon away, just a warm port in her new storm. We hadn't made love. She hadn't asked me to do that. She had only asked me to hold her so she could sleep. My pride wouldn't let me do anything more, although the wrestling match with my desire lasted long after she had fallen asleep. I had pinned desire to the mat where it simmered in fretful sleep, rising again unbidden as I woke to her warm softness.

I knew from the silence that Davy was still sleeping, and felt comforted that he could. Eleana stirred and gazed at me with eyes as blue-gray as the dawn.

I searched her eyes, trying to read the thoughts behind them, hoping to see truth where I knew lies as smooth as the white silk she wore could exist.

She kissed me, softly, reverently. Pulling her lips away, she gazed into my eyes.

I wanted her, and she could see my hunger.

She made the first move, silently removing the fabric that separated us, kissing me again searchingly.

The scent and softness of her body so close to mine was more than I could resist. My mouth found her full breasts, my hands stroked her soft flesh.

I was as scared as I was my first time, but this time not so much of doing it wrong or getting caught, but knowing I could not survive if I let her break my heart again. And I couldn't trust her not to break it again, in so many pieces I would never find them all. I knew she only needed me to take the hurt of Moreno's death away. It was a fair trade. I needed her to ease the pain that losing her had seared into my own heart and soul.

We moved together as so many times before, as if our bodies had been made one for the other, the sound of the waves crashing on the beach blocking the voice of reason in my head, her touch smoothing away all resistance, until the only reason for my being was in the easy rhythm of loving her, loving her, until loving her in tempo with my heart's beat became my soul's desire.

She answered my need so completely that I knew it no longer mattered if she broke my heart again and scattered my soul to the wind like fine grains of quartz sand lifting off the dunes in a morning breeze. I needed her. I would always need her.

Afterwards we both wept. Mine were tears of regret.

Around eleven, we were drawn from the bed by the sounds and smells of Davy cooking breakfast.

"I should go help him," I said.

She smiled, her chameleon eyes now a soft sea-green in the full light of day. "What do we tell him?"

I teased a breast with a kiss as I got out of bed. "I think we should let him draw his own conclusions."

Davy had set the card/dining table with my assortment of garage sale dishes and was spooning scrambled eggs onto plates when we emerged from our intramarital adventure. He gave me a you-old-dog grin, not unlike Tiny's grin last night.

"Coffee's just finishing," he said. "Toast or bagels?"

"Toast," I said and poured Eleana and myself a cup of coffee. "You want juice or milk?"

"I'll take coffee, Dad," Davy said, looking me in the eyes, asserting his adulthood.

I met his eyes and realized he had crossed a tight rope last night, from childhood to manhood, without a net. He drank coffee. He had killed a man. It was time to find out if we liked the same beer, and if he had learned anything about women he could teach me. It was a sobering moment for me to realize he wasn't a child anymore.

It took a while for the conversation to take hold. Davy had a "I'm ready to listen if you're ready to confess" look on his face.

Eleana eased us through the transition. "Your father and I have decided it would be best if we stayed here a few days."

"What about school?" Davy asked.

"I'll talk with your teachers and principal tomorrow," I said.

"Sure, okay," Davy said without a second thought. "Can I use your surf board and wetsuit?"

I smiled at him, seeing a glimpse of his former child, hoping it would survive a while longer. "Use anything you need."

Davy wasn't any more dedicated to school than I had been, except he hadn't turned into the truant I had been. Of course, living in Center City, he didn't have the best surf in the world just down the cliff from his back door the way I'd had, and the truancy laws were more severe nowadays than thirty years ago.

Then, almost every warm spring morning, I faced an irresistible beckon from *Endymion's* wide sea. As I fixed my breakfast before school, I'd look down at the waves and go through the debate. Waves? Algebra? Waves? History? What to do? What to do?

There was usually only one clear choice.

If my father had ever thought to look for me, he'd have known where to find me. But, after my mother died, my father had never looked any further than a bottle. The few times the school bothered him with concerns about my whereabouts, he reminded them that not only was he the meanest drunk in town, he was also the meanest lawyer in the state.

"The boy needs time alone," he would bellow. "Don't you have a heart? Can't people mourn in peace anymore?"

When I showed up for school, I aced any exam they put in front of me. So, for the most part, the adults in my life let me live my youth my way. Sinatra would have been proud of me. But every now and then I wished I hadn't missed that day at school when they taught us how not to dangle participles and split infinitives, whatever they are. I'd also missed a host of other trivia that would have come in handy when Chester and I engaged in armchair challenges with quiz show contestants while we waited on our ladies to dress for dinner. I hated having missed those educational opportunities, only because Chester knew more trivia than I did and I hated to lose.

"You want to join me?" Davy asked, interrupting my lapse down memory lane.

"Yeah, great," I said. Then the doorbell rang.

I glanced at my watch and guessed it was Tiny. He'd probably been dancing on tippee-toes for the last two hours, trying to get up enough courage to knock on the door.

"Welcome," I said as I opened the door. "May I offer you a cup of coffee?"

Tiny nodded at me then spoke to my family. "How you doing, Eleana? Davy?"

There was none of the usual awkwardness associated with a cop entering the premises, but it was obvious Tiny was here on business. After a "just fine" from Eleana and Davy and a cup of coffee for Tiny, he took a seat in my garage sale recliner with the duct tape on its arms. Eleana and Davy plopped down on my garage sale sofa. I turned a folding chair around from the garage sale card/dining table and glanced at their expectant faces.

"I can't remember when I've had this much company in my humble abode," I said.

"It's this way," Tiny said, getting down to business. "The Center City police want all of you to come back for questioning. I left it that I'd keep an eye on you today, and you'd be in touch Monday morning."

"Did they find the other guy, Mike what's-his-name?"

"Mike Sartin," Tiny said.

"Yeah, did they find him?"

Tiny gave me a "we'd better talk outside" look.

"Meet you in front of Fred's in ten minutes," I said.

"Incest," were the first words out of Tiny's mouth.

"Distressed-damsel saving," I defended. "What didn't you want to say in front of Eleana and Davy?"

"Sally's place was broken into. A neighbor up the ridge called it in. Said she heard a noise around five this morning. Didn't call us until almost eight."

"Sally?"

"Except for Lizabeth, no one's seen or heard from Sally."

"So what did you find?" I asked.

"The late Mr. Sartin," said Tiny.

"Sartin?"

"Yeah, probably killed with a .38. Looks like someone shot him elsewhere and dumped him at Sally's. Not much blood. Stiff when we found him."

"Have you told Cramer?"

"No," said Tiny. "I told that Wertheim FBI guy about it. One of his people is watching the autopsy. Thought I'd talk to you before we talk to Cramer. By the looks of things at your place, I assume Eleana and Davy can verify your whereabouts since you left Center City."

"Eleana can verify my every move. You'll have to ask Davy how thin the walls are. I'd get embarrassed. Is that all?"

"No, I thought you'd be interested in something else."

"What's that?" I asked.

"We heard from the coroner on Moreno and the driver."

"And?"

"Looks like Moreno died from an overdose of insulin. Murder weapon, if it was a murder, was a hypodermic."

"Insulin?" I repeated, trying to silence the thought in my head. "I would have picked him for a crack head."

"Yeah, insulin. The way the coroner explained it, his blood work showed low sugar and normal C-peptide, whatever that is. That's when they checked for insulin and found an overload. Enough to do him in fairly quickly. And the funny thing is, his medical records don't say anything about him being a diabetic. In fact, his doctor said he was in the peak of health. The coroner confirmed it. Perfectly healthy, except for him being dead. No high blood pressure, no coronary artery disease, not even a bad prostate. Kind of a shame, ain't it?

"What's a shame, Tiny?

"To die in the peak of health."

"That part's a shame," I said, "but I win the bet."

"Only on a technicality."

"Apply my winnings to what I owe you."

Tiny rolled his eyes and continued, "We went out to the beach to comb for the murder weapon yesterday while you were out damsel saving."

"And you needed a dump truck to haul out all the needles?"

"No. Came to that conclusion before we went that far. Just about the time we started to think about Plan B, we got a call from the state police. It seems they found a diabetic kit along the trajectory of the limo. They're checking for prints now. And one more interesting thing."

"Yeah, what?"

"The driver," Tiny said. "Got the results on him, too. Seems he took a bullet from a .38 before he went over the cliff. Don't know yet if the bullets are from the same gun that did Sartin. They're checking it against the bullet in your ceiling and the bullet in Block."

"You get a time of death on the driver and Moreno?"

"With the driver, there wasn't enough left to tell when he was charred. They know the bullet went in before the charring, and they found him yesterday morning. With Moreno, the coroner figured he'd been dead five to eight hours, give or take an hour or two, by the time they rolled him into the morgue."

"Exactly what time was that?"

"Around ten," Tiny said, confirming my guess on time.

"Ten minus eight is two a.m., ten minus five is five a.m. That's a pretty big time spread."

"Yeah," said Tiny. "Maybe more."

"Why the uncertainty?" I asked.

"Coroner said he was in the water a while, and that can cool a body pretty fast. He's still got some lab tests to run to pin it down. Have you remembered when Sally left her place?"

"Not yet," I said and walked away just as Fred McPeters drove up to his restaurant in his new black Mercedes. Odd, I thought, that Fred and Lizabeth had the same taste in cars.

"Don't do anything stupid," Tiny called after me.

I continued walking, noticing in the glance over my shoulder that Tiny and Fred were both doing their he's-hopeless head shake as they went into Fred's restaurant together.

So what did we have at this point in time? A governor dead with an insulin overdose sometime Friday night or Saturday morning. His driver done with a .38 and burned to a crisp in a fiery crash off Promontory Point near Stan Cramer's place. A fire at the Archives, destroying Moreno's campaign records. One of Moreno's no-show state police backup drivers shot by Davy around eleven p.m. Saturday evening with Oma's gun after he left a bullet in the kitchen ceiling of my ex-house. The other no-show backup driver shot sometime before he was dumped at Sally's this morning, gun unknown. Four deaths and one arson in less than two days, three or more murder weapons altogether.

Oh yeah, the only two diabetics I knew were a seventy-plus-year-old lady by the name of Oma and a sixteen-year-old boy by the name of Davy. And neither of them had played poker with the late governor at Stan Cramer's place Friday night.

What I had was one or more murderers and no obvious motive for any of the four deaths. Or maybe it was just one ambidextrous murderer who carried one pocket full of insulin kits and one full of .38's, and used whatever he/she reached for first. Maybe the murderer was an *Edward Scissorhand* kind of person with guns and hypodermics for hands instead of scissors. This inquiring mind wanted to know.

FOURTEEN

Sunday, May 27, NOON

Back at my shack, I watched Davy ride a wave into shore before going inside to talk with Eleana. He's a fine young man, I told myself. We had done at least one thing right.

Then I opened the door. The pine-cleaner smell indicated she had already scrubbed the kitchen and bathroom. She was now dragging a vacuum through my accumulation of dust bunnies and potato chip fragments. How quickly lovers turn into wives. Even a wealthy career woman like Eleana turned into a cleaning lady when confronted with a man's comfortable bachelor squalor. The Nesting Instinct.

Perhaps I should warn her not to get too comfortable in my nest before she did, I thought. No, let her finish, I answered myself. The place needed a good cleaning. I held my tongue as she backed her way to the door.

When she turned around and noticed me standing there, she turned off the vacuum. "What?"

"Was Moreno a diabetic?" I asked.

"No, why?" She pushed back the blond hair in her eyes the same way Davy did and turned her midday blue-sky gaze on me, her eyes now exactly the same shade as my old blue sweatshirt that she wore, my *favorite* old blue sweatshirt.

"According to the coroner, he died of an insulin overdose."

"Insulin?"

"You know anyone on his staff who's a diabetic? Any of the cops in his guard squad?"

Eleana looked puzzled, then she paced the room. She stopped and stared at me.

"I take it that's a no?"

The fear in her eyes turning them a stormy dark blue-gray. "You don't think?"

"No, I don't think that," I said. I had no intention of thinking of Davy as a suspect in Moreno's murder, putting the killing of the burglar completely out of my mind. "We probably need to talk about it. First let's talk about the fire at the Archives."

"I can't think of anything in those records that would precipitate all this. They're just campaign schedules, photos of Wallie with contributors, things like that."

"Are there any backup records?"

"Everything is indexed in a computer database and copied on microfiche as it's filed. There's a set of microfiche at the Archives Building and another at the State Historical Society."

"Want to take a drive with me?" I asked.

"Where?"

"Back to Center City."

"What about Davy?"

"I'll give Fred a call. Maybe Davy can help bus tables this evening. Or Oma can keep him entertained by feeding him."

"I don't want them to let him out of their sight."

"I'll tell them that," I said, not mentioning the fact that Davy was out of our sight at the moment while he played surfer dude and she played cleaning lady.

"So what did Tiny want?"

I hesitated.

"What, Bill?"

"Sartin's dead," I said. "They found him at Sally's Cliff Road house early this morning."

"Sally?" she asked.

"She hasn't turned up yet."

It took less than an hour for Fred and Oma to show up for baby-sitting duties. Oma brought lunch from the Kitchen with her. After we finished her apple strudel, Oma insisted we tell her everything.

I left out the gory parts, and the private ones. But, by the glint in Fred's surly eyes, it looked as if Tiny had already filled him in about my bare feet.

After lunch, Eleana packed Davy a change of clothes and transferred him to Fred's custody.

"Make sure he gets to Oma's by ten," I said.

"Remind him about his shot, Oma," Eleana said.

"And Oma," I continued, "lights out at eleven. Don't let him stay up watching television all night."

"I'm not a kid," Davy whined.

"When are you coming back?" Oma asked.

"I'll get your car back as soon as I can. We can use Eleana's Lincoln until I get the Corvette fixed."

"Don't fret about that," Oma said. "Bruce's car is all we need. Just take care of this bother. Get those strangers out of our lives. Those newspeople are like wolves."

"I'm working on it," I said.

"I don't like those newspeople and those policemen coming to my Kitchen, especially that Mr. Cramer. He's a mean man, Bill. I can tell. Mr. Cramer is a mean man."

Eleana and I said little to each other on the drive over to Center City, both of us lost in thoughts better not talked about—our past, our future, if any, last night, this morning.

I still had finding Sally at the top of my agenda, but I was at a loss as to how to go about it. All I could do at the moment was hope that wherever she was, she was safe. It was now thirty hours, more or less, since Moreno had washed ashore on Sally's beach. If she wasn't dead, she had figured out where to hide. Sally was a very smart girl. To find her, I'd probably have to figure out who she was hiding from and think like Sally to figure out where she'd go to hide from them. And I'd probably have to have a sex-change operation to come close to thinking like Sally.

But maybe the destroyed Moreno records would give me some clue as to who had done it. Obviously they contained a secret someone didn't want the world to know or they wouldn't have been destroyed. Maybe the same secret someone thought Eleana knew when they sent Block to our house. First thing was to find out whose secret and make sure they had no reason to come back and try again to kill Eleana.

As I drove, I debated with myself whether I should do this myself or whether I should include the cops just in case we came up with real evidence. I settled the debate on the side of the cops. If we identified the murderer through the Moreno records, I'd rather the cops be the ones who collected the evidence and went after their man. Then I could go back to my quietly desperate life.

But I was particular about which cops. I didn't want the Center City boys involved in this because I didn't want to answer any more of their questions. I didn't want the state boys involved because they might be wearing black hats. And Tiny and Gomez wouldn't be any help because they were out of their jurisdiction the minute they crossed the Splendor Bay city limits. So I decided on the Feds and elected Tiny my emissary to the law enforcement empire, running Oma's cell phone bill a little higher.

"Hi, big guy," I said when Tiny answered.

"Hi, yourself. You forget something?"

"Davy's in Fred's care. Then he's going to spend the night with Oma and Bruce."

"I'll have Gomez check on them from time to time."

"That's not all."

"What?"

"I want you to call that George Wertheim FBI fellow. See if one of his agents can meet Eleana and me at the Archives Building. If we find anything, I'd like someone from the FBI to mark the evidence."

"I'll see what I can do," he said.

"Have you heard anything on Sally yet?" I asked.

"Nothing."

"Has Wertheim's coven checked the airport parking lots for her Jaguar? If they have, ask him not to share anything they find with the state cops. If Cramer is behind this, we don't want him getting ahead of us."

"What do you know?" Tiny asked suspiciously.

"Nothing. But dumping a stiff in a lady's living room seems to be a pretty bold move. Of course, if you knew for sure the lady wasn't there, maybe it wasn't so bold. The state cops knew she wasn't there. And who besides another state cop could get the upper hand on a state cop?"

"An FBI cop," Tiny said. "They also knew she wasn't there. Besides, to be factually correct, the stiff was dumped in her kitchen. And just what does that have to do with airports?"

"Nothing. Except, if I were Sally and I suspected some really bold dudes were after me, I'd get out of town. The quickest way to get out of town is to catch a plane. Sally would do a zigzag nobody could follow—San Francisco to Miami to Quebec to Tahiti to Paris or something like that. Sally usually carries her passport and several grand in cash in her purse. That could buy a few airplane tickets. Plus, she has trust funds in half the banks in the world she can get at without leaving any records our FBI can find."

"I hadn't thought of that," Tiny said.

"Just make sure our Feds do. Right now they're probably working on tracing her credit cards. She's smarter than that. They need to be thinking cash. And it might be time for you to tell them about Lizabeth Thorton's little switch-a-roo yesterday."

"You want me to admit I've withheld information?"

"No, tell them you beat it out of me this morning. They'll respect you that way. And thanks, Tiny, for everything, especially for keeping an eye on Davy."

"No problem."

I glanced at Eleana as I hung up. She had a little frown on her pretty face.

"What?" I asked.

"It's nothing," she said in that tone of voice that made it clear it really was something.

"Eleana, please. If you have anything to say, say it."

She took her time in answering, just to irritate me. "You like Sally a lot, don't you?"

I decided to try honesty. "Yeah, I do. And I owe her. Too much not to try to save her life if I still can. She's your cousin. Surely you want to make sure she's safe."

"I see."

"No, I don't think you do," I said, miffed at her tone. "She's my friend, Eleana. She's also my lover. I don't take that lightly.

You were my wife, until you decided you didn't want the job. Twenty years and our son make that a fact of my life. Sally's another fact."

We drove a few more miles in silence.

"What if I asked for my old job back?"

I took my time in answering. "I think it's too soon for us to talk about that. Yesterday you were crying your eyes out over Wallie Moreno."

She sighed, then after a while said, "Is that the only reason?"

"No. I'm sorry Eleana, but this morning can't change all that's happened between us. I don't want you to want me just because I'm handy to help you through your grief. And I have to be honest. Since you resigned the position, I'm considering another applicant for the job."

With that, I went through my calling-Sally routine again. *Nada*, except for me again at the townhouse and bay house. I really needed to change her answering machine messages.

FIFTEEN

Sunday, May 27, 3:15 PM

We went to Eleana's house to make sure it was locked up. I pushed aside the yellow police-line-do-not-cross tape on the front door and crossed into the foyer. Eleana followed me inside. She sighed as she glanced at the mess the cops had made, then trailed after me to the kitchen. Andrew Block's blood had dried to a dark reddish-brown caulk gluing the broken glass to the floor.

Eleana stared at it a moment, then turned away. "I'm going upstairs to pack a few things."

I looked around. Tiny had secured the French doors in the kitchen by nailing them shut with a piece of plywood across them. That was probably all he could do, considering the fact that I had busted the lock all the way through the wood when I'd charged inside. The doors could stay as they were until I had time to call a carpenter to replace them.

The French doors in the den had a circular hole in the pane of glass next to the lock, the hole now filled with a piece of cardboard. Apparently Block had cut the glass using a suction cup as a guide, removed it, reached in, and opened the lock from inside. A cop-mystery novel I had read said you couldn't do that. Guess Block hadn't read that book. I put glass-replacing on my to-do list next to carpenter and added cleaning crew to take care of the mess the cops had made.

The only possible reason Block would have been there was to kill Eleana. The only reason he would want to kill her was because she was Wallie's girlfriend and might know whatever Moreno knew that had gotten him killed. The question was—what did she know? Or what did whoever was behind the killings think she knew?

I should ask Eleana. She seemed to be dealing with her grief quite nicely. But I didn't want to start the inquisition. Grilling Eleana about the details of her relationship with Wallie would be like rubbing salt in an open wound, and knowing the whole story might generate enough scar tissue over that proud flesh to keep that wound from ever healing completely.

But I had no other leads. I had to ask her. Soon, I told myself as I heard Eleana at the top of the back stairs. Then my thoughts shifted to an earlier question—the security alarm.

Why didn't I think of that before? The cops asked about it. Eleana said she'd set it. And I clearly remembered seeing her hand move on the key pad after locking the French doors, before she went upstairs. But the alarm hadn't gone off when I crashed through the doors.

Had Block cut a hole in a window in the den's French doors without setting off the alarm? Then gone to the kitchen doors and punched in the code? Is that how it happened? Did Block have the code? How did he get the code? Maybe Block had come in through the den before Davy went upstairs, before Eleana set the alarm. He could have been there while we were outside eating, while we were in the pool. He could have. . .

Eleana came downstairs carrying two duffel bags. "I have enough for a few days. I have to be back at work by Wednesday. We have auditors coming in."

"Did you set the alarm last night?"

She stared at me, thinking it through. "Yes. . . At least I think I did. I knew you had a key and would know to turn it off if you needed to come in for anything. Yes, I'm sure I set it."

"It didn't go off when I crashed through the kitchen door."

"Oh," she said, meeting my eyes, exploring the possibilities. "Maybe he pulled a breaker outside."

"No, the main power box is in the pool house. I would have heard him. Besides, the house power was on. I'd better check just to make sure the alarm box wasn't tampered with."

I ran upstairs. The breaker was missing from the alarm box.

I felt sick knowing that if Davy hadn't stopped him, Block could have killed my family, and I could have slept through it all only a hundred feet away in the pool house. Then I felt panic, and pure burning hatred. If Davy hadn't killed the bastard, I would be hunting him down this very minute.

Slowly reason returned. How many times could you kill a man, after all? Then I heard Eleana coming upstairs and closed the box.

"Is everything okay?" she asked.

"Yeah," I said. "Let's go check out your archives."

I needed to think about what this meant. Not only had the breaker for the alarm been pulled, but it was missing entirely. I should ask Tiny to make a discrete inquiry of the Center City cops to see what, if anything, had been in Mr. Block's pockets, and where they'd found his prints. And I had another question for Eleana that I didn't want to ask. Had she had given Wallie the code in case his guards had to rescue him from my ex-bed?

I added to the mental list—stop by a hardware store and pick up a breaker for the alarm and look for some kind of lock system to secure the French doors, something that couldn't be opened just by breaking a pane of glass, reaching in, and turning the lock. Maybe break-proof, bulletproof glass. And maybe security gates to go around the house.

"Do you want me to drive the Lincoln over to my office now?" she asked, interrupting my disjointed train of thought.

"No. We'll come back for your car later. You ready?"

The truth was, I didn't want her out of my sight. I was afraid whoever was behind the murders and last night's attack on Eleana might try again. And I couldn't bear the thought she might be harmed. Then I mentally kicked myself for telling myself the truth in front of Eleana. She could read me like a comic book character with little clouds of words floating over his head, especially on those rare occasions when I told myself the truth.

SIXTEEN

Sunday, May 27, 4:00 PM

We found George Wertheim pacing the sidewalk outside the Archives Building. I let Eleana out of the car, trusting her safety to an FBI special agent, and took her garage pass with me to park in the underground lot beneath Liberty Plaza. Located between the State Office Building on the west, the State Capitol on the north, and the State Archives on the east, Liberty Plaza is where the first governor's statute collects pigeon droppings and winos sleep on park benches.

It being Sunday, most of the state's vehicles were parked in the garage. I found a parking place on the third level near the elevator in a long row of white Crown Vics, the vehicles used by the state police and first-line bureaucrats like heads of state agencies. The empty spot was probably Eleana's anyway. She had refused a state car in favor of her own Lincoln. I noticed a Crown Vic parked in Sally's AG slot, which seemed odd because Sally preferred her personal car as well. Maybe she let her secretary use the gift car to run errands.

Eleana and Wertheim were waiting in studied silence on the front steps when I emerged from the street-side garage stairs.

"Your wife said her lawyer told her not to answer any questions," Wertheim reported.

"She told you the truth," I said.

Wertheim extended his hand. "You may not remember me, but I was on the team that brought in your former client, Miller."

Recognition penetrated my soggy brain. Ten years ago. Wertheim had a full head of dark hair then instead of the skimpy gray now, and not near as many crow's feet around the eyes. Johnny Miller was a reservation brave, high on rot-gut whiskey and Indian rights when he declared war on the United States and tried to seize the Federal Building in Center City with nothing more than a bow and arrow. He gave up before anyone was killed. Actually, Johnny passed out before anyone was killed. I negotiated with the US Attorney's office until they agreed to waive Federal charges and let Johnny be tried on a state charge of criminal trespass. Then I talked the Center County DA into a plea bargain, getting a possible five-year sentence down to a six-month stay in the county jail on a misdemeanor trespass.

Johnny used that brief time away from lifelong poverty to get his GED. Then he came by my office to say thanks and tell me about it. Impressed, I talked my firm into giving him a part-time clerk job. Then I talked them into funding his college expenses. And, when he went on to law school, we funded that, too. A little more talking on my part got Johnny's record expunged and he was admitted to the bar. A letter of recommendation from Wertheim helped. Johnny's slate was wiped clean, my brethren lawyers gave the fine, upstanding young man a key to the club, and my job as mentor was done. But, having seen criminal defense work up close as my law clerk, Johnny opted for a life of crime-fighting instead.

"Yeah," I said. "Guess we both had that sweet blush of youth on us then. I should thank you for going to bat for Johnny. But, had I known how he'd get completely reborn, I might not—"

Wertheim laughed. "I bet his joining the DA's office really gave you heartburn. Turn a man around and it might be one-hundred-and-eighty degrees. Now, I'm getting my ass chewed on an hourly basis because I haven't delivered the governor's killer. And the brass want me to find a missing state attorney general, a friend of yours, or so I hear. You know how I should do that?"

"I assume you're checking airports."

"We're working that."

"Why don't we go inside? If we stand here long enough we'll attract pigeons or reporters."

"Results are about the same," Wertheim said. "Lead the way."

Eleana used her card key to open a door. She waved at a guard watching a ball game on a miniature television, then we rode an elevator up to her office on the top floor in silence. As we got off the elevator, I noted that the building had modern, non-opening windows sealing the smoky smell inside and the oxygen outside, not exactly conducive to comfortable research.

"Okay, George, old buddy, this is what I thought we might do. Eleana says they make microfiche copies of all the records as they're filed, and as far as she knows now, the only thing that burned were Moreno's campaign records. There should be a set of microfiche in the building somewhere. They keep another set at the Historical Society. What I think we ought to do is go through the microfiche records here while your troops gather up the other records, just in case the set here is incomplete."

"Sounds like a plan," said Wertheim. "The Archives fire was on my list of things to talk with Mrs. Glasscock about. I was just about to chase you two down when you called me."

"Great minds work alike," I said. "And, given the fact that Moreno's last meal took place at Stan Cramer's house, I don't think we want the state police helping."

"Who told you that?" Wertheim asked, clearly surprised by my revelation.

"Eleana," I said innocently.

Wertheim glanced at Eleana, then at me. "You going to let me ask about that?"

"If you don't get carried away."

Wertheim nodded his agreement.

"Go ahead, Eleana, tell him what you told me."

"There isn't much to tell. Wallie went to a fund-raiser at Stan's place Friday night, dinner and a poker party for a few of the party regulars. Not a big event."

"Who was there?" Wertheim asked.

"I don't know," she said. "I wasn't there."

"So how do you know about the party?" Wertheim probed.

"Wallie called, asked me to have dinner with him at the Mansion. I told him no. Then he told me about the dinner and poker party at Cramer's. He said that since I wouldn't have dinner with him, he'd go on to it instead of sending an aide."

"What time was this?"

"Let's see... I got home around six-thirty. Wallie called a few minutes later, around six-forty-five. Immediately after that,

I drove Davy to a friend's house a few blocks over. He'd left his Land Rover sitting on empty when he came in Thursday night. I checked the clock in my car when I dropped him off because I told him I would be back in an hour and not to start any computer game he couldn't finish. That was at seven. I used that hour to buy groceries."

"Did you talk to Moreno after that call?" Wertheim asked.

Eleana shook her head. "On the way home yesterday, after seeing about the fire, I heard on my car radio that he was dead." She walked over to a window to look out at the plaza below.

Wertheim gave me a questioning look.

I nodded that it was okay to proceed.

"What time was that?" he asked.

She continued to focus on whatever held her attention outside. "I'm not sure. Early afternoon. Bill arrived at the house a few minutes after I did. Maybe he remembers."

Wertheim stared at me.

"I got to our house a little after two," I said.

"When did they call you about the fire?" Wertheim continued with Eleana.

"Around seven a.m. I'm sure there's a record of when they called. You can talk to security."

"You came straight here?" Wertheim asked.

"Yes," Eleana said, then reconsidered, "No. I stopped off at a convenience store to get milk and a breakfast roll. Then I came here. It took about twenty minutes to get here."

"You were here continuously?" Wertheim persisted.

"This is getting old," I said. "What difference does it make what Eleana did yesterday? You ought to be asking Cramer what he was doing to whom Friday night and Saturday morning."

Wertheim met my eyes. "You're telling me I ought to be trying to pin this on him, is that about the size of it?"

"That works for me," I said.

"Funny," Wertheim said, "he's telling me I should be trying to pin it on you."

"Says a lot right there, doesn't it. Obviously, he wants it open and shut before anybody has a chance to dig too deep."

"Maybe he just wants the crime to be solved."

"Moreno wasn't at my poker party Friday night."

"Yeah, but he was dead on your beach Saturday morning."

"Not my beach. Sally Solana's beach. Oh, come on. Cramer is smart enough to know that once you guys get a suspect, you'll manufacture enough evidence to keep from looking like fools. You tag someone else, you'll forget Cramer dropped the ball."

Wertheim glared at me, so I continued.

"You have to admit it was mighty convenient for the backup car to have mechanical problems just when the governor needed backup. And pretty suspicious that one of the backup drivers, one of Cramer's storm troopers, came after Eleana last night. All I want is for you to keep an open mind, so you don't have to explain this to Congress when they take another look at FBI screwups, as they seem to be doing on a regular basis these days."

"Cut the defense-attorney crap," Wertheim barked. "The FBI always keeps an open mind until all the evidence is in."

"Are we talking about the USA FBI?"

Wertheim folded his arms and studied me a moment, making me wonder if I'd gone too far. "What were you doing Friday night and early Saturday morning?"

"Sleeping."

"I heard," he said with a smirk.

"Look, that theory doesn't work. Assuming you could convince a prosecutor to try to convince a jury that I would leave my girlfriend's bed to kill Moreno for boffing my almost ex-wife—"

"Bill!" Eleana shrieked.

"What did I say?"

"You know," she huffed.

"Okay," Wertheim said, "you two can fight this one out later. Let's get this research project over with while there's still enough air to breathe in this place."

Eleana escorted us out of the executive suites and down two floors into the grunt pits—rows of cubicles barely big enough for a desk and chair. She parked us at microfiche readers with several stacks of tapes each.

I was getting sick of seeing picture after picture of Moreno's smiling face when I came across a photo of Smiling Wallie and a small group of his contributors taken at Cramer's home just after the last campaign kickoff, just before I found Wallie in bed with my wife. Among the smiling faces were a couple of dudes I would never have suspected of being Wallie supporters—Chester Thorton and Fred McPeters.

I must have taken too long to click to the next frame, because George Wertheim was nudging my shoulder. "Let me see."

I moved aside and George took my seat.

"So?" he asked.

"One of the guys is Chester Thorton, Sally Solana's brother-in-law. Another is Fred McPeters. Owns a restaurant in Splendor Bay. Neither is known for being a Moreno lover, especially Fred. The five other guys are the richest men in the state."

"Politics makes strange bedfellows," George said.

"So I've heard." I shifted my eyes to Eleana.

She glared back then said, "I've found something."

Eleana moved aside so George could take a look. I scooted in next to him to examine the campaign contributors list. The guys in the photo had given a lot of money to elect Moreno. Even Chester Thorton and Fred McPeters hadn't done too shabby by Old Wallie. Stan Cramer had also given several nice checks, in total almost as much as his yearly salary.

The interesting thing about these kinds of records is they create the appearance of impropriety. All those special prosecutors who use massive amounts of tax dollars to stir a little smoke into fire to burn politicians will tell you the appearance of impropriety is everything. Even a guy like me who would prefer to believe smoke is just smoke had to wonder what all that generosity was about.

"So, Mr. FBI Man, what now?" I asked.

"I'll pack up these tapes and take them with me. Then I'm going to visit with Mr. Cramer about his dinner party. I assume one of Mrs. Glasscock's people will provide documentation of authenticity on these tapes if we need it?

Eleana nodded her head.

Wertheim glanced at me. "What're you going to do?"

"Nothing much. I'm going back to my shack at the beach. I might talk to Fred McPeters. He's my bartender."

"I don't think that's a good idea."

"Why not? I'm about the only person Fred will talk to. Why don't you let me chat with him before your guys go at him and he clams up? If he's knows anything about Wallie and Cramer that you need to know, I'll pass it along."

"What about Thorton?" Wertheim asked.

"Him, I also know. Drinking buddy. But let me talk with his women folk first, just so I'll know if he's telling me straight."

"You don't trust him?"

"Sure, I trust him. He's a fine human being. Known him all my life. But he's a lawyer. Can't expect him to bare his soul."

"His women folk—does that include Miss Solana?"

I shrugged. "I was thinking about talking to her sister, Mrs. Thorton. I don't know where Miss Solana is at the moment."

"I understand Mrs. Thorton pretended to be Miss Solana yesterday? Does it work the other way around? If they're identical, how do you know which one you're talking to?"

I smiled smugly. "Trust me, I can tell them apart. Let me talk to Lizabeth. If I don't get anything, you send your guys in and push her around. If I do, you'll have a head start."

Wertheim gave me that intimidating ray they taught them in FBI school. He wanted me to know he was being a nice guy to let a civilian, and a suspect at that, help with his investigation. The look included a warning that I'd better not think of woodshedding any witnesses in the case.

I stared back and mentally telegraphed my argument. It wasn't likely any of them would willingly talk to the FBI or to any other cops. And they all had enough connections that it would be difficult for him to find a judge who would order a subpoena of parties not obviously involved in the case. I might be able to give him something that would speed up his investigation. Then again, I might entrap myself. Either way, he'd come out ahead. Wertheim wasn't the kind of agent who always played by the rules he'd learned in FBI school. He was much too practical-minded for that. What did he have to lose?

"I'll give you till noon tomorrow," Wertheim said, his eyes indicating he'd read my mind. "After that, I'm hauling anybody who isn't cooperating down to my place."

"You know, Georgie, baby, I love it when you talk dirty."

"And Glasscock, you screw me on this, I'll deliver you to Stan Cramer gift wrapped."

"I don't doubt that for a minute," I said. And I didn't.

SEVENTEEN

Sunday, May 27, 5:45 PM

We saw Wertheim to the front door of the building, then took an interior elevator to the garage. I soon realized Eleana was mad about something. She would huff, then glare at me with sparkling emerald eyes, like she was going to kick me in the family jewels. I opened the car door for her, went around to the driver's side, got in, and started the engine.

She just stood there.

"Okay, Eleana, get in the car."

She glared at me. "Not until you apologize."

"Apologize for what?"

"For that remark about Wallie and me."

"What remark?"

"You know."

"Refresh my memory."

"You know, boffing."

"I should have said 'rutting.' Or is that word offensive as well? How about f—"

"I've had enough of your recriminations. Take me to the house so I can get my car. I'll go to the beach and get Davy. We'll do fine without you. We always have."

"Get in." Now, I was angry. The truth can do that to a guy.

She got in. We slammed doors, went to our respective corners, and slapped on seat belts. I squealed out of the garage. Next thing I knew, I was on a freeway headed in the general direction of Mexico.

"You're going the wrong way," she said when she spoke to me again a half hour later.

Her words pierced the veil of anger that clouded my eyes. "I know," I said. "The wrong way is the way I go."

"I'm sorry, Bill. If I could undo any of it, I would."

"You mind if we stop for dinner?" I asked, realizing that part of the gnawing in my stomach was hunger.

"I'd like that," she said. "Where are we?"

"About three miles from a little seaside inn with a four star restaurant. You didn't leave home without your American Express card, did you?"

She smiled. "May I buy you dinner?"

The place was almost empty. Still, they sent us to the bar to serve our requisite penance. Four star restaurants do that to humble patrons without reservations. Fortunately, bar pretzels were my usual main course or I'd have gotten really drunk. By the time the hostess seated us in the dining room, I had built a nice little bar tab on Eleana's credit card. She was on her third Virgin Mary, watching me like a cat watching a jaybird skirt too close to the ground.

I never should have overconsumed on an empty stomach, but, given the fact it was too late not to overconsume, I decided a California vintage would add just the right touch to the inn's famous seafood cuisine. The waiter brought the wine and took our dinner orders. We still hadn't said ten words to each other. I was thinking this would be one of my drunks where Eleana waited until I was too zonked to notice, took the keys, and left me stranded, until I tried to dissect a crab and sent him flying.

Eleana giggled.

I laughed, too.

Then we laughed together so loud and long that our waiter gave us his undivided attention, asking politely if perhaps he could send our meal to our room.

"We don't have a room," I said, howling at the idea of Eleana and me sharing a room. Nothing good could come of that, not in my present state of inebriation.

"Sir," the waiter continued in the calm voice waiters use to control drunks, "the manager has arranged for you to have a bungalow on the beach, complimentary."

Anything to get us out of here before the now-arriving customers left in disgust, I thought.

"For us?" Eleana squealed.

"The lady seems to think that's a ridiculous idea," I said.

"Oh, Bill?" Eleana said.

"Yes, dear woman?"

"I think we better take them up on their offer. I just pissed my pants." Then she howled with another fit of laughter.

A plump woman at the next table gasped.

"Please, sir?" the waiter pleaded.

"We'll need a doggie bag," I said. I wasn't leaving without my meal. It was their fault for making us wait in the bar.

"No problem." The waiter commenced gathering our plates.

Still giggling, we followed him to the bungalow, but along the way the cool night sea air and trek through treacherous sand robbed the night of frivolity.

"Thank you, kind sir," I said as he opened the door for us, "Please apologize to the management for our behavior. And put a nice tip on the bill for yourself."

Then we were alone inside, and I was suddenly sober.

"Bill," she said, suddenly cautious, "this isn't a good idea."

"You're right," I agreed.

"Yes," she said. "I'll take a quick shower, then we can go. If that's okay with you?"

"Yeah, fine with me," I lied, wanting at that moment to take her into my arms and beg her to forget our transgressions, beg her to not finalize the divorce, beg her to love me again.

"Fine," she said and disappeared into the bathroom.

I settled down to finish my meal while I waited. As things were going, who knew when I would get another one. Eleana's shower lasted my meal and the half of hers I ate. Then it sounded like she was soaking in the tub. So I decided to take a brief nap. A full belly can do that to a guy.

I awakened to a red light on the clock next to the bed. It took me a second to realize the 2:00 meant two a.m. The room was dark. Eleana was asleep next to me. At first I couldn't remember where I was, or how I'd gotten here. Then I remembered. All of it.

It was Monday already. My noon deadline with Wertheim loomed. And I wasn't any nearer an answer to the riddles than when we had parted company, but something worse had happened at midnight. The dreaded day had come. I was a lawyer again. God save us all.

I got out of bed and Eleana stirred. "Go back to sleep," I said, moving to the window to look out at the beach. The sickle of a moon and the stars provided just enough light to see the frothy waves washing onto the sand.

Not a creature was stirring, not even a whale. Just me, restless as I usually was this time of night when I would wake up in my chair and realize that the only noise in my shack was from the waves outside and the static of a signed-off television station inside, and the only worthwhile thing left in my life was my memories of people who had once loved me.

I heard the rustle of sheets, then only the waves as she stood beside me. She circled my waist with her arms, rested her head on my shoulder. "Come back to bed. We'll leave at dawn. Davy's okay. Please."

I wrapped my arms around her and realized I was the only one wearing clothes. "Eleana?"

"Please," she said, pressing against me. She raised her head, her rose-thorn-green eyes meeting mine. "Please."

My body had a mind of its own, and that mind couldn't hold the grudge the mind in my head wanted to keep. I didn't try to stop myself, even though I knew I was getting in too deep without a life jacket, daring the murky waters of her soul to pull me under again.

I picked her up and carried her back to bed and made love to her, true, beautiful, absolute love.

And she had sex with me. Or so I thought. When I lay spent, she kissed my lips with her angel soft lips, stroked my chest with silky fingers, whispered to me with a caressing voice, "I love you, Bill. Only you. I've never loved anyone else."

My body and soul wanted to believe her, more than anything else. But the stubborn, angry mind in my head and my aching heart wouldn't buy it. They just reminded me that I wanted her to hurt as much as she had hurt me.

I pulled away. "It's time we get back to work. Wertheim gave us until noon."

We dressed quickly. She walked to the car without glancing at me and waited silently while I opened her door. She got in and pulled on her seat belt, settling in with only a sigh.

As I drove, locked in the silence of anxiety, I tried to forget what had happened between us, tried to remember I still needed to find Sally. And I needed to figure out who was murdering people and why, before he or she killed again, before he or she killed someone I loved.

What was the motive for the murders? With a governor and the state police involved, it had all the players for a political conspiracy gone wrong, perhaps a falling out among thieves helping themselves to the public coffers. But nothing about murder was ever as simple as it seemed.

What other motives were there? Drugs? Legal or illegal? There's an illegal drug lobby just like there's a legal drug lobby, a tobacco lobby, a gun lobby, a war-machine lobby, an insurance lobby, a power-producers lobby, a big-oil lobby...

Ah, the fiction of public service. Big business was generous in sharing profits with those in power who either overtly assisted their quest for profits or looked the other way as they raped and plundered. A symbiotic relationship of the first order.

But illegal drug murders were usually not as subtle as these. An insulin injection or a single shot in the head with a .38? That was much too subtle. Druggies went for knives for one-on-one killings and Uzis or AK-47s for larger battles. Gored or bullet-riddled bodies were the norm in drug schemes. And money launderers seldom brought out the over-the-counter guns, either. Those guys preferred small personalized car bombs. And if this was money laundering, where did the money come from? Drugs? A Ponzi scheme of some kind—land deals or financial investments? Kickbacks in government contracts?

Yeah. Kickbacks. That was the sort of thing that would appeal to Wallie. He was definitely from the "you grease my palm and I'll grease yours" school of politics. What other school was there? Why else would anyone spend millions on a campaign to win a hundred-thousand-a-year job?

Wallie into public service? I don't think so. If the payola didn't make it worth the trouble, why bother? Politics and payola, the twin sisters of vice that make the world go round. Okay triplets. Politics, payola, and power.

But it wasn't just Wallie. Stan Cramer was also in the tossed salad. Stan didn't seem smart enough to figure out anything too complicated, which probably eliminated money laundering, or Ponzi schemes, maybe even government contract kickbacks if he had to figure it out. But Stan was smart enough to act as a collection agency.

Yeah, Stan had that repoman look about him. What better collector could you want than a guy with a license to carry guns and big sticks? And Stan was real proud of his stick. Easy enough. That issue solved. Wallie got the money. Stan got to hurt people. Both were fulfilled.

And there were the outstanding citizens in the photo with Wallie. There was the butcher whose name is synonymous with meat packing plants, his face where it ought to be—on packs of bacon and baloney in supermarkets everywhere. There was the baker who supplied bread throughout the state. And there was the candlestick maker. Well, maybe not a candlestick maker but close enough. He had a string of small refineries up and down the coast producing carcinogenic petrochemicals for better living. The banker was chairman of a state bank with offices and ATMs all over the place. The last guy in the photo was the largest construction contractor in the state.

So what kind of crime would that group of citizens conspire to do together? And why would guys like them, who had the world by the tail, even want to? Assuming they did, that is.

Beats me. My problem was, I've never understood *mens rhea*, a guilty mind, acting intentionally, knowingly, recklessly in the commission of a crime, at least not well enough to do more than argue it didn't exist in the head of whatever client I was defending. I certainly didn't understand it well enough to figure out why that many rich guys would get into bed together.

And I had another problem with this theory. As much as I didn't want to think about it, Fred and Chester were somehow mixed in with the five other outstanding citizens in those Smiling Wallie pictures. I found it hard to believe either Fred or Chester were involved in any Wallie deal.

Besides, all this thinking about crimes and criminal minds was giving me a headache. This was the line of work I had quit for very good reasons. And it was just the kind of stuff our FBI ought to worry about. Let George do it. He was suited for the work. I would do the work I was suited for—saving damsels.

Then it occurred to me, thinking of criminal minds, that it would be just like Sally to hide out in her townhouse. Who would think of looking for her there? Trying to out think Sally also gave me a headache.

But while I examined the subject of minds and motives, there was one little truth I needed to share with myself. The little digression with Eleana at the seaside inn had made me question my reason for desperately seeking Sally. I now knew I was chasing Sally for all the wrong reasons—because I needed to be the hero again, to prove I could do what other men could not. The last time that need took over, it ruined my life.

EIGHTEEN
Monday, May 28, 5:15 AM

Sally's front porch light was on and the Sunday newspaper was on the stoop, making her place look abandoned. Perhaps as she intended. I parked across the street from her townhouse and glanced at the clock in the dash. Five-fifteen. In a little over six hours, George Wertheim would tug on my leash.

I checked out the street. An early morning jogger huffed past. A car moved slowly down the street.

"Are you going in?" Eleana asked as I took in the predawn ambiance.

"Yeah."

"I'm going with you."

"No, you're not. Move over to the driver's seat. Keep the engine running in case we have to make a hasty exit."

Eleana sighed. "Call her. Let her know you're coming in so she doesn't think you're a burglar and shoot you."

"She hasn't been answering her phone."

"Leave a message. If she's there, she'll hear it and know it's you. And if the burglar alarm goes off, you'll have a verifiable explanation for the police."

"The alarm won't go off," I said. "I know the code."

"She might have changed it," Eleana argued. "If I were worried about killers, I would have changed it."

I stared at Eleana. The voice of reason out of the mouth of a babe. "Okay. But if she doesn't answer, I'm going in. Alone."

Eleana picked up the phone, punched in Sally's number.

"How do you know her number?" I asked.

Eleana smiled as she handed me the phone. "You've forgotten? Sally and I used to be good friends."

"Oh," I said.

Before the recent incest, as Tiny called it, Sally and Eleana had been friends. They would always be first cousins. I had to hand it to me, I sure knew how to pick beautiful, rich women. Now, if I could just learn the art of picking beautiful, rich, faithful women, I'd be a satisfied man.

After four rings, the answering machine picked up with my voice reciting the number, "Please leave a message after the beep."

It beeped and I said, "Sally, this is Bill. I'm outside and I'm coming in the front door. Don't shoot." I glanced at Eleana as I put the phone back in the cradle. "Satisfied?"

"No, but that won't stop you." She opened the car door.

Sally's front door opened the same moment the light in the car came on.

"You're being welcomed," Eleana said. "You still want me to stay in the car?"

It was one of those "Aw Schitt!" moments (Aw Schitt, as in son of Bull Schitt and Damna Schitt). I glanced at Eleana not knowing what answer to give. What is a man supposed to do? A wife in the car, a lover in the townhouse. I didn't really want to leave Eleana in the car by herself on a dark street that hadn't yet come to life, and I didn't want the ladies together in the same room. No good could come of that.

In the few minutes we'd been here, I'd seen only one car and one Gen-X jogger—too young to know jogging on pavement makes for bad knees and a crippled old age, but maybe not too young to be a cop. The car that passed us could have been an unmarked copmobile. It had moved a little slower on Sally's block than before or after, like it was doing a drive-by.

Allowing myself a momentary vision of Sally aiming a gun at my private parts, I decided to be a man about it and face the unknown. Sally had already seen Eleana, and the minute Sally saw my face, she would know I had been unfaithful to her with my wife. Sally had absolutely no problem putting two and two together and getting four point oh, oh, oh, oh, oh. She was accurate to five decimal places, maybe six. That was another talent I had—picking smart women. Smart women can be hazardous to a guy's health.

"Come on," I said. "Maybe you can protect me."

The expression on Sally's face was somewhere between relief to see me and a flash of lightning setting a wild fire. It zapped across the street from her eyes to mine, jolted my spine, and paralyzed my legs. Had Eleana not taken my elbow to guide me to the light, I might have stood there, affixed to the pavement, to this day.

By the time we crossed the street and were entering the street-level gate of Sally's townhouse, her expression had changed to a slow burn, like flames at the edge of a forest fire dying down before going after bigger timber. Her dark eyes crackled like smoldering cinders.

I tried not to look like a tree and grabbed the offensive. "You want to tell me where you've been? I was worried sick," I said sincerely, trying for an approximation of the truth.

She looked at me, then at Eleana, then back at me as her eyes read the score. "I can tell."

I almost caved. But, if I started explaining, I was a goner for sure. So I put on my best lawyer-poker face and went for the bluff. "Eleana was worried sick about you, too. She insisted on helping me look for you, after what happened—"

"What happened?" Sally asked, her eyes darting from my face to Eleana's.

"Don't you know?" Eleana asked. "Wallie and his driver were killed and there was a fire at the Archives Building. And one of his backup drivers broke into my house with a gun and attacked me. Davy managed to get the gun away. Then—"

"Let's go inside," Sally said, glancing up and down the dark street before she closed the door behind us, turned the lock, and punched in the security code. She led us along the trail of light to the library.

Sally's library, in back of the street-front living room, was small but grand—high ceiling, walnut-paneled walls lined with bookcases filled with an impressive collection of first and rare editions, a parquet floor covered with a brightly-colored Chinese silk rug that had made its way across the Pacific sometime during the last century, Imari lamps by the sofa. The computer on the empire desk was the first clue this was a Twenty-First Century house. The screen saver flashed the golden words, "Attorney

General's Office," around a logo with Sally's face in the middle, telling us whose house we were in.

"I've been reading my email," she said, noticing my glance at the computer. "It's been a busy day or two."

"How much do you know?" I asked, looking around. A rumpled quilt was on the sofa. Food and drink containers littered table tops and the floor around the sofa. The place was a mess, in sharp contrast to Sally's usual neat-as-a-pin habitat. The top of her jogging suit carried a dried, avocado-dip stain. Her hair hadn't been combed in awhile. She was seedy, but beautiful.

I summoned the courage to look into her dark eyes. She was as tired and worried as she was angry and disappointed in me, perhaps too tired and worried to kill me. At any other time, I'd have taken her into my arms and tried to comfort her, but now was definitely not the time. I glanced at Eleana. She was taking in the situation as well, even my own internal conflict.

Eleana and Sally, the daughters of half-brothers, were a study in contrast. Eleana's long-legged, blond good looks came from her mother's Swedish genes. Sally's petite Spanish beauty was pure conquistador, undiluted by her auburn-haired movie-star mom's Irish genes.

"I know they torched Wallie's collection at the Archives," Sally said, "and I know they broke into Eleana's house."

"You know they're looking for you?"

"Yes."

"So why haven't you made your whereabouts known?"

"I have my reasons," Sally said, glancing at Eleana. "I could use some coffee. I've been up all night."

Eleana took the hint. "I'll make it, if you two want to talk."

"Yes, thank you," Sally said to Eleana, then turned her dark prosecutor eyes on me. "Bill and I do need to talk."

The two women in my life being so polite to each other made me nervous, especially since the politeness seemed to have that "you bitch" bite to it that I had learned from watching *Dynasty* usually came just before women took to hair-pulling and fingernail-gouging. Not that I had ever had women fight over me, mind you, but I'd watched Alexis and Krystal go at it while pretending I was reading a manly Tom Clancy thriller on my side of the bed. What red-blooded man hadn't peeped at those two gals while pretending he was doing something more significant? Of course, I was no Blake Carrington.

Eleana made a graceful exit to a hallway that led past a powder room, through a butler's pantry, and into the kitchen, leaving me to squirm under Sally's gaze. The image of a fox surrounded by a pack of yelping hounds came to mind. It was obvious to me that Sally could smell my fear. So I ran.

"Let me check the house to make sure we're safe," I said in an effort to cover my cowardliness with an act of bravery, following Eleana, passing her before she reached the kitchen.

"Stay here a second," I said and opened the door slowly.

The kitchen was cast in the gray of early dawn light coming from the skylight.

Sally's townhouse didn't have a backyard. What had been a patio with a lap pool as its focal point had been converted to a solarium with a lap pool as its focal point, the twelve-foot-high surrounding brick walls now supported a glass dome.

I went out to the solarium to look around, checking the door leading to the alley. Locked. The townhouse was secure unless someone dropped through the glass dome from a helicopter. But I didn't think this was that kind of plot.

"It's okay," I said to Eleana. "Just leave the door to the hall open, and don't turn on any lights."

She gave me a you-ninny look and began searching in cabinets for coffee. I went back to face the music.

"If I were to ask the question," Sally asked as she looked up from her computer, "would I be disappointed in your answer?"

I briefly considered pretending I didn't understand the question or playing with semantics like "what is the meaning of disappointed." One look into her eyes told me that was futile.

"Yes," I said, "but I didn't intend it to happen."

"I see," she said, staring at the computer screen.

"Sally," I said, coming to her, touching her face, "please understand."

She brushed my hand away and locked on my eyes. The fire in hers had died down to a smoldering pain. "I understand," she said. "Believe me, I understand."

She turned back to the computer screen and punched a few buttons on the keyboard. "Did you bring a gun?"

"No," I said.

She opened the desk drawer, pulling out a .38 caliber Smith & Wesson Lady Smith, like Oma's except its wooden grip didn't have the silver inlay.

At first I thought she was going to shoot me. I'm not sure that thought didn't cross her mind.

She handed the gun to me. "You're better with these than I am. Now that you're here, I'll answer my email and let the world know where I am."

I looked into her eyes as I took the gun. I could see fatigue and hurt. I wanted to comfort her. I moved toward her.

She raised her hands to stop me. "Let's keep it simple."

"Sally," I said, "I'm sorry." I felt like the heel I was.

She didn't answer, just turned to her computer and started keying in her message.

Eleana came through the door carrying a tray with a coffee pot, three mugs, and some sort of loaf cake. She sized up the situation, focusing on the gun in my hand, then set the tray on the coffee table and began pouring, two blacks and one mostly milk with just enough coffee to color it beige. She took Sally's cup to her desk, leaving mine on the tray, and retreated to the sofa with her coffee-colored milk and set it on an end table. She smiled at us, picked up the new LB Cobb novel lying open on the quilt, tore off the corner of a potato chip bag to mark Sally's place, and settled into a corner of the sofa to read, pretending no interest in my current dilemma.

Both women were in their corners, and I was alone in the center ring of an old Chinese rug thinking I made too tall a target. But it appeared neither of them was anxious for a confrontation on the Bill issue, and I had the gun.

With a sigh of relief, I put the gun down on the coffee table, picked up my cup and took a sip, trying to decide which of the two wing chairs afforded the most protection from a frontal assault. I chose the one farthest from Sally.

Halfway through my first fix of caffeine, my mind began to clear. "You haven't sent that yet, have you?" I asked.

Sally continued pounding the keyboard. "No," she said without looking up. "Why?"

"I have a idea," I said. "There's an FBI agent I trust. Let me call him first, before you alert the world to where you are."

"FBI?"

"Yeah. We have a dead governor, arson at a state office, assault on a state official, and murder of a state police officer. That's enough to make their noses twitch."

"One of the messages I've been working on is a request to the US Attorney for help. I suppose the FBI will be just as good."

I found the phone under a empty chip bag and dialed the beeper number George Wertheim had given me when we left Eleana's office. I waited for the beep, then punched in Sally's number. Three minutes later, Wertheim called back.

"What?" he asked sleepily.

"Bill Glasscock, here," I said. "We have a date today, remember?"

"Where?" Wertheim asked.

"The attorney general's townhouse," I said.

"You found her?"

"Yeah. Alive and well. And keep this to yourself."

NINETEEN

Monday, May 28, 6:30 AM

I focused on Sally. "You want to tell me what happened before he gets here?"

Sally glanced at Eleana. "I'm sorry, dear," she said with icicles on the word 'dear,' "this needs to be a confidential conversation."

"Not at all, dear," Eleana responded with a snowball-cold 'dear,' reducing the cold-war tension a notch. "I'll go make us breakfast." Eleana laid the book aside and stood to stretch.

My eyes, without my permission, followed the rise of her chest, then caressed the rest of her.

Sally's eyes followed mine, and I could feel the heat of her anger. For a minute or more after Eleana left the room, Sally said nothing. Then she said, "I never had a chance, did I?"

I heard the agony in her voice as the stainless blade of betrayal sliced into her heart. I closed my eyes and saw the crimson drops of heart pain, hers and mine. I said nothing. What could I say? That, in a moment of selfish, hurting need, I had betrayed her? That I felt her pain along with my own? That once I had pledged my love to Eleana, there wasn't any left for another?

"When we had the fight," she said, "I planned on taking a drive to get it out of my system then coming back to you."

"Why didn't you?"

"As I was getting into my car, another car came speeding along Cliff Road headed toward the beach access cutoff. Two men were in the front seat. They turned around and followed me, tailgating. They bumped me just as we reached the intersection at Bayside Road. I thought it was accidental and I stopped. Then I checked my rearview mirror and saw Wallie in the backseat, leaning against the door. His eyes were closed."

"Dead?"

"He must have been. I thought at first they'd bumped me because they needed help. When the driver got out, I saw his gun. I knew instantly he planned on using it on me, so I got out of there. They didn't catch up with me until we were in town. I was probably doing a hundred along Main Street. I thought surely Tiny or Gomez would be out patrolling or at the station if I could get there. The men in the car must have thought the same thing, because they stopped the chase before we reached the police station. In my rearview mirror, I saw them turn around. The station was dark. So I kept going."

"Who were the men in the car?"

"I didn't know then, but I recognized them when I checked the news on the Internet and saw photos of the dead cops. The driver's name is Sartin. The other one was Block, the man killed at your house."

"Did you print out those photos?"

"They're here somewhere. But you've seen them."

"No. I saw Block, after Davy shot him, but I've never seen a photo of Sartin. I'm curious, that's all."

That wasn't quite all. I wanted to know if Sartin was the cop in the suit outside Sally's townhouse Saturday afternoon, because I was reasonably sure the cop in the suit was part of Chester Thorton's guard contingency on the hunt last fall. And if Sartin and the suited cop were one and the same, then I needed to talk to Chester real bad.

Sally sorted through the pile of printout on her desk. "Damn, it's here somewhere."

"What time did the bumped-Wallie car bump you?"

She looked at me, stopping her search. "I checked the car clock as I was pulling out of the driveway, before they started the chase. About five-fifteen."

"I guess we now know who killed Wallie, and when. What happened after you outran them?"

"I didn't know what to do. I was afraid to come back to the beach house since you were in no condition to defend us. And I didn't want to come here because this is the first place they would think to look for me. So I kept driving. Around eight, I stopped for breakfast at a truck stop along the Interstate and called Lizabeth. She came and got me, and we left my car parked behind a row of trucks where it wouldn't be noticed. We drove up the coast for a while, talking, and finally decided the safest thing was to try to sneak in here. I was on the floor of the backseat of her car when she drove it into the garage with all the state police around."

"I'm sorry, Sally," I said. "I must have missed something. How did you know the state cops were here?"

"By the time she picked me up, Lizabeth had talked to Chester. He told her Wallie and his driver were dead, that the state police were looking for me. I assumed they would be here waiting for me, but I thought we could sneak in, and that you would come find me and we could figure out what to do. But, I was wrong."

"I've been busy," I said.

"I can tell," she said ruefully.

"I've been evading cops, myself. Somehow, they think I might have had a motive to kill Wallie."

"By the way, how is Eleana?"

"Believe me, Sally," I said, meeting her eyes. "I didn't intend it to happen."

"How did it happen?"

"When they called Eleana about the fire at the Archives Building, she left without waking Davy. He heard the news about Wallie, panicked, and called me. I had to go to him, by which time Eleana had come home and I went looking for you."

Sally gave me a skeptical look. "That was Saturday."

"Yeah. I was parked down the street when Lizabeth drove into your garage, and I followed her home. She said you were okay, but I kept looking for you. I checked all of our places. Nobody had seen you."

"She told me you came by," Sally said, softly, with a tad of forgiveness in her voice.

"How?" I asked, thinking surely she would have expected the cops to wire tap her phone, legally or otherwise.

Sally read my mind. "Don't worry. We've used email, my private account, not the state system. Only the CIA tracks those. As long as you don't use the words 'bomb' and 'President' in the same sentence, you're okay. If Lizabeth doesn't hear from me every two hours, she's supposed to call the city cops."

"I think I saw an unmarked car drive by outside."

Sally nodded. "I think it's a state car. They've been doing that since yesterday afternoon. They must have figured out Lizabeth wasn't me."

I mentally kicked myself. "You really didn't think you could get away with your little switch-a-roo, did you?"

"Why not? You and Chester and Eleana are the only people who can tell us apart. We thought that if the state police believed she was me, and enough neighbors saw me, I mean her, here, the cops wouldn't try to shoot their way in. And if they thought it was me leaving when she left, they'd think I'd gone to her house. We were reasonably sure nobody would try to shoot their way into Thorton House. That would take a lot more explaining than some hyped-up concern for my safety."

I shook my head. "Why didn't she tell me where you were?"

"Because Lizabeth thought that if we hadn't convinced the cops I wasn't here, your continuing to look for me would convince them."

I scratched my head. Nice plan. All of it make a certain amount of sense in the perverted logic women use. "Why didn't you just hire a security guard?"

"Why do that? If I'm not here, why would I need one? Besides, most of them are off-duty cops. You know how cops talk. If I had a security guard here, the state cops would know for sure I was here."

Dang. It almost made sense. "I'm surprised they haven't tried to be more forceful," I said just as the doorbell rang. I glanced at Sally. "It looks like we've run out of time."

Then I heard Eleana's kick on the kitchen door. I went to open it for her, and cleared the coffee table so she could set down the tray of eggs, bacon, toast, and an assortment of spreads.

Eleana glanced at me as the bell rang again. "Wertheim? I'll get another plate."

I started for the door and remembered the gun. I retrieved it from the coffee table and slipped it into my pants pocket. Never can tell. "Don't either of you say anything to him unless

I tell you it's okay," I warned, "at least not until I'm sure I can trust him."

"Yes," Sally said, "you are the expert on trust, aren't you?"

I checked the peephole. "You alone?" I asked as I opened the door, sticking my head out to check the street. FBI guys seemed to travel in packs.

"Yeah, I thought I'd wait about calling this in."

Except Wertheim. He seemed to be the dominate dog who only summoned his pack when he was outnumbered. "Come on in," I said and led him to the library.

Eleana and Sally were seated in opposite corners of the sofa, balancing plates on their laps. Both smiled brightly at Wertheim.

"Please," Sally said, pointing to the empty wing chair. "Have a seat, have breakfast. Eleana was kind enough to make it."

The initial shock on Wertheim's face turned to a you-old-dog grin as he glanced at me. I was getting a lot of those lately.

"Yes, thank you," Wertheim said.

Eleana put down her plate and fixed one for Wertheim. "A fresh pot of coffee should be ready, Bill. Would you bring it and a cup for Mr. Wertheim?"

"Always pleased to serve," I said. Eleana had taken over as hostess in Sally's house and Sally didn't seem to mind. Was she that upset by recent events?

When I returned, Eleana had a plate ready for me. We ate in silence, except for the click of silver against china and the occasional crunch of toast.

Every now and then Wertheim glanced at the women, then at me, and let go with a grin. Finally, he put his plate down and cleared his throat. "We have things to talk about, don't we, Miss Solana."

"Do we?" Sally asked.

"Yes," Wertheim said, "we've been looking for you."

"I've been right here," she said innocently.

"So I see. But I'd like you to tell me how you got here, and everything that's happened since you left your beach house."

"It's not a beach house, Mr. Wertheim," she said. "It's a bayview house."

"I stand corrected, Madam Attorney General," he said and glanced at me for support.

I shrugged. When it came to pinning Sally to the mat, it was every man for himself. Besides, I was on her tag-team, the least I could do under the circumstances.

"Did you see anything when you left your bayview house Saturday morning?" Wertheim continued.

Sally glanced at me and I nodded. She proceeded to tell him the same story she had told me about seeing Wallie, apparently dead, with his backup drivers.

Then Wertheim asked her the question I hadn't had time to ask. "Why do you think they killed the governor?"

"Here, let me show you," Sally said, going to her computer. She clicked her mouse a few times and the printer started. A minute later she handed me the letter she had written to the Department of Justice. I read it and handed it to Wertheim who did the same.

"What's the basis of your suspicions?" he asked.

"The files are at my office," she said.

Wertheim eyed her, first to make sure she was leveling with him, and then, I realized by the jealousy that flared between my eyes, because he was enjoying the view.

"I suppose you want to freshen up before we drive over to your office," he said, staring at her chest.

Sally examined the food-stained shirt then smiled at George. "I suppose this isn't the sophisticated look the citizens of our state expect from their attorney general."

Sally glanced at Eleana. "Would you care to join me? You can borrow anything I have that's long enough for you."

Eleana gave Sally an expression of pure joy at the offered olive branch.

Again I thought "Aw Schitt." No good could come of this, no good at all. Just what I needed—the girls making up while trying on clothes, comparing notes and giggling about my abilities compared to their other conquests. No doubt, they would dream up an appropriate punishment for dear old Bill for letting them seduce me.

After the ladies left the room, I warmed George Wertheim's coffee and poured myself another cup.

"You going to tell me how you do it?" he asked with the fairly common you-old-dog grin plastered across his face.

"I'm a Mormon," I said.

"How do I convert?" George asked.

"It's a baptism by fire," I said, leaving Wertheim with the coffee to go find one of the lawyer suits I kept in Sally's guest room closet to wear when she wanted to buy me dinner at some place fancier than Moe's.

TWENTY

Monday, May 28, 8:15 AM

We drove over to the State Office Building in two cars, Sally with George Wertheim and Eleana with me. While getting out of the car, I remembered the gun. The metal detector at the guard check would cause a stir. "Wait a second," I said, pulling Sally's .38 out of my pocket.

I leaned across Eleana to open the glove compartment, accidentally brushing her breast. She flinched as if I had hurt her. Before I could apologize, she was out of the car, tugging on Sally's short skirt, trying to hide some of her long legs.

"I like you in short skirts," I said.

"Pig," she said with a smile.

Wertheim and Sally waited for us in the garage elevator. I caught him checking out Eleana's legs as we walked toward them. Then he stared straight ahead, all FBI-business-like. Dang, why doesn't he get his own women and leave mine alone.

Wertheim showed his badge to the guard.

The guard ignored him and focused on Sally. "How're you doing this morning, Miss Solana?" the guard asked, smiling like he meant it.

"Fine, William, and you?"

"Can't complain," he said, waving us around the metal detector. "Have a nice day, ma'am."

Gee. I could have gotten past him with the gun. All it took was the right connections.

Then I noticed the too-friendly way George Wertheim took Sally's elbow to escort her into the elevator. Sally smiled up at him. Damn her.

Eleana checked my face and frowned at what she saw.

Damn women. Damn Wertheim. Just what I needed in my life, another archetype—*Dirty Harry*—strong, silent, cop who speaks softly, looks you in the eyes, winks as he blows you away.

With these happy mixed-doubles thoughts in mind, we converged on Sally's kingdom. After a friendly hello to her front-office staff, she unlocked her door and swept into her inner sanctum with the three of us on her heels. She stopped in mid-stride and screamed—high-pitched, off key.

Files were scattered everywhere. Law books were toppled from their cases. Desk drawers and credenza pilfered. Sofa and chairs ripped opened.

Instantly, Wertheim took charge. He pushed us back out of the room, closed the door, and pulled out his badge.

"FBI. Everyone, sit tight," he announced with the badge held high. Then he nodded at the secretary outside Sally's office. "Call the local FBI first, then call the Chief of Center City PD. When you get them on the phone, I'll talk to them. Nobody goes anywhere until we're done."

Thirty minutes later, FBI suits swarmed through the Attorney General's office. The way George did it, being in charge meant letting the other guys do the dirty work. Of course, he probably knew as well as I did that whatever evidence had been in Sally's office was long gone. The first order of business was to get the story out of Sally's mouth, then worry about piecing together enough evidence to nab the perpetrator.

The thing I didn't like about Georgie boy being in charge was that he seemed to view his role, at least in part, as being Sally's white knight. I wasn't sure I was ready for another Sir Lancelot to take over my job in the damsel-saving department. Of course, I was definitely sure I didn't want George to take on my role as Eleana's white knight. I wondered how Brigham Young would have handled the situation.

Leaving grunt agents to sort out the mess and interview Sally's staff, Sally, George, and I retired to Eleana's office in the Archives Building across Liberty Plaza from Sally's office. Eleana's secretary brought coffee in then left us. Eleana and I took the ends of a loveseat and Sally took one of the club chairs across from us. George, down on his knees in front of Sally, holding her hands as Prince Charming had after fitting Cinderella with the glass slipper, started the questioning.

"You sure you're all right?" The look on his face was that of a man gazing at the girl of his dreams. The fool!

Leave her alone, I wanted to shout, but that would not be the wise thing to do under the circumstances. It really teed me off that I had broken her heart a few hours ago and here Sally was, already taking comfort from another man. If she was trying to make me jealous, it was working. Maybe I hadn't meant all that much to her. How could women tell me they love me and then let the next guy who happened along comfort them?

I glanced at Eleana.

Eleana looked back with cat-green eyes and shrugged.

I knew it. She and Sally had cooked this up while they were getting dressed for the office. Sally was getting even with me, and Eleana was getting off scot-free after having seduced me.

And old Georgie boy was eating it up. I expected him to pull the glass slipper off and lick Sally's toes any minute now.

"Hmm, hmm, hmm," I cleared my throat loudly. "Can we get on with it?"

Wertheim glared at me, then patted Sally's hand again, taking the chair next to her. "Whenever you're ready, Sally."

Sally? When the hell did they get on first name basis?

"I'm fine, George," she said, "really I am."

I could swear she batted her eyes at him. The bitch!

Eleana reached over, took my hand, bringing it to her lap, and closed her other hand over it. She smiled like the canary she'd swallowed was giving her indigestion.

"Okay, Sally," I said, "exactly what did you have?"

She glanced at me, then focused on George. "It started with an email to Stan Cramer that someone forwarded to me. Others followed. The first one aroused my curiosity, the others were enough to trigger an investigation."

"About what?" George asked in a just-the-facts-ma'am voice.

"That's just it. They were vague, like, 'You're falling down on the job,' and, 'Any shortages, you pay.' Like Stan Cramer was on the hook to somebody."

"Who forwarded it?" I asked. "They identify the sender, don't they?"

Sally sighed her you-idiot sigh. "The first one was forwarded from a computer assigned to a secretary in Stan's office who had left the payroll. No one had closed that account. We're certain it wasn't her. She went on maternity leave a month before it was sent and hasn't come back. We've checked her out thoroughly."

"What about the sender code on the original email," I asked, "the one that went to Stan?"

"That belonged to a clerk in the state treasurer's office who was seriously injured in a car wreck. He's paralyzed and has been on disability leave ever since the wreck. He isn't in any condition to have sent it and he didn't have access to an internal computer."

"The others?" George asked.

"Sent from inside computers, at night. We thought the original sender must be someone in the controller's office or computer services—both have access to passwords—alerting my offices anonymously, but we could never pin it down."

"Who was in those buildings at the time they were sent?" George asked. "Don't people need a pass to get in?"

"You saw what happened this morning," Sally said. "If the guards recognize someone, they usually wave them past the metal detector. And they only check IDs after five. Someone could have come in during the day and stayed late."

"The building guards are state police, aren't they?" I asked.

Sally rolled her eyes. ""Yes, Bill, they are. And we have copies of the guard rosters for the nights in question. They work in pairs—one at the desk and one checking the building—and none of the same pairs were on duty more than one of the nights emails were sent."

"Sartin or Block on any of your lists?" I asked.

"I don't know," Sally said. "Until this weekend, neither of them made it to my radar screen."

"Okay," George said. "I'll get our computer experts involved. I presume that there are backup tapes of emails."

Sally smiled and shook her head. "Sorry, George. We pulled the tapes immediately. They were in my office."

"Shit," George said. "Sorry."

Sally smiled at George. "Don't look so gloomy. My emails are automatically forwarded to my home computer so I can look at them at night. I've saved those."

"Good," George said, sounding relieved and smiling back just like he had gotten one of Sally's special gifts.

"And you said they were copies of email to Stan Cramer," Eleana said. "They might be stored on his computer as well."

Sally shook her head. "Afraid not. They were deleted, and computer security was unable to recover them from his hard drive. There's a memo about that in my files. Or was."

"Hey gang. I hate to sound like a defense attorney, but a few vaguely threatening emails to Stan Cramer do not make a case against Stan or anyone else."

Sally gave me another you-idiot glance. "I know that. We looked behind the words, at what Stan Cramer might have been involved in that would evoke threats. The treasurer's office has done a complete audit of the state police books going back five years, and we've come up with nothing, no misuse of funds, no subcontracts that look out of the ordinary, none of the stuff that would speak of malfeasance in public office."

"Did you check his bank records?" I asked.

"Yes, Bill. "There have been a number of large deposits to the local account where his payroll check is deposited, from a Swiss bank account. But we can't get the Swiss bankers to tell us where the money originates."

"Maybe we can get a little more cooperation out of the Swiss," George said, like Dirty Harry would have said it.

Sure, I thought, the FBI and who else. Obviously old George hadn't tried to get anything out of Swiss bankers before. "Have you talked to Cramer?"

"No, Bill. We didn't want to alert him to our investigation until we found a factual basis to bring an accusation."

"What seems funny to me is that someone is blackmailing Stan Cramer and he's the one getting the money."

"Yes, Bill. That's my problem."

George got up to pace the office. "Have you thought about the possibility that a former employee might be trying to get back at him?"

"We've come up with nothing there," Sally said.

"What about the deposits to his account?" asked George. "Any routine in when he receives them or in the amounts."

"Most are around the first of the month. There might be a legitimate reason. They could be from a trust fund. Mine is through a Swiss bank."

"What's his background?" I asked. "Everybody knows you're rich, but does anyone know where he came from?"

"He joined the state police right out of high school," said Sally. "He didn't do much beyond average in the ranks until he was assigned to guard Wallie during his first campaign. He received a few quick promotions after that. Wallie appointed him state police chief when he was elected to his second term."

"Who did his background check?" George asked.

"Our office did," Sally said. "There wasn't anything that would cause a stir with the press or the voters, and nobody in the legislature asked any questions, so we didn't spend a lot of time on it. But there might be a memo-to-file that would help."

"Thanks," George said meaningfully, taking his seat.

Sally smiled at him, meaningfully.

"When did he acquire the Promontory Point house?" I barked meaningfully enough they managed to peel their eyes off each other and look at me. "What did he do to afford a place like that. Did he marry rich?"

"Hardly," said Sally, "Mrs. Cramer was an... uh... an entertainer... in a strip joint when he married her. That's when he bought the house. It cost three million dollars."

"Wow!" I said. "I should have been a policeman."

George glanced at Eleana. "I guess we better look at those archives records a little closer."

"What archives records?" Sally asked.

"Oh, I forgot to mention it," George said, sincerely apologetic. "We went through microfiche copies of the paper records destroyed in the Archives Building fire."

"And?" Sally asked, looking curiously at Eleana.

"There are records of campaign contributions to Wallie from Cramer and others," George answered for Eleana.

"What others?" Sally asked.

"Chester Thorton and Fred McPeters for two," I said.

"What?" Sally said. "Chester and Fred hated Wallie. Neither of them would have given him a dime. Lizabeth would never have approved Chester making a campaign donation to Wallie."

"I would have thought so, too," I said, eyeing Sally, thinking to myself that her words sounded off key. "But apparently neither of them hated Wallie enough not to have their picture made with him. That was in those files as well."

"None of this makes any sense," Sally said.

"Tell her what Wallie told you Friday," I said to Eleana.

"He didn't tell me anything," Eleana said. "Wallie called me to see if I would go to dinner with him."

"And?" Sally asked.

"When I said I couldn't, he told me he was going out to a dinner and poker party at Cramer's house at Promontory Point."

"The next step is to talk to Stan," said George, "see if he can give us the guest list for his poker party. I'll put my people to looking into where his money was coming from and going to. What I'd like to do, Sally, is have my people work with your people on whether any of the individuals at the poker party had anything improper going with any state agency. But first, I'd like to take agents to your house to copy your computer files."

"Certainly," Sally said. "I'll tell my staff to cooperate fully. As to my computer files, the answer is yes, but only if I go with you, and only if you let me copy the files."

"I don't understand," George said, clearly surprised at her new-found resistance to his charms.

"That's not negotiable," Sally said, suddenly the tough-as-nails lawyer I knew she could be. "Otherwise, you'll have to get a warrant, and I don't think you have probable cause to get one. I have a number of things I need to take care of here this morning, but I could meet you at my townhouse this afternoon, if you're agreeable to my terms."

I stared at Sally. Now she had me curious.

She caught my look. "I have my private files on that computer, my tax returns, and..."

George raised his eyebrows. "You haven't been downloading dirty pictures off the Internet, have you?"

"Damn it," she blurted, then collected herself and continued in her soft, sweet voice that she'd been using on George, "Poetry. I write poetry, all right! It's personal, that's all."

Well, that just goes to show you. All this time I had thought of Sally as a feisty, tough-as-nails, ambition-knows-no-end female prosecutor, warrior-princess protector of the public trust and me. And here she had the soft heart of an Elizabeth Barrett Browning to go with the soft feet of a Cinderella.

George Wertheim must have been as impressed as I was. He reached over, picked up her hand, and said, "I'd love to read your poetry, but only if you want me to."

Can our FBI pick 'em or what?

TWENTY-ONE

Monday, May 28, 1:00 PM

As far as I could tell, the only new information to come out of the morning's inquiry was that Stan Cramer was a recently wealthy man, cause unknown, who might possibly be involved in shady dealings, kind unknown; Sally was a poet; and George Wertheim now had a lust on for Sally. Curiouser and curiouser.

However, it appeared I was no longer a target of the FBI's investigation into Moreno's murder, a good thing, and Stan Cramer would have enough on his mind that he might just forget about me and mine entirely.

With Sally safely in George Wertheim's custody and Eleana at my side, we drove back to our, correction, Eleana's house. I tried not to fret about George beating my time with Sally. At least, I told myself, at the end of the morning, I was still even when it came to woman count. Now was not the time to ask myself any of those deeper questions like whether I could ever again live with the deceitful woman at my side, or whether I would regret choosing Eleana over Sally. Nor was it the time to ask myself how I could have believed Sally's feelings for me were anything more than pity, in the best lamp light, or a case of settling for the man at hand, in the brightest daylight.

Besides, I consoled myself, if things didn't work out between Eleana and me and between Sally and her new white knight, there was always the possibility Sally and I, being creatures of habit, would find the familiar more comforting than the unknown. We had, after all, taken comfort from each other for a few months. Nice comfort. I liked her, liked her a lot. Times like these, I wished I really was a Mormon.

***

Eleana and I went by Davy's school and spoke with his teachers and the principal. Davy had two exams left to complete the school year, but everyone agreed that, under the circumstances, he could take makeup exams during the summer after he had recovered from the trauma.

Back at the house, nothing had changed. And neither of us wanted to take time to do anything about cleaning up the mess. Eleana's primary goal was getting back to Splendor Bay to see about Davy. I raided the refrigerator while Eleana packed a few more things she thought she needed, like towels without holes in them and dishes without chips in them, then I helped her load them into the trunk of her Lincoln. She led the way as we wove our way through city streets to the highway.

As I drove, I listened to another few rounds of Sinatra—"The Girl That I Marry," "The Things We Did Last Summer," "Lost in the Stars." I sang along when we got to "My Way," then got misty-eyed on "Ain'tcha Ever Comin' Back." I now knew what I should give Oma for Christmas—a new CD. Possibly update her to Willie Nelson.

While I drove, wishing I had a bottle of Scotch to help me through Frank's love-gone-wrong songs, I mulled over the assortment of facts that I'd gathered the past two days.

None of them added up to murder. For murder you need opportunity and means. It helped to have motive. And motive was such an individual thing. For a postal clerk having a bad-letter day, one more rude customer was enough. For LA commuters, a traffic jam was enough. The only thing I felt certain of was that whoever had killed Moreno had a reason I would buy if I were on the jury. Heck, I'd buy any excuse for killing Wallie, even eating too many fake-fat potato chips.

Another thing I didn't understand was the means part. Usually a murderer hit on a technique that worked and stuck to it. How a murderer could be subtle enough to use a hypodermic on Moreno and blow out the brains of his driver was a mystery.

But, it wasn't my mystery any more. George Wertheim and the able, willing, and ready Center City coven of FBI were on the case. I could safely contemplate going back into my early-retirement and let some other dude deal with the many major and minor sins and sinners.

I wanted my simple life back, to catch a few waves with Davy, to feel the sea spray on my face as I jogged on the beach, to watch the sun set beyond the edge of the ocean that marked the end of the world I could see from my beach shack. Simple things. And not so simple. Get reacquainted with my son, maybe see where this new thing with Eleana would lead since we were both free agents at the moment and the peace pipe had been smoked, in a manner of speaking.

I had let my focus drift, so it took a few seconds for me to realize Eleana's car had moved out ahead. I saw her car in the distance, cresting the next ridge. We'd be at the Splendor Bay exit shortly. I put crime solving on hold while I focused on driving. The winding cliff-hugging Bay Highway was a tough stretch of road, even sober.

By the time I reached the exit, she was out of sight. I turned onto Bay Highway and picked up speed, greatly exceeding the barely-safe legal limit, expecting any minute I would catch up with her.

Just after I rounded a hairpin curve, a state cop pulled up on my rear bumper, blue lights flashing. Darn. I hadn't even smelled him. I was definitely losing my touch.

Doing the good-citizen thing, even tempted as I was to find out how fast Oma's new Caddy could cruise, I slowed down and put on the blinkers to indicate I intended to pull over. It took me a couple of minutes to find a stretch of road with a wide-enough shoulder for the Caddy.

When I did, the cops pulled in behind me like it was ticket time. But before either of them got out, they pulled back onto the road and roared away at lightning speed, lights flashing, sirens blaring.

I shrugged and counted my blessings, then felt that first tingle of fear. Eleana?

A vision of her car diving off the side of the cliff in a fiery crash flashed in my mind. Oh God, let it not be Eleana.

I spun gravel pulling back onto the pavement.

As I crested the next hill, I saw Eleana's car snared in a guard rail, the front crumpled back to the wheels. The state cruiser that had pulled me over was parked sideways in the road blocking traffic. One cop waved down traffic on the other side of the wreck, one cop peeked inside Eleana's car.

I slammed on the brakes, stopping just inches from the car in front of me, and took off running.

The cop standing beside Eleana's Lincoln tried to stop me. I shoved him out of the way and jerked on the front passenger door. It refused to budge.

I tried the rear door. Same.

"Help me," I yelled at the cop.

He just stood there.

The driver's side of her car was wedged against the guard rail and the passenger side was so crumpled that the doors wouldn't open. Eleana was covered in an airbag. I could see blood. Smoke billowed from the front of the car.

"For God's sake, help me," I shouted at the cop.

A guy from one of the stopped cars came running up with a tire iron and tapped on the rear window with it.

Finally, with the public yelling at him to help, the cop sprang into action, grabbed the tire iron from the citizen, and gave the rear window one substantial blow, breaking it into a web of small pieces.

I climbed onto the trunk, kicked the mesh of window glass into the backseat, and climbed through the car to Eleana. She was wedged between the steering wheel and her seat.

I tried to lower her seat to give me room to slide her out from under the wheel. The buttons were frozen. Wisps of smoke floated into the passenger compartment from under the dash. I pushed the collapsed airbag back into the steering column, released the seat belt, and slid it off.

Her arm appeared broken. A bone pierced the skin of her thigh, which was bleeding profusely. A cut on her forehead was also bleeding heavily.

"Eleana, can you hear me?"

"Bill?" Her eyes fluttered. Then she drifted away.

"I have to get you out," I said, and eased her from beneath the steering wheel.

She moaned.

"I'm sorry, darling. I have to get you out."

The cop came through the rear window. "Guide her legs," he said. "Lift her up, and I'll take her."

With my arms under her neck and hips, I lifted her over the seat back. He put one hand under her neck and the other arm under her back as I held her hips and legs.

As we moved her past the seat back, I looked out to see Tiny on the trunk of the car.

Tiny helped the state cop get her onto a backboard. Medics carried her to the ambulance. The cop crawled out.

I was right behind him. Tiny pulled me free of the now smoke-filled passenger compartment.

I ran to the rescue squad Bronco and crawled in beside her. Just as they closed us inside, I heard an explosion and looked out to see Eleana's car burst into flames. Tiny and the state cops were holding people back.

We passed the Channel 12 news van heading to the crash as we sped off to Splendor Bay Hospital.

I watched helplessly and prayed as a medic worked over Eleana. The ambulance came to a screeching halt at ER. Hospital staff pulled her out and moved her to a gurney. They ran with her to the emergency room. I followed on their heels.

"OR-2," bellowed a nurse just inside the door. "Move aside, sir," she yelled as I tried to touch Eleana's hand. Then they disappeared into an elevator with her.

Minutes later, I don't remember exactly how long, someone led me to a waiting room. Tiny soon joined me.

"What happened?" he asked.

"I don't know. Maybe the state cops do. They pulled me over, then took off again when they got the call."

"I got it, too," he said. "A driver with a cell phone called it in. Said it looked like someone ran her off the road deliberately."

"Did they give a description?"

"Not much. A late model white Crown Vic, like the state police use, but without lights or logo. Didn't get a tag number."

"What's taking so long?" I asked.

"Don't worry, Bill. She's tough. She'll make it."

"God, I don't think I can survive losing her again."

"Is there anything I can do?" Tiny asked.

"Yeah. Find Davy and bring him here."

"Will you be all right?"

"Yeah. Just go find Davy."

Tiny was almost to the door when Oma and Fred walked in. Oma took one look at my face and gathered me in her arms. I cried like a baby.

"There, there," she said as she patted my back.

I know a man's not supposed to cry, but there comes a time when the hurt and worry are too great for any other form of expression. The hurt of losing Eleana to Moreno came out in those tears, and the fear of losing her again, the anguish of knowing Davy might lose his mother, the long buried grief I still felt over losing my own mother when I was his age. It all came out. Men shouldn't cry, but losing a woman we love will turn the best of us into infants. So I sobbed, and Oma made soothing mother sounds, and Fred looked embarrassed.

Then Tiny came back with Davy, and Oma went through the process again with him.

Eventually the bawling was done. Worry took hold as we watched the clock click the minutes into hours.

We were all sitting quietly, each lost in our own thoughts, when a doctor in scrubs walked through the door.

"Mr. Glasscock?" he addressed the room.

I stood up, quickly joined by Davy.

Tiny, Fred, and Oma were right behind us.

"Yes?"

He sighed.

My heart sank. Davy grabbed my arm.

"No, no," said the doctor. "It's not that. It's..."

"What?"

He glanced at Tiny, Fred, Oma, and Davy's anxious faces, then back at me. "Perhaps we should talk privately, Mr. Glasscock."

"What?" I demanded.

"Your wife has several broken bones, and there's the blow to her head, but she's stable. You can see her now, for a minute. But the baby..."

It took a moment for me to hear anything other than Eleana was alive. Then the full message hit.

"The baby?" Oma and I said together, locking eyes.

"The baby?" Tiny echoed.

TWENTY-TWO

Monday, May 28, 6:00 PM

Eleana was hooked to tubes and electronic equipment, her fair skin a deathly gray, but she was breathing. I assured myself of that fact by touching the warm skin of her cheek.

"It's unlikely she'll be awake before morning," the nurse said. "She's highly sedated."

Davy assured himself his mother was still among the living by touching her hand. He patted me on the shoulder. "I'll wait for you outside, Dad."

I picked up the hand Davy had touched and pressed it to my lips. "I love you," I said. "Please don't die."

Her eyes moved beneath the lids as if she'd heard me. I held her hand and asked for a divine favor, then I left to find Davy. He and Tiny were at the nurses' station at the end of the hall.

"I'll drive you home," Tiny said. "Fred retrieved Oma's car and took it back to the Kitchen. We'd better go out the back. Those newspeople are in the front lobby. They're starting to piece together Wallie's death, the archives fire, Eleana's accident."

"Into what?"

"So far it's just one of those crazy-patch quilts."

"You and Davy are welcome to come home with me for dinner," Tiny said as he pulled the cruiser to a stop at Fred's restaurant, "Mary Louise won't mind."

"Thanks, Tiny, but not tonight," I said. "I may call you later on for a ride back to the hospital."

Davy and I walked the rest of the way to my beach shack in silence. My thoughts were too much of a jumble to put them into words. I needed to pull myself together, to take care of Davy. He might be as big as a man on the outside, but I knew he was still a boy on the inside. Over the last few days he had been through a lot more than any kid should, and now this.

"Are you hungry?" I asked when we were inside, not knowing how to ask "Are you hurting?"

"I'm fine," he said, going to the television to flip on his instrument of self-hypnosis.

"Did you take your shot?" I asked as we both stood there in front of the TV and watched the six o'clock news commentator say, "And now for area news."

"Dad, please. It's not due until ten. I'm not a baby. And you're not my mother."

At that moment the picture of Eleana's burning car flashed on the screen. Our eyes met, each of us realizing what he had just said, and all it meant. He came to me and wrapped his arm around my shoulders. I hugged him as we both bawled again.

"Buy you dinner at Fred's?" I asked as we sniffed back tears.

"I need to wash the saltwater off. I was surfing when Tiny..."

Davy turned quickly and retreated to the safety of the shower, where his tears could be washed down the drain.

I watched the rest of the news. Ten new state prisons were being built, the contracts already awarded to everyone's surprise, especially those government contractors who weren't asked to bid. Very expensive new homes for crackheads, drug dealers, carjackers, convenience-store-clerk killers—the criminals the public will spend tax dollars to support, which is why the politicians and crime fighters always make them the big ticket cases. A warring faction of some African nation was exterminating some other faction, which could be solved with donations to the Red Cross. Some basic food supply was contaminated with some new strain of Ecoli and some weight-loss drug caused birth defects, both of which could be solved with a larger budget for the FDA. And terrorist had taken over another embassy. No one knew what to do. And so it goes.

Fred glanced up from his booth in the bar and waved us over.

"You two all right?" he asked in his usual gruff voice.

"Yeah," I said, "thanks for asking." Fred didn't mean to be gruff, but he didn't know how to be anything else.

"It's been a hell of a few days, hasn't it?" he continued.

"Yeah, you could say that," I said.

"What do you want for dinner, Davy?" Fred asked. "Whatever, it's on the house."

Davy smiled at Fred with his sixteen-year-old appetite in full bloom. "The seafood platter and strawberry cheesecake."

"You got it." Fred motioned for a waitress. "How about a pound of king crab legs on the side?"

Davy nodded eagerly.

"And you?" Fred asked me after he gave Davy's order.

"Same," I said.

"Same for the old guy," Fred said. "And Scotch for the old guy and a root beer for the young man."

We ate our meals with Fred chattering away about how he was thinking of expanding. Fred wasn't a chattering kind of guy, so I was wondering if he was trying to take our minds off our troubles or whether there was some meaning behind his words. By the time Davy finished his cheesecake and half of mine, Fred was on his third Scotch and I was on my second.

"If you're feeling up to it, Davy," Fred said, "Juan could use help busing tables in the dining room. There's some money in it for you if you want to help him out for a while."

"Sure," Davy said, and he stacked the plates at our table.

Fred waited until Davy disappeared into the kitchen. "I need to talk to you."

"About what?" I asked.

"About Wallie Moreno."

"What about Wallie?"

"If I tell you, can we call it attorney-client privilege?"

"Or something," I said. "Today's your lucky day. My suspension has been lifted. I am a lawyer again. We can call it privileged if you think you're talking to your lawyer in confidence instead of to your drinking buddy."

"That's what I think," Fred said, grinning ever so slightly. "I think I'm talking to my lawyer about an important legal matter. Your bar tab enough of a retainer?"

"Fine," I said. "What is it you want to tell me?"

"Moreno was blackmailing me."

"What could he possibly blackmail you about?"

"You know," Fred said, "about that conviction."

"But that's common knowledge."

"Maybe. Around here. You and Tiny know it, and maybe a few other people, but the state liquor control board doesn't. If I had put it on the license application, they would have denied."

"You would have done all right with the restaurant."

"What's a restaurant without a bar? What's a bar without a wholesale liquor supply? And once you go wholesale, it only makes sense to go retail. Besides the store here, I have a whole string of liquor stores across the state, different names."

"I never would have guessed," I said. "You ought to try bragging so we'll respect you."

"How do you think I support two ex-wives? On this place?"

I shrugged. I guess I hadn't thought about it. Fred was even more unlucky in love than I was. Neither of his marriages to big-chested waitresses had lasted much longer than the honeymoon. After the second one, Fred gave up on wives and stuck to fooling around with the help in the storeroom.

"What are we talking about here, Fred?"

"A few hundred grand a year to Moreno for hush money."

"And another felony conviction if they find out you lied on your liquor license application."

"Yeah," Fred said. "I figure with Moreno dead, cops everywhere will be turning over every pebble. If they find out, I'm going to need a lawyer."

"You didn't kill him, did you, Fred?"

"No, but who knows what the cops might decide if they discovered the payoff," said Fred. "I'd be suspect number one."

"Better you than me. So, who do you think did it?"

"Lots of people had reason, but I figure it's somebody local."

"Why local?" I asked.

"Don't know," Fred said, "Just feels like it must be somebody who knows where to find quiet spots to dump bodies in the middle of the night."

"You have anybody in particular in mind?"

"You might want to talk to Chester Thorton."

"Why Chester?" I asked.

"Wallie was blackmailing Chester, too."

"How do you know?"

"'Cause one day I dropped a check off at Cramer's place. Saw one of Chester's checks on his desk."

"Cramer?"

"Yeah, we dropped the money with Stan."

"You sure it was Chester's check?"

"He's signed enough bar tabs around here."

"You sure Chester's check was to Wallie?"

"No, not exactly. It was made out to a bank account number like mine was. I don't know which number, it could have been to a different account. But it was signed by Chester Thorton. I just assumed it was to Wallie, like mine was."

"When was this?" I asked.

"Couple of months ago," Fred said.

"Were you at Stan's poker party the other night?"

"No, but Chester might have been."

"How do you know?" I asked.

"He was here having drinks Friday at happy hour. Said he might go to a poker party later on. You heard about any other poker parties Friday night?"

"You wouldn't happen to know what Wallie was blackmailing Chester over, would you?"

Fred met my eyes and lied to me. "Can't say as I do. I try to stay out of other people's business."

"Good policy," I said. "You think Davy has earned a twenty yet? I want to go back over to the hospital to see Eleana."

Fred pulled keys and a wad of cash from his pocket, handing me the keys and a couple of twenties. "Take my Mercedes. Drop the keys at the cash register when you're done with it. I retrieved Mom's Caddy. Lucky somebody didn't drive off in it instead of pulling it over to the side of the road."

"Yeah, lucky," I said.

"I found a gun in the glove compartment," Fred continued. "Mom said it wasn't the one she loaned you, so I put it in the glove compartment of the Mercedes."

I answered his unspoken question. "Belongs to Sally. Oma's gun is in an evidence bag from the shooting at my house the other night. I'll make sure she gets it back when they're through playing evidence games with it."

"If I were you," said Fred, "after all that's happened, I'd keep Sally's gun in my pocket."

"If I were you, I wouldn't tell anybody else what you told me. Sally has an investigation going about how Stan lives so well on a cop's salary. With any luck, he won't have kept very good records, and since she only started the probe to get at Wallie, she might forget about it once they get Wallie buried."

"Thanks for the warning."

"And Fred?"

"Yeah?"

"When I do lawyering, I charge five hundred an hour."

"Well," Fred said, "that's about the going rate for a good whore these days."

"Cracks like that are one of the reasons I malpracticed on my last client."

"And you got disbarred," Fred said.

"No, I was suspended, a temporary thing," I said. "Not permanent, as in disbarred. I got a much needed vacation out of it and I get to play lawyer again. And with his new lawyer, my ex-client got ten years in the slammer."

"I liked you better as the town drunk than as a lawyer."

"I liked me better, too."

I found Davy in the kitchen and gave him Fred's forty dollars. Walking out, we bumped into Chester and Lizabeth Thorton.

"Bill," said Lizabeth, gathering me into a hug, "we're so sorry about Eleana. If there's anything—"

"Yes," said Chester. "Anything at all. You want us to call in a top notch specialist? I've got a friend at the Mayo Clinic who'll get us the best."

"Thanks, Chester," I said. "I'll keep that in mind."

"How're you holding up, son?" Chester said to Davy, draping his big arm around Davy's shoulder in a grandfatherly hug.

"Fine," said Davy, letting Chester leave the arm in place.

Chester had taught Davy to fish, fussed over his achievements, bought him lavish birthday gifts. They had become even closer the past year during my alcoholic absence.

"You sure are," said Chester. "Your dad's lucky to have such a fine son. I'll be at the beach this week, if you feel up to fishing."

Davy nodded, then glanced at me.

"I guess we'll see you later," I said. "Davy and I are headed over to the hospital to visit Eleana."

"Give her our love," said Lizabeth.

"You tell her we're praying for her," said Chester.

I nodded and started to walk away.

"Oh, Bill," Chester said.

I turned.

"I... never mind, I'll catch you later," he said, giving me a pat on the shoulder.

"Maybe tomorrow," I said. "There's something I want to talk to you about, too."

Davy and I loaded into Fred's Mercedes and drove over to the hospital, me thinking about Chester the whole way. There was a lot I needed to talk with him about.

Campaign contributions. Blackmail. Murder.

And I dreaded it. How had he allowed himself to get mired in Wallie Moreno's misdeeds? Chester was too smart for that. But sometimes even a lawyer needs a lawyer to restate the rules. I should at least warn him that he might need one. But I suspected he already knew that.

I checked in with the nurse on duty. "I'm Bill Glasscock. I'd like to see my wife, Eleana."

"Oh, yes, Mr. Glasscock, we were about to call you."

I must have looked the alarm I felt because she continued, "She's fine. She's awake, asking for you. I told her I'd tell you."

"Thank you," I said, as Davy and I moved past her.

"Oh, no, just you, Mr. Glasscock. Just one visitor at a time."

Davy looked as if she had slapped him.

"Please, let him see his mother, so he'll know she's okay."

The nurse studied Davy's pleading eyes. "Just a second for the boy. And only a minute for you."

Eleana opened her eyes and smiled at us.

Davy took his mother's hand and started telling her how worried he had been and how glad he was she was okay.

I stood back and used the moment to examine her. Her color was better but she had a large purple blotch on her forehead around the butterfly bandage holding the cut together. Her right arm and leg were in casts, her right leg hooked to a traction device. The airbag and seatbelt may have saved her life, but she had been severely battered.

After Davy left, Eleana met my eyes. "I'm sorry. I should have told you about the baby."

"Now isn't the time."

"I'm so sorry, about us."

"Did you see the other driver?" I changed the subject. I didn't want to think about Wallie Moreno planting his bad seed in my wife's loins.

"No," she said, "the car came up behind and bumped me, pushing me to the edge of the road. I was too busy trying to control the car to look at the driver."

"We'll talk about it tomorrow."

"Bill?"

"Yes."

"The baby. Is the baby okay?"

"You need your rest," I said, realizing they hadn't told Eleana her baby was in danger.

Her pregnancy had survived the accident and surgery, but her doctors felt she would miscarry soon. And they would terminate her pregnancy if her life was in danger. I'd made that decision for her, even knowing she would never agree herself. Sacrificing Wallie Moreno's baby for Eleana's life had not been a hard choice for me to make.

"Is the baby okay?" she pleaded, her left hand moving across the small mound made by the child inside her.

"For now," I said.

She looked away, tears on her cheeks.

Eleana was four months pregnant. Moreno's child was a girl. The pre-surgery ultrasounds had shown that.

I should have known. The fuller, tender breasts, the fuller waist, her refusal to take a pill when she was upset by Wallie's death, her passing on alcohol, drinking milk.

But I hadn't suspected my wife would have a child with another man. Of course, I hadn't even suspected the other man until I walked in on their moment of passion.

The child Eleana and I had lost the year Davy was ten was a girl. A beautiful, perfect-in-every-way baby, except for the missing part of her heart.

We named her Angela, knowing from the ultrasounds before her birth that she wouldn't survive her first day without Eleana's blood supply, wouldn't survive any attempt at a transplant even if another baby's heart were available. Neither of us had known how to help the other get past the grief. I buried myself in my work; Eleana planted a garden where her perfect rose, *Angela*, now grew from our baby's ashes.

Losing our baby seemed like the end of a struggle we couldn't win. Davy had come so easily, so unexpectedly while we were weighing the issue of the '80's, a child or a career for Eleana. He was God's gift to the indecisive.

When Davy was two, we started trying to have a second child. Nothing happened. The doctors said give it time, let nature take her course. So we waited on nature. But as Eleana reached her mid-thirties we realized Mother Nature was a no show.

The doctors examined, poked, prodded. Our private parts appeared normal and operational, but nothing happened. Then we tried "assisted reproduction," her eggs and my sperm united in a glass dish, in vitro fertilization, IVF. Eight eggs were fertilized, two placed in her womb, one attached, and nine months later Angela was born. Our other six embryos were still frozen, waiting on our decision to give them life or death.

After Angela's death, we were too devastated to try immediately, too afraid we'd condemn another child. Then we were too far apart as we each found ways to hide from our loss.

At first, Eleana filled her empty time with her rose garden, and when that wasn't enough, by volunteering for one charity or political thing or another, finding fulfillment in coordinating political campaigns. Somehow she had come to work in Wallie Moreno's last campaign. When Wallie was elected, he appointed her head of the State Archives Office. To the victor's camp go the spoils. To their beds go the victor.

I was too busy playing lawyer to notice when she became more than Moreno's political supporter. But I'll never forget the night I left one of her fund-raising parties to find some unpolluted air and solitude in the pool house.

It was like a breath of slaughterhouse air when I found my wife and Moreno together in a lover's embrace. I turned and ran from the house, tucking a bottle of Scotch under my arm. A few weeks later I showed up at Oma's door in Splendor Bay. I'm not sure how I got there. By then, I'd had too many bottles to remember.

But time heals all but the wounds that penetrate vital organs like the heart and those pesky sores you pick at until they abscess. No doubt Eleana would recover from her injuries, and she would recover from whatever her feelings for Moreno had been. But if she lost this child, I knew with a familiar certainty, that wound would never heal. Losing a child is a deeper blade into the heart than losing a lover. Been there, done that, worn-out that shirt.

But if Moreno's child survived, where did that leave us? The past two days had forced me to realize Eleana was more important to me than I'd ever wanted her to be again. I knew I could get past the hurt of her adultery if I would stop picking at that scabby sore. I had allowed myself to think about drifting into whatever relationship she wanted us to have, spouse or occasional lover and protector, whatever. I was comfortable with the idea, perhaps even eager to give us another chance. But her lover's child?

Would Wallie Moreno's face on Eleana's child always be too painful a reminder of her betrayal?

I now knew the motive behind her seduction plan that had worked so well. She wanted me to play daddy to Wallie Moreno's orphan. That might be too much for even me to ask of myself.

TWENTY-THREE

Monday, May 28, 10:00 PM

I gathered Davy from the sofa in the waiting room where he was glued to a ballgame on television and we went home.

He took his injection and we watched the remainder of the game. Neither of us had much to say. I was too busy replaying the day's events on the movie screen in my mind to be much of a listener, even if Davy had wanted to talk.

When the late news came on, we watched the replay of Eleana's car fire and the latest version of the ongoing investigation into the deaths of Moreno and his drivers. At least one reporter, namely Pam Baby, had put together the coincidence of Moreno being found on the beach below Sally's home where I was in residence, Block's subsequent death in Eleana's Center City home where I was in residence, and Sartin being found dead in Sally's Splendor Bay home where, fortunately, I was no longer in residence.

"Sources close to the investigation say prominent attorney Bill Glasscock is not a suspect at this time," declared Pam.

"Dad?" Davy said, alarmed.

"Don't worry," I said, slightly worried. Obviously my kiss on Wonderwoman Pam's tattooed lips had made an impression on her. "Everybody is a suspect. She's just mouthing off for fun and profit."

I watched an interview of Sally, seated in front of a bookcase full of law books. She announced the murders were now under investigation by the FBI, that all state agencies were cooperating fully, and the Lieutenant Governor would serve in Wallie's place until a special election could be held. She refused to comment on whether she'd run for governor in the special election.

Lieutenant Governor. That's what they called it. We had one of those just like Texas did. Why hadn't I thought of that? Maybe because I didn't vote in state elections anymore, and only in federal elections when somebody like John Kennedy ran, and I was still waiting for that to happen again. I should call Tiny and tell him none of us had won the bet.

The final news blurb before the weather report told of the coming state occasion. Tomorrow, our late, great Governor Moreno would have a funeral of grand proportions, to be attended by no less than the Vice-President of the United States, maybe a couple of ex-Presidents, a few US Senators thrown in for good measure, and everyone who is anyone in state government.

Davy went to bed, and I sat there in my duct-tape recliner, feet up, the television volume turned down so all I could hear was the subdued laughter of the *Tonight* show audience. I closed my eyes and sifted through the cobweb of recent events for a thread of logic. There was none.

Suddenly I felt panic. Someone had tried to kill Eleana twice, and so far this killer had been very successful with his/her other targets. I picked up the phone and called Tiny.

"Eleana may still be in danger."

"We're on top of it," Tiny said. "The same thought occurred to me, so I sent Gomez over to stand guard. And I called that FBI guy, Wertheim. He's sending over some special agents. We need help keeping the press out of there anyway. Just as soon as you hang up, I'll go relieve Gomez. You try to get some sleep."

"Thanks, Tiny. By the way, none of us won the bet on Wallie's replacement. It's the lieutenant governor. Like in Texas."

"I heard. Get some sleep. We'll look after Eleana."

"Goodnight," I said.

It was late. I was tired. So I contemplated the idea of trusting Eleana's fate to Tiny. But no way could I sleep. I checked on Davy, looking with pride at my sleeping son. Chester was right. He was a fine young man. Then I locked the front door behind me and walked the mile to the hospital.

***

Tiny and George were chatting near the elevator when I got out on Eleana's floor.

"Short nap," Tiny said, looking at his watch.

"I couldn't sleep," I said.

Wertheim offered his hand. "Sorry about your wife."

"Yeah, thanks for your concern," I said. I glanced over at the young man at the nurse's station. "Your guy?"

"Didn't think you'd mind."

"I'm very appreciative. I trust you have everything squared away about Sally's evidence."

Wertheim looked at the ceiling and sucked in a breath.

"She's okay, isn't she?" I asked, alarmed.

"Yeah, Sally's fine. But when we got to her place to check the computer, it was missing. I parked her at a hotel tonight with agents on guard while we dusted her townhouse."

Yep, Sally had a new white knight, all right. "Looks like somebody doesn't want you to investigate," I said. "You been to Promontory Point?"

"It took a while to get a warrant," Wertheim said. "I had to calm Sally down enough to get an affidavit from her as to the nature of the missing evidence. Then I had to convince a judge to sign a warrant naming the state police chief. Not many judges want their name on the line in case we're wrong about Cramer."

"Can he be trusted?" I asked, nodding toward the young Fed flirting with a nurse.

"Holds the marksmanship trophy. I have another agent outside your wife's room, another by the exit stairs, one in the waiting room, and you walked past one in the lobby."

"Gomez is parked at the emergency room door," Tiny volunteered. Splendor Bay PD was doing its part.

"In that case," I said, "let's go serve your warrant."

"Sorry," Tiny said and thrust back his shoulders. "We can't risk taking a civilian along."

"Listen, Tiny," I said, pointing to Eleana's room, "my primary goal in life at the moment is to find the bastard who hurt her. I'll go with you and be nice, or I'll go on my own and you can try to protect Cramer from me."

George Wertheim glanced at Tiny.

Tiny nodded.

"You have a gun?" Wertheim asked me.

I patted my pants pocket. "Sally loaned me one this morning. You didn't think I was this glad to see you, did you?"

"Let's go," he said. "And you stay the hell out of the way until we get the place secured."

Tiny squeezed into the passenger side of the front. I took the backseat of George's government-issue sedan.

"How do you know Cramer hasn't flown the coop?" I asked over George's shoulder.

"A little birdie told me," George said.

"What little birdie?" I quizzed.

"The little birdie who has done his yard work for the last couple of days," George said. "We've had Cramer under surveillance since the shooting at your Center City house."

It took me a second to put two and two together. "Does that mean he didn't personally run Eleana off the road?"

"Cramer's accounted for," George said, "but maybe one of his storm troopers did it."

We drove on a couple of miles and were just starting up the ridge when Tiny asked George the next question, cop to cop. "Who do you think is behind this?"

"I don't know yet," George said.

"My guess is drugs or wetback smuggling," Tiny volunteered. "That's the primary criminal activity in this part of the state."

"Too easy an answer," George said.

"I like easy answers," Tiny said.

George made a hundred-and-eighty-degree curve for the last lap up to Promontory Point.

"So why would Cramer kill a governor, a few of his own good men, and go after the ladies?" I asked as George straightened out the car, which had an unbelievably good suspension system if no other remarkable attributes. "Doesn't sound like the kind of thing that would keep a drug deal, or any other deal, quiet."

Tiny shrugged.

"That is a mystery," George said, "isn't it?"

"Yeah," I said, "a real whodunit."

We waited while George went through the radio check routine with the three other cars of special agents scattered along the road and the agent playing yardman and watchdog from a domestic-staff apartment above the garage. That made a total of eight agents, counting George, and one Splendor Bay PD officer to serve a warrant. Plenty of white hats. Maybe they were afraid of Stan's stick.

According to the watchdog-yardman agent who had a clear view of the master suite from his servant's quarters at the back of the house, Stan and wife had arrived home at seven and moved about the house until lights out at ten. According to one of the agents who had tailed them all day, they had been on a shopping spree in Center City. There had been a phone call to the house around nine, the caller not on the line long enough for the FBI to run a trace. The only traffic along this road since seven had been local, nobody stopping or turning around in the driveway.

It took ten minutes for the FBI guys to hold their meeting and decide to serve the warrant by the official FBI book—ring the front door bell first, then if you don't get an answer in three seconds, shoot your way in. I got the impression all government decisions were made by committees. That way, it's harder to point the fickle finger of blame when something goes wrong.

With that decided, all the guys with badges and official issue guns proceeded with their plan to converge on the front door in SWAT fashion. Me, they left in the back seat of George's car. Of course, I didn't stay put like I was told. I'm not good with verbal instructions. For me, it's fine print or nothing.

I hung back as the heavily armed Feds moved in on the house in precision dance steps—six steps this way, six more steps that way, then dash across to the other side of the yard, sort of like weaving a cop braid. Cute.

What I couldn't understand was how guys dancing this way and that across a front lawn made any less of a target than guys running in a straight line to the door. But I was willing to concede some government survey proved that to be true.

At any rate, it took them another few minutes of braid-weaving dance steps to make it to the front door. Being a coward by nature, I held my place behind the largest tree and waited to see if a gun battle was part of the evening's entertainment.

They didn't need to ring the front door bell. The door was standing wide open, a fact that had been obscured by the shadows, or so they later explained to each other. I personally think they forgot to look. I was surprised that particular turn of events didn't bring on another meeting, but all that happened was a few shrugs as they glanced at each other wondering what to do next.

George, being in charge, ducked his head and barged right inside the dark house, followed by the other Feds and a minute later by Tiny. Tiny wasn't a fool, either.

I waited another minute, listening for gun fire to erupt. Nothing happened. When all the lights came on, I left the security of my front-row tree and followed the cops inside.

Stan Cramer's place at Promontory Point was a lot bigger than it appeared from the road. The rooms in the adobe-style mansion were of lavish proportions and furnished just about the way you would expect a newly rich cop with an ex-stripper wife to furnish it. Expensive cheap. To their credit, the black velvet Elvis behind the bar was a signed original.

Looking around at the flamboyant furnishings as we moved to the back of the house, a few things were soon clear: (a) Stan had done all right for himself, (b) somebody should have gotten suspicious before now about his success, and (c) for a cop, he sure had let somebody take him by surprise.

We found Stan, at peace with the world if not with his maker, in his combination shower/sauna in the master bath, wearing an undershirt and jeans. He had apparently decided to take a bite off the business end of the .38 Special still clutched in his right hand. His wife had been shot in the head, in the bed, possibly while asleep since her eyes were closed, possibly while watching television, which was still on.

It looked like a classic spousal murder/suicide—the husband shoots the wife and himself when he realizes he's never going to win this game of trials and tribulations but doesn't know how to stop fighting. I guess being the perpetrator of a recent murder spree could do that to a fellow.

"How the hell did this happen?" George yelled at the young Hispanic yardman-watchdog special agent, who had apparently taken more interest in watching the yard than in watching Stan.

Soon agents were swarming the place looking for scientific clues to the Cramers' apparent murder/suicide. Calls were being made to forensic investigators from pocket cell phones, beepers were buzzing. Probably one of the calls was for a body wagon, because Splendor Bay's overworked ambulance showed up a half-hour later to cart the bodies off to the funeral home, which seemed to be getting a heck of a lot of business this week.

The cops were noisy, noisy, busy, busy all around the now hushed and peaceful Cramers. I was somewhere between the two states of being. Perhaps pensive and unobtrusive were the words. Not being much of a scientist myself, I stayed out of the way while the other guys gathered their evidence. Not being much of a talker, I stayed quiet, trying not to be noticed.

As the agents swarmed about, wearing latex gloves and filling plastic and paper bags with bits of this and that, I relaxed on the sofa in Stan's media room, an alcove separated by a wide arch from the main living area. I busied myself looking at the photos on the walls with one eye and watching the cops at play with the other, occasionally casting both eyes on a rerun of the evening's lawyers-yelling show on Stan's wall-sized television.

I soon realized two things. I should offer myself up as a legal expert on criminal law in this obviously high-profile case of a dead governor which had all those other lawyers rudely interrupting each other speculating on whether I was or was not the culprit. I could idly speculate as well as the next lawyer and just as loudly. And, it was a shame we couldn't bring back the Salem witch trials so those guys and gals of the bar could have full-time jobs burning the subjects of their what-if debates at the stake. Surely they would find more satisfaction in that than in mere character assassination. Boards of legal ethics guys, where are you tonight? And second, why would anyone buy one of those grainy big-screen TVs anyway?

Yeah, and number three, Stan Cramer really loved sticks.

The walls were littered with team shots and shots of Stan sliding into home, or cracking a bat, or collecting a trophy, or shaking hands with his opposition. What I found interesting about the photos was that in every one that involved Stan doing things with his arms, he was using the left one.

No doubt about it, Stan was a lefty. So, I wondered, why had he used his right hand to blow his brains out?

And why was he wearing a T-shirt and jeans in a shower? Didn't want to be found naked and dead? Wanted to be neat? Why not wake the wife up and make her get in the shower with him so there wouldn't be blood on the bed?

I tried not to make too much of these observations as I watched the hustle-bustle of the murder investigation from my quiet alcove. They would either figure it out or decide not to figure it out.

It didn't take long for me to conclude from the comments of the special agents that they had decided not to figure it out. Stan was the most obvious answer to five homicides, an arson, a burglary, an attempted murder, and his own theoretical suicide. Eight crimes and a mortal sin solved for the price of one investigation. Cops liked nothing better than to solve crimes and get them off the books, fair and square or with a little help from a fortuitous event or from the evidence locker, all in Lady Justice's name, of course. It gives their public relations department something to brag about and their chiefs something to show the public when they ask for more money to support their wars on crime. Unsolved crimes don't do much but get police chiefs fired and special agents demoted.

So my money was on these guys calling it solved. That way, the FBI and the Splendor Bay PD got credit for good police work, Stan got blamed, the rest of state copdom could claim the buck stopped there with a single sick individual in their ranks, and the citizens could feel safe and protected again. The murderer was dead. Long live the murderer.

If that was their decision, I had two choices. I could buy whatever story the FBI came up with about Stan Cramer being the sole perpetrator of all crimes and go on about my ordinary life, trusting that whoever was behind the murders would leave my family alone. After all, if the crimes were declared solved, what right-thinking murderer would risk killing again and unsolving them?

Or I could say, "Wait a second, fellows. Stan was left-handed and look who he played ball with. His ball-playing friend had a motive."

What then? Sit around and wait for the killer to come after my family while the cops debated whether or not they wanted to pursue it? Take the starring role in my home-movie version of *Conspiracy Theory*?

All things considered, it seemed to me the best of the two choices was for me to buy whatever story the *Federales* handed me, hope the killer felt secure enough not to kill again, and quietly settle my own personal score with the son of a bitch handing Stan his trophy.

Frankly, I didn't give a damn whether anyone ever pinned Moreno's murder on Stan's ball-playing friend or not. For killing Moreno and Stan he probably deserved a medal, and killing the other cops might also have been a favor to the world. Murdering Stan's wife, maybe not. She was probably an innocent beneficiary of Stan's labors of love. Still, I felt no need to avenge her death. For hurting Eleana, on the other hand, I would see that the bastard hurt real bad. But first, I had to be sure he was the one.

Tiny started in my direction. I met him in the doorway. "George about done?" I asked. "I need a ride home."

"Yeah," Tiny said, "he sent me to find you."

"Well," I said, "it looks like justice has been served."

"Yeah," Tiny said, "it looks like Stan was behind it."

"Whatever you guys decide is fine with me," I said. "How about the next time you find a stiff on the beach, you don't ask me any questions?"

"Works for me," Tiny said.

TWENTY-FOUR

Tuesday, May 29, 3:00 AM

It was three in the morning when Tiny dropped me off at Fred's Fine Seafood. As I walked down the beach to my shack, I marveled at how the star-studded sky and the waves lapping the shoreline in foamy crests could exist night after night, year after year, millennium after millennium, ever the same, never much bothered by humankind's little dramas.

I stood there gazing at the stars, listening to the sea, smelling the ocean air. We were nothing but minor amusements for the gods, if the gods even took notice of us at all, nothing more than the amusement humans experience when we noticed the struggles of ants fighting over a mound.

It couldn't matter much in the scheme of the universe that six people were dead and my wife had been severely injured, or why, or even who had done the deeds. I tried to tell myself that if it didn't matter to the gods, it shouldn't matter to me, except I didn't much like the fact that Eleana had been hurt.

A personal problem. The only one of the dead I knew personally I had wished dead, and the others I didn't care one way or the other whether they lived or died. If I wanted retribution, I should focus on inflicting the amount of pain necessary to avenge Eleana's injuries, nothing more. Just solve the personal problem. Anything more and I would be back to solving the problems of the world. That wasn't my job any more.

Then I asked myself, as I took a deep breath of clean sea air, if I really believed my current line of Bull Schitt, why couldn't I let things be? Why couldn't I accept the official version of events? This would be an even easier story to buy than the one about how the lone 1960's Russian traveler, Lee Harvey Oswald, single-handedly brought down the President of the United States.

Yeah, if I could buy that tall tale, then I could buy this one. Any doubts I had, I'd keep to myself. If the cops thought it was over, I'd let it be over. I owed that much to my son and his mother. I wasn't going to solve the crimes and enter the witness protection program. Not me. Playing the lead in *Conspiracy Theory* was not my gig.

I entered my abode and checked to make sure Davy was safe. He stirred when I opened the door to his small room.

"Dad?"

"It's okay, Davy," I said. "I'm just restless."

"Mom?" he asked.

"Mom's okay," I said. "We'll talk in the morning."

He turned over and went back to sleep.

I went to my bedroom and settled in, snuggling into the pillow that held Eleana's scent. The images of Stan and his wife in death wormed through my mind. Someone had killed Stan for a reason, had killed his wife because she was a witness to that reason. Had they tried to kill Eleana because she was a witness to something Wallie was involved in? Some transaction between Wallie and Stan the women knew about? What was he involved in that would lead to six murders? Could I be sure it really was over? Go to sleep, I told myself. Inquiring minds don't really need to know.

Davy knocked on my door at eight. He had pancakes and coffee ready when I came out.

"Want to catch some waves?" he asked.

"Okay."

"Dad?"

"Yes?"

"About Mom…"

"I'll call in a few minutes, but I'm sure she's okay."

"I already did," he said. "They said she was better."

"Good."

"What I wanted to ask was… about the baby?"

I stared at him, my man-child, my pride, my joy. I hadn't thought to consider what the baby might mean to him. His sibling, if not my child. He was too old to be jealous about a new baby. He was also old enough to know I wasn't the father, and how I might feel about that.

"It just seemed like you two might get back together," Davy continued, "and I was wondering… with the baby..."

"I don't know," I answered truthfully, meeting his like-mine eyes. "I'll have to see what your mother wants."

Davy nodded. "You know, she stopped seeing him. He kept calling her, but she wouldn't see him."

"No, I didn't know." I hadn't seen any society page photos of them together for a while, but I rarely read the Center City society pages anymore.

"She misses you."

I looked at my son. What sixteen-year-old didn't want his parents together? It was certainly worth a little white lie.

"Let's check out those waves."

Davy was still riding surf and I was back at the shack, exhausted from the morning's battle with the forces of nature, changing into clothes to wear to the hospital, when the phone rang.

"Bill?" Sally said tentatively.

"Yes?"

"I heard about the wreck and I'm so sorry," she said, almost sincerely. "How is Eleana?"

"She'll make it," I said.

"Uh, Bill?"

"Yes?"

"I have a favor to ask."

"What?"

"Would you accompany me to Wallie's funeral today?"

I was dumbfounded. I was speechless. Pay my respects to Wallie Moreno? She had to be out of her frigging mind.

"Please, Bill," she said. "I know how you feel about him, but I have to go. Two pairs of eyes would be better than one."

"For what?"

"You know the FBI think they've solved all crimes?"

"Yeah, I was there," I said.

"I'm not as convinced as George seems to be that Stan Cramer is the one and only answer," Sally said. "I thought maybe whoever is behind it might show up at Wallie's funeral, and—"

"And you thought that with my ESP I would figure out who, if anyone, in the church full of mourners is killing people?"

"I thought maybe we could compare notes afterwards and figure out something that way."

"Why don't you ask George? You two could work the loose ends together. It's his case. And I'm sure he would like nothing better than to get into your mind."

"He doesn't want to be seen at a public event."

"Neither do I. You know, Sally, this could be dangerous. If Stan isn't the answer, there's a killer out there who might get nervous if he thought he hadn't gotten away with it."

"It's my job to see justice is done."

"Leave me out of it. Justice can do for herself. I have enough on my plate right now."

"Please, Bill. Just think about it. Please."

I sighed, straining to hear any voice of reason in my head, yet knowing I would crumble. I'd always been a sucker for a woman saying "Please." Besides, I was curious about who might pay their respects to Old Wallie. The only people I'd expect to show up for Wallie's funeral were either (a) people who might profit from his death one way or another, or (b) people who might profit from the publicity surrounding his funeral, or (c) people who didn't have the nuggets to say no to (a) or (b) people. I placed Sally in category (b). I was in category (c).

"I'm going to check on Eleana this morning. I'm not making any promises, but if I can talk myself into it, I'll pick you up at one-thirty. If I'm not there by one-forty, go on without me."

"Thank you, Bill."

When Davy and I arrived at the hospital at ten, Eleana's doctor was standing at the nurses' station filling out charts. "Oh, Mr. Glasscock," he said, "glad I caught you."

"Is she okay?" I asked, alarmed by his serious tone of voice.

"She's doing well." He glanced at Davy uneasily.

"Go on, visit with your mother?" I suggested to Davy.

Davy gave me his stubborn look.

"I'll be along in a few minutes," I urged.

When Davy was out of range, the doctor began. "So far your wife has shown no sign of a spontaneous abortion, but we can't be sure the fetus is undamaged, either from the trauma of the accident or from the medications we gave your wife during surgery and afterwards. We did a series of ultrasounds this morning and the staff obstetrician is reviewing them now. I think you should talk with Dr. Andrea, so you can make an informed decision on whether we induce an abortion or let nature take its course."

"Is Eleana's life in danger if the pregnancy continues?" That was the only criteria Eleana would accept, if that.

"Not at the moment, but you should consider the possibility of a damaged baby."

I nodded. "When can I talk with Dr. Andrea?"

"Let me check." He picked up the phone. A few uh-huh's later he said, "She can see you now. She has an office on the third floor. Take the elevator and go to the nurses' station. They can direct you from there."

The third floor was the maternity ward, with a glass-walled new-baby nursery just off the elevator. In spite of my desire to stay focused, I was drawn to the window where two new fathers stood cooing to infants unaware of their existence.

I had forgotten how small they were, how pink and cuddly, and how much of a sucker I was for a baby. The middle baby in front yawned, opened her navy blue eyes, and looked me over. She had a full head of blond hair, like Angela and Davy had at birth. Then she smiled. I swear it was a smile. She smiled, yawned again, closed her eyes, and squirmed into a contented sleeping bundle as she drew her legs and arms up into a little ball. I felt a strong desire to pick her up, hold her to my chest, and smell her new baby flesh. Reluctantly, I went on my way.

Dr. Andrea motioned me to a chair on the visitor's side of her desk. She took the chair next to me and picked up a folder, pulling out ultrasound photos of a human in utero.

"This is the umbilical cord," she said, pointing to a string of bright dots in a photo. "It's still firmly attached to the wall of the uterus, so we're not concerned that blood flow has been compromised or that there's been oxygen deprivation. And the placenta is intact, no breaks or leakage, hence no danger of infection. But that doesn't mean the trauma to the mother did not impact the fetus. The thing we are most concerned about is the effect of the medications during surgery and afterwards. They all carry strong warnings against use by pregnant women. They can cause a wide range of birth defects. But, with the surgery and the extent of her injuries, we had no choice but to use them."

"Is that the baby?" I asked, recognizing a human profile.

She traced with a paperclip. "Her forehead, nose, mouth." She moved the clip. "And her belly, that's a knee, that's a hand."

"Ah," I said, looking at a baby. Unbelievable. Four months.

Doctor Andrea caught my focus. "They latch onto their thumbs as soon as there's enough finger definition. At birth, they have sucking down to a fine art."

The memory of Eleana with Davy at her breast floated past my mind's eye. "Did you check for internal injuries?" I asked, surprised at my concern for this baby.

"Here's one of the brain. Everything appears to be normal." She pulled out others. "The internal organs. Everything normal for this stage of development." She picked up another. "Obviously a girl. And long legs."

"Like her mother," I said.

"Why don't you read these?" Dr. Andrea said, handing me the patient warnings. "They explain the potential harm and why we're concerned with allowing the pregnancy to continue."

I squinted and read the drug-company flyers written in microdot print that made me suspect the drug companies didn't really want anyone to read the potential adverse effects. They could cause liver, kidney, and brain damage in adults. In a fetus, the additional problems included damage to the thymus and other glands, blindness, hearing loss, limb defects.

"Is this a now or never thing?" I asked. "Can't we give her a little time and see what happens? Aren't there tests?

"We can monitor the baby's growth, check on organ and limb development, but such things as glandular damage, blindness, hearing loss, and a number of other things may not be evident until birth, or afterwards. If there's been trauma to the baby's brain from the collision, it could be minor enough that we can't detect it with the ultrasound now, yet she could demonstrate cerebral palsy or retardation. Those conditions are usually not evident until the child fails to develop the proper motor or verbal skills at the appropriate time. The long term effects of the drugs are totally unpredictable. She might develop cancer or another serious problem."

"But you don't see any signs of any injury now?"

"We can't really determine everything that could go wrong."

"Doctor, we lost a baby, after trying for years to get pregnant. Both of us would have gladly taken that child in any condition rather than lose her. Eleana is forty-two years old. The prospects for having another child are not favorable. And she's a Catholic."

"I understand your reluctance to terminate the pregnancy, but the decision won't become any easier by waiting," Dr. Andrea said. "If we detect damage later, it may be too late to abort."

It should be an easy decision for me. I could tell them to go ahead and end the life of Wallie Moreno's child, then tell Eleana I had done it to protect her life. She wouldn't get over the loss of the baby, but she might believe me. And that would be the end of it. No Wallie, no Wallie baby.

But I couldn't. I kept seeing the baby in the nursery, that toothless smile. That infant was a stranger's child, yet if they sent her home with us, I knew I could love her and protect her as if she were my own. In the final analysis, it didn't really matter who had donated the sperm or the egg. Even if I couldn't be a father to her, I could at least not take her life.

"No abortion," I said. "Not unless Eleana's life is in danger. Or my wife is well enough to make an informed decision."

On the way out I stopped to look at the baby girl in the bassinet in the middle of the front row. Again she opened her eyes and stared at me like she could read my mind. I cooed at her like a fool. That little girl would probably have that effect on men all her life.

Eleana looked better, even though the bruise on her forehead was a now a dark purple. She and Davy were talking.

"Where have you been?" she asked.

"On the third floor," I said.

"Oh?" She gave me a worried look.

I touched her hair, then kissed her lips softly. "Dr. Andrea showed me baby pictures."

Eleana's sea-green eyes searched mine. Before I could tell her about my chat with the doctor, Mary Louise, carrying a flower arrangement, burst into the room with Tiny on her heels.

"Bill!" Mary Louise exclaimed. "I was hoping we'd see you." Then she turned her concerned mother-of-four face toward Eleana. "And how are you doing, Eleana?"

"Much better," Eleana said, examining the flowers. "They're lovely. Thank you, Mary Louise."

"The baby?" Mary Louise probed, concern in her mother-of-four voice.

Eleana glanced at me and all eyes followed.

"So far, she's okay. I met with the doctor a few minutes ago and she showed me the ultrasounds. We have a tough little girl."

Just then the nurse showed up and frowned at us.

"They're not fond of visitors," I said.

"Oh, I'm sorry," said Mary Louise. "We'll leave."

"No, no," I said. "Eleana's probably getting sick of me. You stay and I'll get coffee. Want to come, Tiny?"

"Okay," he said.

"And Mary Louise, would you do me a favor?"

"Sure, Bill. What?"

"Would you drop Davy off at Oma's after your visit? He can help her wait tables. I have errands to run this afternoon, but I should be home before dark."

Inside the elevator, Tiny said, "I never expected you and Eleana to get back together."

"Neither did I."

"Sounds like you've been leaving your shoes under her bed for a while now. I'm surprised Sally didn't shoot you."

I glanced at Tiny. Did I level with him, tell him it wasn't my baby? Did I say nothing? Or did I lie to him, let him respect my ability to keep two women at the same time?

I went for his respect. I lied.

"Divorce can turn into one of those love-hate relationships. We tried to discuss the property settlement without our lawyers. She started yelling at me and the only way I could shut her up was to kiss her. One thing led to another. Now we're going to have a daughter."

"So the divorce is off?"

"I guess," I said as we got off the elevator. "Oh, would you mind checking on Davy? If he runs out of anything to do at Oma's, he can go bus tables for Fred. I may be late getting home."

"Where are you going?" he asked suspiciously.

"Center City."

"What for?"

Again I was faced with the choice—lie or tell the truth. There would be TV news coverage and I was escorting the Attorney General to Wallie's farewell party. I would get found out so I told the truth. "Sally asked me to accompany her to Wallie's funeral. And I need to go by her place and get my stuff."

"Shit, Bill!" Tiny said, disgust in his voice. "Can't you keep your pecker in your pants ten minutes? You're going to blow it again. Think of Davy and Eleana, and the baby."

"I had planned on keeping my fly zipped. I just want to pay my final respects to our late, great governor. In fact, I want to make sure he's in the ground and covered over. I'd be even happier if they would let me drive a wooden stake through his heart."

"Bill," Tiny said, "one of these days you're going to get in so deep nobody can pull you out."

TWENTY-FIVE

Tuesday, May 29, 1:15 PM

I arrived at Sally's in time to change into one of my righteous lawyer's suits and a pair of spit-shined wingtips that I kept in her guest room closet. I wanted to look nice when I waved goodbye to Wallie and thanked him for my daughter.

Sally was a study in grace as she eased into the room, bringing me a glass of wine. She placed the glass on a chest near me, lay down across the bed, and propped herself up on an elbow, watching me button my shirt and put in the gold cuff links she'd given me at Christmas.

I picked up the glass and took a sip, glancing at her through the mirror on the closet door. She wore an almost-too-low-cut-for-church, body-clinging black jersey number, straight out of a 1930's movie. Her slender ankles peeked out below the long and tight skirt, making me think of female parts higher up. Not many women wore high heels like she did anymore. She was a beautiful woman. Any fool could see that. I felt the first stirring of desire and ducked into the closet to choose a tie.

Sally's voice trailed after me. "I talked to Tiny."

"Yeah? How does this look?" I asked, showing her a maroon and navy paisley silk tie, another Sally gift.

"He said Eleana is pregnant," she accused.

I studied the tie. So what was the answer? Should I tell her the truth, that Eleana was pregnant with Wallie Moreno's child and I hadn't cheated on her with my wife when she believed I was being faithful to her? Or should I lie to her and tell her I was the father of Eleana's child, that I had never been faithful to her? Would it make any difference in whether she ever trusted me again? I said nothing.

"When is the baby due?"

I met her eyes. "October," I said, mentally counting five months into the future.

"Oh," she said, counting four months back, reading her mental calender on my whereabouts last winter when I was supposedly faithful to her.

"I'm ready," I said.

"Let me get my hat and gloves," she said.

Wallie's funeral was what one would expect for a governor. The biggest church in the center of Center City welcomed all who had an invitation, with valet parking provided at curbside so that each of the many important people who were allowed in could have their important cars put in the proper pecking order for traveling to the cemetery behind the Governor's Mansion afterwards. Wallie had what he had always wanted—center stage with all his betters and full press coverage.

The crowd of ordinary citizens were held at bay across the street by uniformed police. The free and noisy press were lined up along the steps yelling and jostling each other like little children around an ice-cream truck when any mourner of note appeared, treating the event like a Hollywood premier.

I handed the keys to Fred's Mercedes to the valet and came around to open Sally's door.

As we started up the steps to the church, Pam of Channel 12 thrust a microphone into Sally's face and yelled, "Madam Attorney General, how do you feel about Governor Moreno's death? There's a rumor you will run for the vacant office."

Sally paused and smiled sweetly and sadly for the camera. "I'm greatly saddened, as we all are, at the governor's untimely death. He was a great man and accomplished much for our state. We will all miss him. For now, I'm more concerned that the Attorney General's office run smoothly. It is much too soon for anyone to think about filling Governor Moreno's shoes."

"Thank you, Madam Attorney General," Pam said in somber television tones while eyeing me. "That was Attorney General Sally Solana, accompanied by prominent attorney Bill Glasscock on this solemn occasion. The governor's body was found Saturday morning near Ms. Solana's home in Splendor Bay where

Mr. Glasscock was a house guest. A state police officer was found dead in Ms. Solana's home on Sunday morning. Another state police officer was killed in Mr. Glasscock Center City home Saturday night. And just yesterday, Mrs. Glasscock, a recent companion of Governor Moreno's, was grievously injured in an automobile crash outside Splendor Bay."

Pam must have remembered my beach kiss, I told myself.

Sally gave her speech three more times to other reporters as we ascended the stairs. Each recited a similar spiel about our complicated relationship to their viewing audiences.

Entering the candle-lit foyer of the church, I prayed everyone who saw the broadcasts would be too kind to tell Eleana about my appearance as Sally's consort, at least not tell her before I had a chance to tell her myself. Hopefully, I could convince Eleana my intentions were honorable, that I hadn't cheated on my wife with my lover. Yet.

We moved into the sanctuary with Sally leaning against me, holding onto my arm, her perfume driving me to distraction, and I continued to think about God. I asked Him, when you dreamed up this sex stuff, why did you make all these rules about one to a customer? Life is hard enough without these kinds of choices. Had there been no choices, no rules, I would have taken Sally right there in the midst of the other high-tone mourners and full press coverage. Instead, with Eleana heavy on my mind, I crossed my self and prayed. Forgive me, Father, for I have sinned, and for Heaven's sake, lead me not into temptation anymore. Amen.

Nobody can give a funeral like the Catholics, I thought as I looked around the stained-glass and statue-endowed sanctuary, remembering my own hour-long, down-on-the-knees wedding twenty years before in the same church. All Eleana and I had at our wedding were a couple of priests chanting Latin, a dozen altar boys balancing candles while singing falsetto, lots of pretty girls in satin and lace, an equal number of young men in tuxes and studs, and about four hundred close friends of the Solana family in fancy dress.

Ours was just a brief, song-filled, the-show-must-go-on production number compared to Wallie's somber, grandiloquent send-off. What with eulogies by the Vice President, both state Senators, the Lieutenant Governor, two former governors, and chants by the priest, we said good-bye to Wallie and wished him well in the hereafter for the better part of two hours. Another half-hour was expended for the procession drive and getting properly parked on the street behind the Governor's Mansion. We spent another thirty minutes on the ashes-to-ashes and throwing dirt on him part of the event in the small cemetery where the state's first families are buried. All of it received impressive media coverage.

Finally, assured that Wallie was in the ground for good and could do no more harm, we went about our business. While tramping back to the car, I bet myself twenty that if Wallie had known he would get this much press, he'd have died sooner. Realizing there was no way to determine a winner on this kind of bet, I called it even and got on with seeing Sally to her door.

Back in the car, Sally asked, "What's your take on it?"

"I would say he's dead and buried." I maneuvered the car onto High Street. "What do you think?"

"Damn it, Bill! I mean about who was there. George showed me the photos of campaign contributors you guys found in the Archives. All but Stan, Fred, and Chester were at the funeral."

"Well, Stan is dead, and Fred didn't like Wallie much." I made a right turn on red without a full stop, then glanced in the rearview mirror to check for cops. "You'll have to ask Chester why he wasn't at the party. He's your brother-in-law."

"That's not what I mean."

"What do you mean?" I noticed a white Ford Crown Victoria a few cars back. A cop? A tail?

"Did any of them seem suspicious to you?" Sally asked.

"You mean any of the mourners?"

The Crown Vic moved up a car, now only two behind us.

"Yes!" she said, tired of my game. "Any of the mourners in the photos with Wallie."

The Crown Vic turned onto a side street.

"I didn't see any of them laugh out loud, if that's what you mean," I said, beginning to pay attention to Sally. "Nobody behaved any more hypocritically in their expressions of grief than anyone else. For what it's worth, you do the grief thing like a pro. I especially admired your little sniffle."

"Hollywood is in my blood. Actually, all those flowers triggered my allergies."

"I would hate to think you grieve for Wallie."

"Right," she said. "Just so you know, in a couple of days, I'm going to announce an investigation into corruption in state agencies. I thought I'd do that before I announce my candidacy. I promised George I wouldn't turn it into a murder investigation. Just a probe into bribery of Wallie's handpicked people, to take the glow off our acting governor's chances."

"You really want to get yourself killed just to prove you'd make a tough-on-crime governor? Why risk it? You can win the election without getting into that casket of maggots."

"I need to show the voters I'm the best candidate."

"Who else are they going to vote for? In case you haven't heard, grumpy old white guys are out of favor these days."

"I think an investigation would give me an edge," she said. "The publicity can't hurt me and it'll taint the opposition."

"It's not worth it. You can buy all the publicity you need. Think about it. Beautiful, Hispanic lady governor, the first of her people, the Eva Perón of our state. Half the state will vote for you, everyone who voted for Wallie because his last name was Moreno, plus all the Anglo, Afro, and Asian women will swing over on the feminist issues. Us skirt-chasers will vote for you, too, 'cause you're a babe. You can't ask for more."

"Stop it, Bill. I've had enough of your bigot act. This is important to me. And it's something I need to do. Not just to win the election, but because it's my job as AG."

"There you have it." I took my right hand off the wheel and placed it over her small gloved hands resting in her lab. "If it's your job, then damn, you'd better be a man about it. Show 'em you have balls. Make us proud of you. Even if it gets you killed. But I'm really going to miss you."

"I can't look the other way," she said, pleading for my understanding. "You know as well as I do that Stan Cramer didn't kill all of them. I think he killed Wallie because Wallie was putting pressure on him, but I don't buy that he did the other killings."

"Right. So Stan killed Wallie because Wallie nags him about something. Okay. But it won't do you any good to put another nail in Wallie's coffin. He's in the ground already. I saw it happen. And Stan is dead, too. Just let this whole mess die with them."

"But that's not all of it."

"Leave it alone!" I shouted, surprising myself with my concern for her welfare.

"You wouldn't if it were you."

"You've forgotten that I'm usually on the side of the bad guys. Convicting criminals is not my game. I get them off."

"You were always on the side of justice," she said. "Sometimes you were wrong about the people you thought were innocent. But you can't look the other way. That's who you are."

"Sally, please, if I were in your pumps, I'd let it drop. You don't need the issue."

"I can't let them scare me off."

"What do you mean?" I asked, wondering if someone had threatened her.

"Sartin. The only reason I can think of that they'd dump his body at my house is the killer intended it as a warning."

"It would be wise to take it as such."

"You're not home free, you know," she said, like a poker player ready to drop a royal flush on my pair of deuces.

"How do you know?"

"Because an old friend of yours, Johnny Miller, in the Center County DA's office called me today. They have the ballistics results. They also wonder if Cramer was really behind it at all. The gun Davy shot Block with is the gun used to kill Moreno's driver who burned in the crash. He wants to sort out how you came into possession of that particular murder weapon."

"What?" I can't describe the range of emotions that raced through me on learning Oma's gun was used in a murder just a few hours before she gave it to me. Fear was part of what I felt. But not for myself. How had Oma come into possession of a murder weapon? Bewildered, I pretended a calm I didn't feel.

"The gun is registered to Oma and your name was added to a permit to carry Saturday morning, after the murders," Sally continued. "Your prints, as well as Davy's prints, are on her gun. They know Davy is a diabetic since you made such a big deal about it when they tried to question him. They want to talk to you about the shooting on the theory you might have killed Wallie using Davy's insulin, then killed the driver with Oma's gun. You had access to both, hence means. You had opportunity, and you have motive. Obviously, you're still very fond of Eleana, and have been all along."

"So? Why did they call you?" I asked, knowing exactly why. The Center City cop, Carson, had gotten his feelings hurt and had to prove his manhood. He had now gotten the attention of the Center County DA's office, which made this more of a problem I should worry about. I might even have to put on my lawyer suit of armor.

Or maybe not. They would have a hard time placing me anywhere near the limo driver or Sartin at the time of their deaths. Of course, I would have a hard time proving I wasn't there without Sally's alibi. But Oma would verify when she'd given me the gun. No, I told myself, the Center County DA's office had too many holes in their case or they would have been after me sooner. Besides, the DA's office wasn't about to cross a state attorney general who was the leading candidate for governor. Was this her point? That I still needed her to alibi me.

"Miller wants to give you an opportunity to explain it."

"Whose gun killed Sartin?" I asked, in my defense.

"He didn't say. Perhaps you two could discuss it."

"What's there to discuss? I went by Oma's Saturday looking for you. While I was there, Davy called to tell me Eleana was missing. Oma insisted I take the gun with me since nobody knew what was going down. I didn't take possession of the gun until after the murders. Ask Oma. Besides, she keeps it on the shelf below the cash register. Anybody could have borrowed it while she was serving a customer. She wouldn't have missed it until a robber walked in."

Sally met my eyes. "Maybe Miller will be satisfied with that answer, but you'll have to talk to him."

"Can we do that tomorrow?" I said as I pulled up to the curb in front of her townhouse. "I need to get back."

"It might be better if you took care of him today. Tomorrow everyone will be back at work, trying to get their name in the paper with new news. Reporters will need new stories. It's easier to stop these things before somebody leaks the investigation and the press stick their collective noses into it."

She was right, of course. Maybe that's what I should do. Talk to Johnny, have him put in a good word for me, and be done with it.

"Okay." I looked at the car clock. Five-fifteen. "I'll give him an hour. And you better hope he buys my story. Otherwise the other candidates are going to be asking why a certain lady attorney general hangs out with a certain murder suspect."

She batted her baby browns at me. "Can I help it if you pulled the wool over my eyes? What girl wouldn't be led astray by a handsome, silver-tongued devil like you?"

I bit my silver tongue on an obscene retort. No more sexy repartee with Sally, no more sex with Sally, I thought sadly as I followed her inside. The straight-and-narrow was again my road.

TWENTY-SIX

Tuesday, May 29, 5:40 PM

Johnny had gained at least fifty pounds over the past few years, and he looked at least ten years older than his thirty-five. Obviously, Johnny had found the life of an Assistant DA to be a hard one with few satisfying moments, as I had.

Lady Justice's battle robes are multi-shades of gray, and battles with shadows and windmills rarely result in illusions of truth or victory. I know. I had done my time as an Assistant DA, until the manly need to earn a living to support a wife in the luxury to which she'd been born called me to the opposition camp.

Johnny refused Sally's offer of liquor and asked for a soda instead. Either he had stayed on the wagon, had an ulcer, or was showing off for my benefit. I decided to join him on the wagon and asked for a soda, too. Sally raised her eyebrows.

I shrugged. I thought about quipping that expectant parents shouldn't drink, but now was not the time to make her mad. I needed her alibi.

The pleasantries over and refreshments dispensed, Johnny addressed the business at hand, making it clear that this wasn't just a friendly gathering of acquainted members of the bar. "Sally tell you about the tests on the gun?"

"Yeah," I said, "what happened to the other ADA? I thought it was her case."

"Bodanzky's on maternity leave. She had a nine-pound boy Sunday night. So why don't you tell me how we came up with those results?"

"You subbed the work to the lowest bidder?"

"Cut the crap, Bill," Johnny said.

I wondered if he'd ever met Tiny. They were starting to sound alike. A lot of people were saying "cut the crap" to me these days. Crap was my usual routine. I might have to find a new act. Sincerity? Yeah. I could fake sincerity. So I tried sincerity on Johnny, gave him the same explanation I'd given Sally earlier.

"I decided to stay over in the pool house so Davy and I could take in a ball game on Sunday. I asked Davy to bring the gun in from the car and put it in a drawer in the kitchen. You know about the struggle he had with Block and all that."

"Let me see if I've got it straight? Davy struggles with Block. Block's gun discharges into the ceiling. You break into your house, knock them apart. Block drops his gun. While you're on the floor, Block picks up his gun. Davy pulls a gun out of a kitchen drawer and outdraws him. Is that about the size of it?"

"A burglar breaks, enters, and gets shot. Poetic, isn't it?"

Johnny stared at me long enough to make me wonder if I'd gotten all my prints off Block's gun. My prints on Oma's gun didn't mean anything. Everybody's prints were on Oma's gun.

"Davy shot him in fear of imminent harm," I argued, hoping I'd put Block's gun into the hand that had fired the bullet into the ceiling so there wasn't a powder residue problem to explain.

"You expect me to believe Oma keeps a loaded gun where anybody can get at it, and loans her gun to just anybody who walks in the door?"

I couldn't tell by Johnny's sidestep whether he had decided to do me a favor and believe me or whether he was going to let the matter ride until he had me in an outright lie.

"That's where she keeps it," I said. "And I'm not just anybody when it comes to being someone Oma might loan a gun to. She's like a mother to me. Davy called. Eleana was missing. He'd heard about Moreno turning up dead on the beach and was afraid his mother was in danger. So was I. We didn't know what was going down, so I took the gun to town."

Johnny just stared at me.

"Well, why don't you ask Oma what happened? If you don't think it's possible someone might have borrowed the gun, then come out for breakfast at the Kitchen and see for yourself. It gets pretty hectic during meal time. Oma and Bruce McPeters wait on customers themselves. You don't expect senior citizens to keep up with every move everyone makes. Somebody at the counter could have grabbed her gun, then put it back without either of them noticing."

"There's another problem," Johnny said. "Moreno was killed with an insulin injection. Davy's a diabetic."

"So is Oma, and millions of other people. It's a growing problem in this country. They mention it on the evening news about twice a week, the nights when they're not worrying us about heart disease and cancer and impotence and terrorists. Maybe the killer grabbed her kit when he grabbed the gun. Did anyone check for prints on the insulin kit?"

"Yeah," Johnny said.

"And?"

"According to the FBI lab, no prints."

"There you are," I said, "absolutely nothing to link it to Davy or me, or Oma. Besides Davy and his mother were at home in Center City when Moreno and his driver were killed. And I bet Oma was sound asleep next to Old Man McPeters in downtown Splendor Bay."

"There's something else," Johnny said.

"What?" I heard a "gotcha" in his voice.

"The last phone call from Moreno's personal line at the Mansion on Friday was made to your home in Center City at six-forty p.m. Can you explain that?"

"He called my wife," I said. "They saw each other socially after we separated. And her state office reported to his office. You'll have to ask her about that conversation after she recovers. You'll recall someone ran her off the road, after they tried to kill her at her house, after they torched the Archives, after they killed Wallie and his driver."

Johnny shrugged and gave me a that-sounds-like-something-a-jealous-husband-would-do stare. "You there when he called?"

"No, Johnny, I wasn't. I was in Splendor Bay, at Sally's."

Johnny glanced at me. His stoic-Indian-Chief you-old-dog expression wasn't as smirking as Tiny's or Davy's or Wertheim's, but his eyes held the same look. Then he addressed Sally. "Where were you Friday night and Saturday morning?"

"Bill and I were together *all night*, and Bill was asleep when I left my bay house," Sally said, then launched into her story.

"Why didn't you share this information with our office?" Johnny asked when she finished, impressed with his new facts, as I had been when I first heard the story.

While he was being impressed, I asked myself whether she had said Block or Sartin had gotten out of the car with a gun when she told the story this time? I remembered her saying Sartin before. I should check what George wrote down before she gave another statement, help her get her story correct, fix any minor misstatements, woodshed the witness, as it were.

Here I was, a lawyer again for less than a day, and already contemplating subornation of perjury, after tampering with evidence Saturday night. Of course, I wasn't a lawyer Saturday night, and lying to the police before they wrote it down might not count. Someday, I would have to research that particular ethical issue.

"Mr. Wertheim, with the FBI, took my statement. I had assumed the FBI shared information with the Center City police, and they were sharing with your office."

I'd better check her statement, I told myself. I sure didn't want our state's attorney general committing perjury.

"They never *shared* with me," said Johnny.

"I'm sure it's an oversight," Sally said smoothly. "A lot has happened. If you'll give George Wertheim a call, he can verify that he was informed and perhaps bring you up to date on all the facts surrounding the governor's death."

"I don't mean to rush you, Johnny," I said as he pulled a notebook out of his pocket, "but if we're done here, I need to get back to Splendor Bay. Good seeing you."

Johnny frowned at me, not pleased with getting the bum's rush from his old mentor. But he put the notebook back into his pocket. At that moment, I wasn't as concerned about his feelings as I was about making sure he didn't write down anything Sally had said. Let him think it was his bad memory when he read the written statement she'd given Wertheim.

Johnny glanced at Sally, then back at me. I watched his eyes as he came to terms with the situation. He didn't have much of a case against either Davy or me, and this particular potential governor and current attorney general was not going to give the DA's office permission to go after her lover. The case would have to get a lot better to make it worth his trouble.

"Yeah, I'm done. For now, assuming everything checks out." Johnny put down his glass and got up to leave.

"Wait up a second," I said. "I'll see you to your car."

Sally gave me a dirty look.

I didn't blink. She had alibied me.

I trailed Johnny out of her study, but turned back when she said, "Bill, you wanted a copy of the Internet news photos?"

"I'm glad you remembered," I said, taking the file folder she was holding. Instead of looking at the photos, I met her eyes and pleaded for forgiveness for running out on her.

She stared back unforgiving.

"You might want to get hold of a copy of the statement you gave Wertheim and see exactly what you told him," I whispered. "You might have been confused when you told Johnny who drove the car and who got out with a gun."

She looked at me, alarmed.

"You're welcome," I said to her, then followed Johnny out.

I glanced back at Sally as she stood in her doorway looking after us. I sighed, regretting my haste.

The truth was, I was afraid to be alone with her because I doubted I would be any better at resisting carnal temptation with Sally than I had been with Eleana. I knew if I stayed, we would talk about the case, then about us. Talk would lead to other things. Other things would lead to me hating myself in the morning. I would have to confess to Eleana. Then I would have two women who couldn't trust me. For reasons I couldn't explain, even to myself, I had decided to return to my marriage bed and never leave again, even if I had to chain Eleana to the bedpost to keep her faithful.

As we reached Johnny's car, he said, "I was sorry to hear about your wife."

"Thanks, Johnny," I said, knowing he meant it.

"If there's anything—"

"Thanks for asking, but no."

Johnny shrugged.

"She's going to make it," I said, meeting his eyes to acknowledge his concern, "but there is something."

"What?" Johnny asked.

"Help me figure this out," I said to my old law clerk.

Johnny raised his eyebrows.

"Have you got, or can you get, telephone records on a few people?"

"Probably," Johnny said. "Why?"

"Because the FBI are satisfied with the status quo, but there's one thing that bugs me. I'd like to know who called Stan Cramer's house just before his death. I'd also like to know how much talking Wallie and Stan did with a few other guys over the last year or so." I gave him the names.

"I'll see what I can do. But no promises."

"And the gun that killed Sartin, the state cop somebody dumped at Sally's Splendor Bay house?"

"Yeah?"

"We can assume it wasn't Oma's gun or Block's gun since both of those guns were in an evidence locker by then, right?"

Johnny nodded slowly.

"Check with Tiny Sanders of the Splendor Bay PD and George Wertheim of the FBI. See what they have in the way of ballistics on the Sartin and Cramers death bullets. My way of looking at it, there's at least one unaccounted-for gun out there. Find the gun, find the owner, maybe you'll find the killer."

Johnny shook his head. "The Sartin and Cramers murders are out of my jurisdiction. You need to take that one back to the Splendor Bay PD or the FBI."

"They don't want to know," I said.

Johnny shrugged. "Take my advice, Bill. Best I can tell, you've skidded into home base. If I were you, I'd stay down until the umpire called me safe."

TWENTY-SEVEN

Tuesday, May 29, 6:45 PM

I went through the facts as I knew them on the drive back to Splendor Bay, trying to put two and two together to get four. I kept coming up with three. Chester, Fred, and, as much as I hated to think about it, Sally.

I wouldn't let myself count to five. I knew kids could be devious when it came to getting what they wanted, and I knew Davy wanted his parents together more than just about anything, but Davy wasn't on my list and never would be. And Oma, the other diabetic I knew, no way, no how, was she a killer.

Fred wasn't even high on the list as a possible killer because he was, after all, one of those little guys who had done the two-finger pledge with me to "be square, do my best, do my duty, to God and my Country," back in our Cub Scout days. And I couldn't think what Wallie might have done to provoke him.

Fred's only reason for killing Moreno was many years further in the past than my reason for killing him. The blackmail thing about the liquor license probably meant more to Wallie than it did to Fred. Wallie would have seen it as proof he was an invincible king collecting his percentage from the serfs. Fred would look at it no differently than a payoff to a health department inspector, a minor cost of doing business. The other reason one man might kill another was missing. All Fred's women belong to somebody else anyway, so he didn't have any women for Wallie to steal. If Fred hadn't killed Wallie, why would he kill the others. And why would he try to kill Eleana?

Sally? Well Sally might have killed Wallie because she (a) hated him, (b) wanted his job, (c) hated men when she ran into him early Saturday morning after her fight with me, or (d) all of the above. The problem I had with her being the killer was I couldn't recall her being anywhere near Oma's Kitchen on Friday, so she lacked opportunity to steal Oma's gun and insulin kit. And even if she had stolen them, why did she choose one over the other as a murder weapon?

The insulin shot was iffy. She would have to be up-close and personal with Wallie with a hypodermic needle in her hand. She didn't like him well enough to get that up-close and personal. Even if she had managed that part of it, I couldn't see how she could take on Wallie with his driver in the car, then blast the driver, then talk Block and/or Sartin into helping her dispose of the bodies. But then, Sartin had been found at her Splendor Bay house after Block was out of the picture. Maybe she had done him in. I only had her word for where she was when I thought she was missing. I had no idea where Sally was at the time Sartin or the Cramers died. Maybe she had another .38 besides the one she gave me. Maybe the gun she'd given me, now in the glove compartment of Fred's Mercedes that I was driving, was the gun that had killed Sartin. And it would be my word against Sally's as to how I had come into possession of that gun. Good thing Johnny turned me down on looking for another gun!

Dumping Sartin at Sally's? Someone a lot bigger than Sally had carried him in. Chester was big enough, but maybe not strong enough at his age. So was Stan Cramer. So was Fred, and Tiny, and me, and Davy, and around and around the circle went.

The misstated driver's name? A minor detail, one of those misstatements that slip out unbidden, the kind of thing Sally did occasionally, the kind of thing a determined prosecutor could turn into a winning case.

And what about Chester? I had nothing to link Chester to any of it. He had been at Oma's for Friday lunch and again on Saturday morning, supposedly looking for Sally. He could have taken the gun and insulin kit on Friday, put the gun back on Saturday. And he might have been at the poker party. But I only had Fred's guess on that.

That was all I could come up with for Chester. I was bothered by how he knew Sally was missing early Saturday morning before anybody else did, but the "why" on Chester had me stumped.

Chester's reason for making the campaign contributions was probably the same as Fred's—it made good business sense. Give a little, get a lot. The Solana empire was a business after all.

Hmm. Such a mystery. The trouble with trying to come up with a theory about who had done what to whom was I didn't have enough motive or opportunity to go around.

I could see why Sally, Fred, or Chester might want to kill Wallie, but I didn't see why any combination of them would kill all the recently departed or why they would gang up in a vigilante committee. Besides, it seemed to me that if Fred, Sally, or Chester had killed Wallie, and killed Wallie's driver in the process, any of them would have done the efficient thing and sent Moreno and his driver over the cliff in the same vehicle, then gone home. Not one of them had the patience to lug a body around half the night even with help.

My basic problem was I didn't have enough suspects with specific motives to go around. My guess was, the only reason the various cops hadn't hauled Davy or me in for further questioning was that they didn't have enough suspects to go around, either. Maybe I should follow the advice I'd given Sally and Johnny had given me. Let it be. Keep up my cordial relations with the various authorities involved in these cases—Johnny in the Center County DA's office, George Wertheim in the FBI office, and my old Cub Scout den brother, Tiny, in the Splendor Bay PD—while staying away from Sally to make sure I did no wrong in the carnal sin department.

Yeah, that's what I should do. But it wouldn't hurt to discretely check out the chaps with Chester and Fred in Wallie's campaign photos. It didn't have to be someone local, just someone with a big enough motive. There was no such thing as private information anymore. Anyone with a credit card could get any information they wanted on anyone else, and the government could get it for free. Orwell was right but early—Big Brother and email marketers had their finger on every websurfer world wide. So that's what I would do. Tomorrow. A little quiet research at home out of harm's way.

Tonight I would spend actual and quality time with my wife and son.

***

Davy was watching a *Home Improvement* rerun.

"How's it going?" I asked, pulling a beer from the refrigerator.

Silence.

I pulled the tab to open the can. "Did you see your mother this afternoon?"

Silence.

I took a sip. "What do you want me to fix for dinner?"

Silence.

"Is something wrong? Davy?"

Silence. Rage.

I set the beer down. "Okay, spill it. What's bothering you?"

Silence. Rage. Aimed at me, I noticed, from his pointedly disgusted looks in my direction.

"Damn it, Davy! What's your problem?"

"How could you?" he yelled.

"How could I what?" I asked calmly.

"*Her!* I saw you with *her* on the news."

I turned off the television. "Okay, Davy. Let's talk."

"How could you go back to *her*? He's dead. Now you and Mom can be together."

I sat down next to Davy. I wasn't sure how to explain the situation with Sally. "It's just business" didn't even play to my own ears. "She's trying to find Moreno's killer, trying to find the people who did this to your mother. I am, too. We thought if we went to the funeral together that would give us two pairs of eyes to check out the people we suspect."

I paused to see if I'd had any effect on him. Not much.

"Sally knows I love your mother, that it's over between us. Now that there's a chance your mother and I might get back together, I wouldn't do anything to screw that up. You have to trust me on this one, Davy."

"But what if Mom finds out?" Davy said, a deep hurt in his voice. "She'll make you leave again."

"Davy, I intend to be completely honest with your mother. I'll tell her what I did, and she'll understand."

"But she's so sick," Davy said, his eyes full of tears. "If she finds out, she might lose the baby."

I hated myself for doing this to my kid. Damn, I should have held firm with Sally. I put my arm around Davy's shoulder. A few pats and he sniffed his feelings under control.

"You never said what you want for dinner."

"I'd like to go check on Mom first," he said. "Then maybe we could get a pizza."

"Give me a minute to change into some jeans," I said, grateful for the peace offering.

Gomez stood guard outside the nurses' station when Davy and I arrived. I gave him a quizzical look.

"Tiny thought it wouldn't hurt," he said. "Until the Feds get it all tied up with a nice neat bow. Besides, I've had to chase off three TV news crews today."

"Thanks, Gomez, I appreciate your help. But what makes Tiny think it's not all wrapped and tied?"

"He's been talking to an Assistant DA over in Center City. Johnny Miller. Know him?"

"Yeah," I said, "I know him."

"Well, this Miller dude has a problem with the evidence not matching up."

"Tell Tiny I'll be over in the morning. We can thrash it out then. Right now, Davy and I want to visit with Eleana."

"Sure," Gomez said, "I'll tell him."

Eleana smiled when we entered the room. Davy went over to her bed and kissed his mother. I followed his lead. She was happy to see us and talked about how well she was feeling. They had promised to move her to a room with a television and a phone tomorrow so she could rejoin the world. She worried about what was going on in her office. She talked about needing to thank people for sending flowers.

After a few minutes of her chatter, Davy looked at us with a you-two-need-to-be-alone expression and said, "I'll head on over to the pizza parlor and play pinball until you get there."

Eleana and I smiled at our worldly-wise son. He was giving us every chance to work on getting reacquainted.

"I'll be over in a little bit," I said and pulled the visitor chair up close to the bed.

"I start physical therapy on Thursday," she said. "Although I can't imagine how that's possible with a broken arm and leg."

"I'm anxious to see that, too. Are you really feeling better?"

"It might be the drugs, but the worst part of it is my arm. It's been itching like crazy today."

"That means it's healing," I said, repeating something I'd been told when I broke a leg as a kid. Who knew?

Eleana nodded, letting the conversation die.

I thought about asking her if the doctors had said anything more about the baby, but decided she'd mention it if they had. Then I took the plunge. "I need to tell you something."

"What?" she asked, alarmed.

"It's nothing. But I wanted to tell you before anyone else did. I went to Moreno's funeral today. It made the news."

"Why? Why did you go? Why did it make the news?"

"I went because Sally asked me to. It made the news because I was with her. They took note of the fact that I was her escort."

"I see," she said.

I heard the hurt in her voice. "No, it's not what you think. She's continuing the investigation into Wallie's and Cramer's little game. She asked me to go with her just to have a second set of eyes to look over the people on her list of suspects."

"Why didn't Sally ask Mr. Wertheim?" Eleana asked curtly. "They seemed to have hit it off."

"She asked him. He didn't want to be seen in public. It might blow his cover or something."

"She could have gone alone."

"Yes," I said, "but there's a self-serving reason I went."

"What?"

I met her truth-seeking eyes. "I thought my being seen with Sally might deflect some of the suspicion that keeps following me around." Then I told her about the meeting with Johnny Miller. "He had questions."

"What kinds of questions?"

"About the gun. Where I got it. That kind of thing."

"What did you tell him?"

"The truth. That Oma gave it to me when I borrowed her car to come looking for you, that I asked Davy to move it inside to a drawer in the kitchen when he parked the car, that he grabbed it to protect us."

"Yes," she said, "that is the truth."

I nodded. Our version of the truth. Who's to say what the truth really is. Davy fired the gun perhaps thinking he was saving our lives, perhaps rendering the last blow. A mere technicality.

"Tiny keeps asking me if Moreno told you who would be at the poker party," I said.

"Wallie didn't mention any names."

"Why did he call?" I asked, testing the truth of what Davy had told me earlier, that Eleana had not seen Moreno recently.

She sighed. "He wanted to talk about us."

"And?"

"I told him there was no 'us.'"

I locked on her eyes, searching. It felt like truth. Truth enough that I didn't want to probe any deeper. "I think the reason you were forced off the road was the killer thinks you know something that would identify him. That means he thinks Wallie talked to you about something in that phone call, or you were with Wallie when he met with the killer."

"I can't think of anything," she said. "I hadn't even made the connection about the campaign contributors until we went through the Archives records."

"Let's go over the list. Maybe you can remember something."

Eleana shook her head. "I'm sorry, Bill. I've been thinking about it, but I keep drawing a blank. I've seen them all at one dinner or another, but I can't remember Wallie saying anything more than 'hello' to any of them."

"Wallie never talked with you about any of them?" Like in our bed when you gave him the security code, I thought.

"He never mentioned any of them to me. Besides, I haven't been out with Wallie in months, haven't talked with him about much of anything in months. There was nothing between us when he died, not in the way you think."

I looked into her eyes again, wanting to believe it was the truth but knowing it had to be another Eleana lie.

"We were friends in the beginning," she continued. "We weren't really that later. In between never should have happened."

"Eleana, I've seen you photographed together in the papers. You've gone to plenty of parties with him."

"I haven't felt like partying the past few months. Besides, you just told me you were photographed with Sally today and you expect me to believe that it was innocent."

"That's different."

"How is it different? I went to campaign events. Wallie did, too. Sometimes he asked me to accompany him to dinner and I did. He was someone I could talk to. That's all it was."

"Damn it, Eleana! Don't lie to me. I'm the guy who saw you two in bed together. That wasn't just politics or talking. And you're pregnant. You don't expect me to believe you got that way by yourself."

"No," she said, "I don't expect you to believe anything I say. That night with Wallie was a foolish mistake on my part. I was lonely, I'd had too much to drink, he was insistent, you had ignored me all night, for months even. All you thought about were your cases. I didn't think you cared. And I'm sorry I hurt you. If I could wipe that moment from our lives, I would. But I can't. We both have to live with it."

"I'm not sure I can," I snapped.

"I see. Well, you should know this. I love you. And if you had given me one sign you still loved me, it never would have happened. I'm sorry it did happen. I ask your forgiveness. But if you can't forgive me, I don't think there's any reason for us to even try to make a new start. I can't carry that burden for the rest of my life."

"Eleana, I'm sorry," I said, repentant.

"Are you? I wouldn't know it. Every conversation leads back to this. I have every right to be hurt, too. You ran off in the middle of the night and I didn't hear one word from you for a month. Then I find out you're at the beach living with my cousin. My cousin, for God's sake! And you're still seeing her."

Eleana burst into tears and I tried to comfort her. "Eleana, please. I'm sorry. Calm down."

"Calm down? You son of a bitch!" she screamed. "Leave me alone. Just leave me alone."

"I'm sorry," I pleaded, as the nurse came into the room.

"Please, Mr. Glasscock, you'll have to leave."

"But—"

"Now, Mr. Glasscock. Your wife shouldn't be upset."

I left, feeling like the fool, the heel I am. Damn. Damn. Damn. Damn. I am such a fool.

Fleeing her room, I ran smack into Gomez.

"Is she okay?" Gomez asked.

"I hope," I said

"What set her off?"

"Me. My magic touch with women."

"She see you on the news with Sally?"

"No," I said. "Like a fool, I confessed."

"You got to expect it. You go messing around on a woman, and she's going to get pissed."

"Tell me about it," I said to the only man in town who had less experience with women than Tiny. "Listen, Gomez. I'm going over to the pizza parlor to have dinner with Davy. Would you give me a call over there if there's any problem?"

"Sure thing," he said. "What's your cell phone number?"

"Sorry," I said, "I don't do cell phones anymore. There's a phone at the pizza joint. Afterwards, I'm going back to my beach shack. Call me immediately if the nurses act concerned. Damn! I'll never forgive myself if anything happens to the baby."

"Yeah," Gomez said, grinning at me. "Congratulations. I guess I'm going to have to start calling you Swordsman instead of Fragile Dick."

"Fragile Dick is fine," I said.

"Nah," he said, "I respect you, man. I respect you. I hope that when I'm as old as you I can keep two women happy."

"That, Gomez," I said, pointing to Eleana's room, "is not a happy woman."

"Nah," he said, "I've seen her smile at you. She's happy. She just don't like sharing."

"Nobody does," I said, "nobody does."

TWENTY-EIGHT

Tuesday, May 29, 8:30 PM

Davy read my expression when I walked in. He frowned at me then finished off his pin ball game and came over to the table where I had plopped down. "What happened?"

"I told your mother about today. It upset her."

"Is she okay?" he asked, concerned, accusing.

"I think so. Gomez said he'd call if—"

"What happened?"

"Look, Davy, I don't want to talk about this, okay? It's between your mother and me."

"No," he said, his voice firmer than ever before, deep, manly.

I stared at my son, startled by what I saw in his eyes.

"It's about all of us," he said with conviction. "I wish you two would grow up and quit playing games. You're supposed to be the adults. You love each other. Can't you just be happy?"

"Davy." I put my hand out to touch him.

He shrugged my hand away and stared at me with an expression somewhere between disgust and pity. "Oh, grow up," he said and walked out the door.

Grow up. How do you do that when you're forty-six-years old and you've screwed up your entire life?

I left the pizza parlor. At the end of the boardwalk, I paused long enough to debate with myself whether I should go to my beach shack where I figured Davy had gone and talk it out or give him some time to get over it. I turned away from Davy and began an aimless stroll up the beach, watching the sun set.

The sunset was one of those heartbreaking, flaming, purple, fuchsia, ruby, orange sunsets, one of those sunsets where you don't think you've ever seen anything as beautiful before, no matter how many times you've seen a heartbreakingly beautiful sunset before.

I looked out and he was still there, my teenage ghost riding the waves, still playing the male lead in my version of *Beach Blanket Bingo.* Eleana and I were the ever-young stars in the movie in my mind, pretending we still had another life ahead of us if this one didn't work out, that we still had time to get it right if we'd just give it one more try.

"*You love each other. Can't you just be happy*?" our son had yelled at me. God, I wanted to. I wanted to be happy with Eleana. I wanted to hold her in my arms night after night, to tell her for the rest of our lives how much I loved her, how much I needed her. And I couldn't even do that right.

"You're a real shit, Fragile Dick," I said to my teenage ghost when he came gliding in on the waves. "A stupid, whiny, kid, not worth the trouble of me beating the shit out of you."

"*You don't have the guts,*" my teenage ghost answered. "*Besides you're old, and a drunk. Yeah, you heard me, you're a dilapidated old drunk. Your brain is so soggy you can't even figure out who tried to kill your wife.*"

"I can figure it out," I yelled at him as he took off running up the beach.

"*Yeah,*" he called back, "*maybe you don't want to, because you know you don't have the guts to do anything about it. That's it, you're a coward. A coward and a drunk, and useless.*"

"I'll show you who's a coward," I said as I took off chasing my ghost up the beach. "If I catch you, you stupid little shit, I'm going to beat the hell out of you."

I ran. Just like the gingerbread man, I ran as fast as I could, but I never caught me. A mile or so up the beach I finally gave up the chase and collapsed in the sand.

I lay there, spread-eagle, feeling myself sink into the damp sand, filling my lungs with misty air, watching stars fill the night sky, feeling that comforting certainty that I was glued to this planet, would not fall into that vast sea of twinkling suns. I felt the water move the sand beneath my feet as the tide came in, wetting my sneakers and the legs of my jeans. I took a deep breath and willed myself to stand. I glanced around.

In the starlight I could see that I had collapsed in almost the same spot on the beach where they had found Moreno. I looked up to the dark shadow of Sally's house. Back to where it had started.

How did it happen? I asked my ghost.

Figure it out yourself, Fragile Dick answered, wading back out into the surf, leaving me alone with my adult self.

Sally said the car with Sartin, Block, and Wallie had passed her house heading in the direction of the Cliff Road bay access. Sally's house was about halfway between the Cliff Road bay access and the Bayside Road bay access. They had turned around and chased her into town and stopped. Wallie was found here on the beach less than three hours later. How?

Was he dumped here or was he dumped in the water and washed up here? It would have been simpler to put him in the limo with his driver and send them both on a ride to hell. Why were Block and Sartin driving around with a dead Wallie in the back seat? Not the most efficient way to dispose of a body. But murderers seldom do efficiency analyses.

I turned and watched Fragile Dick catch another wave. As the whitecaps tumbled in, crashed, and became foamy ripples in the beach sand, I noticed seaweed floating in with the waves. The current moved it up the beach in the direction of the Cliff Road bay access. I closed my eyes and remembered the surf rides. Waves always move me up the shoreline in the direction of the Cliff Road access.

So they couldn't have dumped Wallie into the water at the Cliff Road access. That was the wrong direction for the current to wash him ashore here. Either they dumped Wallie on the beach right here, or they put him in the water near the Bayside Road intersection, or they might have dropped him from a boat. Chances were, they dumped him here, after Sally spotted them at five-fifteen a.m. Maybe as a first warning to Sally. Had she stumbled onto something really big with her investigation? Was she still in danger?

Don't get sidetracked with a conspiracy theory, I told myself. Keep thinking. If they had driven along the beach from Cliff

Road access, they would have left tracks from that direction. I hadn't seen the cops look for tracks. I should ask Tiny, I thought as I jogged up the beach to the Cliff Road access.

The night fog rolled in just as the bay access came into view. I slowed to a walk, trying to stay out of the water. A few yards later, I realized there was less than four feet between the cliff face and the water. They couldn't have driven a vehicle along here with this level of tide, at least not in the Ford that Sally had reported seeing. It would have sunk in the sand. Unless the tide level was lower. That was something else I'd have to check—the tide level at five-fifteen a.m. Saturday morning?

Two more things for my mental list—tire tracks and tide level. Make that three things—check the docks and see if anybody missed a boat Friday night or Saturday morning. And ask Chester. Chester had a boat, a nice little fifty-foot sailing craft he used as a fishing boat. Item four—check Chester's boat.

The fog was now so thick I could barely tell where I was headed so I turned back. Fifth thing—was there an early morning fog? How easily could anyone actually see anyone else do anything on the beach that morning?

On the way back, I stumbled on the foot of the stairs to Sally's place and paused to rest. I hadn't been back to her house since they discovered Wallie's body, not even to check out the facts on Sartin's killing. Remiss I had been. Busy I had been. Should I do it now or go make friends with Davy?

Maybe I should give him more time to cool off, I told myself as I launched my climb up the stairs to Sally's deck.

My coffee cup was still on the railing where I'd set it while watching the cops on the beach. So were Sally's opera binoculars and the can from my breakfast beer.

Gomez must have done the evidence collecting on Sartin, I thought as I moved across the deck to the kitchen door.

The patio door to the kitchen was locked from the inside, the bolt in place. I peered in but could see nothing in the dark interior of the house.

I followed the deck around the side of the house to the driveway. My Corvette sat where I'd left her. I really should try to get Baby down to a brake shop, since it didn't look as if I'd have time to do the brake job myself anytime soon. The keys to the house and to Baby were in my pocket. No time like the present for a roller-coaster ride down the cliff. But first, I chickened, maybe I should see where they'd dumped Sartin.

I turned the knob on the front door as I inserted the key. The key wasn't needed. The front door was unlocked.

Strange, I thought. Tiny always locks up, even nails doors shut if he has to. I pictured the French doors to my house as Exhibit A. He must have trusted Gomez to lock up for him and Gomez forgot. Or maybe someone else had come along and unlocked the door. I eased the door open and listened.

Who had a key? Sally. Lizabeth. Chester. Me. And the maid. And Sally left one with Oma for when I lost mine. Oma kept it under the counter with her gun and her insulin. And Fred kept one in the cash register at the restaurant for when I got so drunk he had to drive me home. Heck, who didn't have a key by now? Simple enough. Somebody had been by to check on the house and had forgotten to lock the door. Probably Chester checking on it for Sally. Chester never locked doors. Not a biggie, Fragile Dick. Get over it.

I pushed the door a little further, wide enough to step inside and paused, listening. No sound from inside.

I took a cautious step into the entrance, listening to the silence, listening to the dark. It didn't feel empty, but I didn't hear anything, just had a feeling that I wasn't alone.

I reached for the light switch by the door then heard it. Breathing. And a moan.

I flipped the light switch and heard the swish the same instant, just before I felt the blow. I'm a fool to have let it happen, I told myself as I fell into darkness.

TWENTY-NINE

Tuesday, May 29, 9:30 PM

I opened my eyes. Tiny loomed over me, his big face inches from mine as he checked my focus. "You all right?"

"What?"

"Who hit you?"

"What happened?"

"Don't you know?" Tiny quizzed.

"No, not really. Someone slugged me. Now you're yelling at me. What else, I don't know."

"You want me to call an ambulance or can you make it out to the patrol car?" Tiny continued his quizzing.

"I'm okay," I said. "Just give me a minute to get my bearings. What are you doing here anyway?"

"One of the neighbors saw the light and called it in. I guess I should be asking you the same question?"

"I came to get Baby. Thought I'd check on the house while I was here. The front door was unlocked."

"Nah," Tiny said, "I locked it when we left the other day. I checked it just this morning."

"Trust me, Tiny. It was unlocked. And someone was in here. When I opened the door, I got that feeling. You know, the one where you hear that scary Hitchcock music in your head and the hairs on your chest stand up."

"You mean the hair on the back of your neck?"

"No. The hair on your chest. Oh, that's right. You don't have chest hair."

"Bill!"

"I was about to turn on the light and heard a moan. As I switched on the light, somebody clobbered me. Have you checked the place?"

"Stay there," he whispered.

I rubbed my head and got up, following Tiny.

He turned around and hissed, "I told you to stay put."

"I am," I mouthed. "Here."

Tiny glared at me. Then we heard it. Clearly a moan. In Sally's study.

"On the count of three," Tiny whispered, pulling the gun from his holster. He moved into place beside the door and turned around to look at me.

"After you," I mouthed.

Tiny said, "Aw shit," and kicked the door open, jumping in with the gun held out in front of him in both hands like the cops do on TV, making the world's biggest target.

Not hearing any immediate gunfire, I reached in and flipped the switch. Let there be light.

Fred was on the floor, next to Sally's computer desk. Sally's face greeted us from the screen saver. Whoever had clobbered Fred and me hadn't made away with this computer, which they had probably figured had some of the same stuff on it as her townhouse computer. But, whoever he was or they were, was ahead of us, thinking outside the box that Tiny and I and the FBI had been thinking in.

"Now what the hell is he doing here?" Tiny asked, hands on his hips as he stared down at Fred.

"Playing video games?"

I dropped to the floor to look for bleeding wounds, seeing none. "He's breathing if that means anything," I said. "Let's get him to the hospital."

"You grab his legs," Tiny said. "I'll carry the heavy end."

The ER doctor reported that Fred might have a concussion to go with the nice bruise at the base of his skull. I didn't, have a concussion that is. Just a bruise on my crown where whatever had hit me glanced off. My fault for leading with my head.

After it became clear we would have to wait a while to talk to Fred, we prevailed on the doctor to move him to intensive care so Gomez could stand watch over him and Eleana at the same time.

Then Tiny and I headed back to Sally's place to look for evidence. The paradigm had shifted, we agreed on the drive back, whatever a paradigm was. I thought it was a theoretical framework. Tiny thought it had to do with electricity. We placed our bets and agreed to look for a dictionary when we got back to Sally's.

Whatever the definition was, our perpetrator had shifted *modus operandi*, which we agreed translated into "means of operation," or something like that. The killer, assuming it was the same person and not a burglar, had switched weapons again, from a gun to a blunt object. Maybe he or she or they had run out of guns after leaving the .38 in Cramer's right hand.

Tiny thought it would be nice if the object that had been used on Fred and me was still at the scene, even nicer if we found the perpetrator's prints.

Fat chance, I thought. While we were dealing with a creative killer who could make do with whatever deadly objects were at hand, I didn't think we were dealing with a dumb killer. Fingerprints would make our game of divine the perpetrator much too easy. And nothing about murder is ever easy.

We were at the front door, ready to go in with Tiny's portable small-town-cop evidence collection kit. He glanced at me. "Any point in taking prints from the door knob?"

"Not unless you want another set of mine," I said, thinking maybe Tiny wasn't the best cop to handle the evidence collecting. But I didn't expect to find much, so maybe he'd do.

Sally's big view-of-the-bay house was as we had left it before the run to the hospital with Fred. The only object out of place was the Oriental rug in the foyer that I had disarrayed in my unconscious fall.

From there we moved into the living area and found no unidentified or identified blunt objects lying about in other than their appointed places.

Tiny put on his latex gloves and dusted the large sculptures, then a smallish cast iron tomb cat that Lizabeth had bought for Sally as a souvenir of a recent trip to Egypt. He lifted a few prints around its neck and stuck the cat into a paper bag which he labeled as "Solana house cat."

I plopped myself down on a sofa while Tiny went about his evidence collecting. He gathered up a couple of brass-whatnots on the table behind the sofa, but none of them made the bruise on my head. This I know for a fact since Tiny insisted on checking each of them against the growing lump in the center of my thinning spot before he bagged them.

"Why don't you do the bedroom door knob for prints?" I suggested. "Neither of us touched that. You just kicked it in. Get the computer 'on' button and keyboard. And the mouse."

"Good idea," Tiny said.

"Do the computer first," I said. "I want to see what game Fred was playing." I was betting that any prints would turn out to be either Fred's or Sally's, or the maid's, or mine, but it made Tiny feel important to be doing something useful.

Finally, Tiny finished and let me get on with my computer investigation while he lifted prints from the door.

The computer asked for a password. No problem. I tried Solana. That didn't work. I tried Sally. That didn't work. I tried Jaguar. I tried all of Sally's phone numbers—both lines at each house, car, the office, the beeper. I tried her car license tag number. I tried her date of birth, various combinations of her social security number, her bank card pin number, my bank card pin number, my first name, my last name, my middle name, which for the record is Lenoir (don't ask), my car tag numbers, my birth date, my social security number, my phone number. None of them worked. Frustrated to the point that I considered picking up the phone and calling her, which would be just as humiliating as asking for directions, I typed "AwSchitt!"

That worked.

"I'm done here," Tiny said.

"I've just started," I said, pulling up files. "Have a seat. This may take a while."

Tiny pulled up a chair and breathed over my shoulder as I read and closed various files, mostly drafts of letters about routine office stuff she had crafted at home while I watched a ball game. I was about to give up hope when I hit pay dirt.

"Wow!" Tiny said.

"Wow is right," I said.

Sally had dirty pictures on her computer. Three of them. Naked lovers locked in a heated embrace. Looked like they were stilled frames from a video camera tape. And a lot more stuff she hadn't told Wertheim or me about. No wonder she had wanted to copy her townhouse computer files for him. He'd be unhappy when he learned there wasn't a single line of poetry. There was, however, a list of every action taken in the Stan Cramer investigation, by whom, when, and the result, as well as an attachment that included all the emails she had talked about.

I found a blank CD and started copying files.

"Tell you what, Tiny," I said as I shut down the computer.

"What?"

"I'll unplug all the cables if you'll cart this thing out to the back seat of the cruiser. I think you can tag it as evidence in the Moreno murder investigation."

"You want to tell me what you have?" Tiny asked, glancing at the CD case in my hand.

"Be happy to, as soon as you get the computer to the car. I'll explain the whole thing as I understand it. Then you and I need to decide what to do about it."

"Works for me," Tiny said.

"Want a beer?" I asked, when he was back in the house.

"I'm on duty."

"I'll write you a note."

"Okay," he said, following me to the kitchen.

I pulled two beers out and handed him one, taking a seat across from him at the cook's table. That's when I noticed the dried blood on a rug by the patio door.

"Is that where they dumped Sartin?"

"Yeah," Tiny said.

"Not much blood, is there?"

"That's why we think he was shot somewhere else. And, that lividity thing, you know, where the blood settles. It settled on his side. We found him on his back."

"You talked to the coroner about that?" I asked.

"Yeah, he's the one that noticed the lividity, said the dude was dead several hours before they tagged him. Why?"

"Just wondered?" I said. "Strange."

"What's strange?"

"Why didn't the killer and/or killers bring him in the front door? Had to lug him around the deck if they brought him in from the driveway, or up the stairs if they brought him up from the beach. Easier to bring him in the front door."

"Yeah, I wondered about that myself," Tiny said. "But you know how it is with stiffs."

"How is it?"

"You take them where you find them."

"Seems to be the case with a lot of things," I said. "But I guess we know one thing for sure."

"What's that?" Tiny asked.

"Sally didn't cart Sartin in here."

"How do you know that?"

"Number one, she's not big enough to carry him. Number two, she really liked that rug."

Tiny glanced at the rug and nodded. Any man who lives with a woman knows that makes perfect sense. Putting the toilet seat down and not getting dirt on rugs were the two big things a man had to learn in order to live with a woman. No way would Sally dump a bleeding body on her favorite rug.

"You going to tell me what you were doing up here?"

"I told you. I came to get my car."

"Yeah," he said, "but I don't believe you."

"You've never been an easy one to fool."

"So, you going to tell me?" Tiny probed.

"Nothing to tell. I took a run along the beach, decided to come on up and get my car while I was in the neighborhood."

"Why where you looking in the house? Why didn't you just get in the car and drive off?"

"Lost my nerve. Baby needs new brake shoes, if you recall. Thought maybe I'd get a beer to steady my nerves before I drove down the cliff. One thing led to another and here we are. Together again, again."

"You know, it's up to us to solve this thing."

"Yeah," I said. "Wertheim has his good conduct medal, probably even got promoted. The FBI has again saved the citizens from the criminal masterminds of the world. He's probably happy with his nice little package, so he's not going to look any further. Besides, he's busy courting Sally."

"You didn't tell me about that."

"Slipped my mind," I said.

"Well, since all your damsels have law enforcement men watching over them, what do you suggest we do next?"

"We'll burn that bridge when we get to it," I said.

"Sounds like a plan to me," Tiny said. "So tell me, besides dirty pictures, what was in those computer files you copied."

"Be patient my good man, be patient," I said. "Let's take a drive down to your office, lock up that computer, and I'll tell you what I think it all means."

We unloaded the computer at the station, locking it in the storage closet that contained office supplies instead of in the evidence room. According to Tiny, lots of things disappeared out of the evidence room, but nothing had ever disappeared out of the supplies closet.

"You should buy better quality pens if you want the help to take them home," I said.

"Don't you think it's time for guys our age to be in bed."

"Yeah. Drop me off at Fred's. I'll walk the rest of the way."

THIRTY

Tuesday, May 29, 11:45 PM

I tried to enter the shack quietly. Davy was asleep on the sofa with the television on static. I turned it off and covered him with the quilt Eleana had draped across one arm of the sofa to hide the tear in the upholstery. Wives.

Asleep, he looked so young. My boy. I touched his cheek, feeling the soft, unshaven face of a boy trying hard to be a man.

He felt cool to the touch. Too cool. Pale. Deathly white.

Fearful, I turned his face to me. That's when I saw the blood on his neck, into his hairline.

"Oh, no," I said, panic sitting in. I patted his cheeks trying to wake him, terror moving through my spine.

He didn't stir.

I checked for a pulse. Rapid pulse. Shallow breathing. I raised an eye. Dilated. Shock? Concussion? God, what have I done? I should never have let him come home alone.

"Davy, wake up. Wake up, son!"

I shook him but he didn't stir. The blow? Diabetic shock? One could lead to the other.

Oh, my God! Think, Bill. Think.

Call 911. Check for diabetic shock. Too much insulin? Too much sugar? If it was too much insulin, an injection would kill him, he needed sugar immediately. If the blood sugar was too high, he needed an insulin injection immediately. I didn't have time to wait for help. He could die before the medics got here or I could get him to the hospital.

His diabetic supplies were in his duffel bag. I ran to his makeshift room in my office to find his insulin kit and turned on the light. My computer was gone. The bedding, Davy's clothes, and my files were scattered around the room.

I tossed things aside until I found Davy's bag on top of the phone, which was on the floor and off the hook. Now was not the time to worry about destroying evidence.

I dialed 911. "Help me. This is Bill Glasscock, down the beach from Fred's Seafood. Number seven, Beach Road. Get an ambulance here immediately. My son's injured and he's in a diabetic coma."

"Stay on the line, please."

"I can't stay on the line and help him. Get an ambulance here immediately. I'll leave the phone off the hook so you can get an address trace. Number seven, Beach Road. Hurry."

I ran back to the living room with the diabetic kit. What next? Yes. Blood test first.

I pulled out the Lancet razor and punched a hole in his finger. A drop, then two, squeezed out onto the test strip. Count to ten. Read the strip. Sugar. Too high. Davy had forgotten his shot. Damn, I should have reminded him. I should have come home with him. My fault.

I jerked the cap off the hypodermic syringe and injected the insulin. Count to ten. Check his pulse. Still too fast. Check his eyes. Count to ten. Check his pulse. Better?

"Davy, please, Davy," I pleaded with him, "Talk to me, son, talk to me. Answer me, Davy."

Nothing. I closed my eyes, fighting off the terror. Focus, damn it. Focus. I patted his cheeks again, rubbed his arms, checked his pulse. Slower? Breathing? Regular?

But how do I bring him out of it? God, why wasn't I here? Please God, don't punish him for my sins.

"Davy, please, talk to me."

Nothing. I pulled him into my arms. "God, please, help me," I pleaded as I held my son, knowing that Davy could be breathing normally, his pulse strong, yet be comatose, perhaps no longer Davy. I felt the sting of tears, knowing I could have already lost him. I should have been here to protect him instead of running away, chasing Fragile Dick up the beach, playing cops with Tiny. I should have been acting the part of a grownup.

I could hear the sirens in the distance, coming closer. "Please, God, don't take him," I pleaded.

Nothing.

"Please. I'll grow up. I'll do better. Don't take my son."

At that moment Davy moaned.

"Davy, speak to me," I cried, fear turning to hope.

Davy's eyes fluttered then closing again.

I heard the rescue squad at the door. "It's open," I yelled, holding Davy. "In here. Help me!"

"Ohoo, Oh," Davy said, opening his eyes, seeing me for the first time. "Dad?"

"Thank you, God," I said, "thank you."

"We'll take it from here," the medic said.

I moved aside. "Be careful. He has a bruise at the base of his skull, and he's in diabetic shock. I've given him an insulin injection."

I stood back while they checked Davy's vital signs, moved him carefully, and strapped him onto the stretcher. I followed them to the rescue squad Bronco and climbed in the front seat with the driver while the other medic worked on Davy in the back, hooking him to an IV.

When we reached the emergency room, doctors examined him, took him up to a room in the critical care unit, put him into a bed, and hooked him to various monitoring devices.

I collapsed into the chair beside Davy's bed, too tired to sleep, too afraid to take my eyes off my son even with the nurses making bedside checks every few minutes, and too afraid to face Eleana, who would rightly blame me for what had happened to Davy. I should have been there, being a father to our son. I blamed me, too. But I blamed someone else more.

I sat there, looking at Davy's face, watching his chest rise and fall. He was breathing normally, regaining his color. I thanked God and medical science that he would be okay while plotting how to get even with the person who had done this to my son.

Slugging Fred and me was one thing. We were poking our noses into somebody else's business. But Davy was just a kid, minding his own business, in his own home. This time the killer of governors and state cops had gone too far.

The person who had slugged Davy did so before Davy had time to give himself his injection, and had almost killed him in the process.

The new *modus operandi,* taps on the head with a blunt object, indicated whoever was doing this didn't really want to kill Fred or me or Davy. We were on a different list than the guys getting .38 slugs and hypodermic needles.

Whoever had slugged us liked us better, wanted only to put us out long enough to get on with the business at hand, which seemed to be stealing computers containing Sally's files.

Enough already! Time to put a stop to it.

Vengeance is mine, said the Lord.

Fine, I told the Lord. You can have the son of a bitch. After I get through with him.

THIRTY-ONE

Wednesday, May 30, 7:00 AM

The doctor made rounds at seven, and we discussed Davy's condition. They wanted to keep him under observation another twenty-four hours to make sure nothing unexpected showed up.

We had been lucky, or blessed. Davy's sugar level was stabilizing and the damage, while perhaps cumulative over his lifetime, was something he would recover from now. The blow to his head was at the base of his skull, sufficient to knock him out, a minor concussion perhaps, but no fracture. Something he would get over.

But, had I arrived home a few minutes later, the prognosis might not be as good. Davy's insulin injection had been due at ten p.m. Within thirty minutes of missing it, he would have been irritable, perhaps had a headache, possibly dizzy. There would have been enough symptoms that, had he been conscious, he would have known what was happening and he would have taken his shot.

The obvious conclusion was that Davy had been slugged no later than ten-thirty, but it could have been sooner, while I was running on the beach, while I was getting hit on the head at Sally's, while Tiny and I were taking Fred to the hospital, or while we were playing cop. I hadn't arrive home until almost midnight. By then, Davy was in acute distress.

The Doctor left orders to move Davy to a regular room and to make sure he had breakfast. I made sure the orders were followed, then, while Davy ate, I headed to the cafeteria and ran into Tiny as I stepped off the elevator.

"Why didn't you call me?" he asked.

"I take it you heard."

"Yeah. Saw the 911 call sheet when I got to the station this morning. You going to file a police report?"

"Sure, for all the good it will do."

"Why don't we do that now?"

"Thought I would get a cup of coffee, then check on Eleana."

"You going to tell her about Davy?" Tiny asked.

"Not yet," I said. "Thought I'd wait until they let Davy out of the bed and take him in with me. Let her know he's okay."

"Have you checked on Fred?" Tiny asked.

"No. Want to grab breakfast at Oma's first? Tell her what Fred's been up to?"

"Let's check on Fred first," said Tiny.

We went up to Fred's room. He was out of danger and in a surly mood, demanding to be released.

"Offer him a sponge bath," I suggested to the pretty nurse.

"Keep him here," Tiny ordered.

Outside the room, Tiny called the station, asked Gomez to come over and stand guard again.

I went to the counter to chat with Oma while Tiny staked out a booth. Oma was more concerned about Davy than she was about Fred. Fred was where he shouldn't have been, and he'd been hit on the head a few times before without any serious consequences, at least none any of us could detect. He had always been hardheaded.

"Do I look as bad as you do?" Tiny asked, giving me the once-over when I slid into the booth across from him.

"Worse," I said. "You never were what they call handsome, and you haven't aged as well as I have."

"That's because I've had you for a friend. You could turn a saint gray-headed. You, on the other hand, lucked out and got me to take care of you."

"Lucky me," I said, then called from the booth, "Oma, two of your Country Specials. Tiny's starving."

While we ate, I told Tiny the whole story. About Davy almost dying because of a blow that, I was guessing, wasn't intended to do more than knock him out. In almost the same spot as the blow to Fred's head. Both of them were glancing blows to the base of the skull, where mine might have landed had I not led into Sally's foyer head first. Point being, whoever had been hitting people on the head last night didn't intend to kill us, otherwise he would have used the bullet end of one of his many .38's.

"He?" Tiny said.

"Yeah," I said. "Somebody big enough to carry a six-foot, one-hundred-sixty pound kid from the front door to the sofa at my place. Somebody big enough to move Sartin's body around at Sally's. Know any Amazons around here?"

"I don't even know any women around here who exercise," Tiny said. "You sure it wasn't Fred?"

"Like he slugged Davy, then slugged me, then hit himself on the head. How did he get rid of whatever he hit himself on the head with?"

"Did Davy see who hit him?"

"He said he was in my office playing computer games when somebody knocked on the front door. Davy opened up and no one was there, so he stuck his head out and looked around. That's when whoever was there clobbered him. Next thing he knows, I'm trying to wake him up from the sofa. He doesn't remember getting there by himself."

"It could be one of the state police, someone we don't know about yet. Cramer and those drivers might not have been the only ones into whatever they were into."

"Those guys would have used bullets. It's somebody who didn't really want to kill us. Funny how you keep showing up after the fact."

"Well, I know it's not me," said Tiny.

"Chester is the only one on my list who might like us enough not to kill us. Especially Fred. If he killed Fred, where would he get his booze?"

"Sounds right," said Tiny. "So who turned on the television?"

"Somebody who watches a lot of television," I guessed.

"That would be you," Tiny said.

"It's someone into collecting computers. Probably the same someone who collected Sally's computers took mine. Maybe he thinks Sally sent me emails."

"So we're looking for a computer nerd?"

"We're looking for someone interested in Sally's emails. And someone big enough to lug around a man-size bodies. Besides you and me, and Fred and Davy, who are out for the count, the only guy I know around here big enough and who had access to Oma's gun and a key to both of Sally's houses is Chester."

"I can't believe it's Chester," Tiny said. "Why in the hell would he do something like this? You don't really think it's Chester, do you?"

"He played poker Friday night. But I hope I'm wrong."

Tiny and I finished breakfast and loaded into the cruiser to go to the hospital to check on Davy, Eleana, and Fred. Davy was looking much better, and the nurses said he could visit his mother if we went through the wheelchair routine.

I headed for Eleana's room pushing Davy while Tiny went to Fred's room to make sure they hadn't turned him loose before we could talk to him. On the way, Davy and I worked on the lie we would tell his mother to keep her from going ballistic when she saw him in the wheelchair.

"Oh, my God," Eleana yelled. "What happened?"

"He's okay, Eleana," I said. "He forgot to take his shot, got dizzy, fell and hit his head. I heard the noise and gave him his shot. He's okay. I brought him in so you could see for yourself. No concussion or anything. They'll probably let him go home later today, in the morning at the latest."

"You should have watched him," she said.

"I know," I apologized. "I'll do better."

"It's not Dad's fault," Davy said. "He reminded me, then I started playing a computer game and forgot."

"I've told you about that before," Eleana said, shifting her disapproval to Davy.

He did the smart thing. He wheeled his chair over next to his mother's bed, kissed her cheek, and gave her that grin she'd never been able to resist.

"I've done wrong," he said as he patted her hand. "I apologize. Let's forget about it, huh?"

Eleana laughed, then glanced at me. I met her eyes, hopefully with a sufficient apology in mine.

She smiled and I wanted to pull her into my arms and never let her go. I moved in between Davy and the bedside table, bent over to kiss her lips, lightly, but she wrapped her good arm around my neck and pulled me to her, welcoming me home with a real kiss I felt to my toes.

"I love you," I said.

"I love you, too," she said.

I kissed her again.

"Will you two cut the mushy stuff," Davy said.

"Hmm, hmm," Tiny interrupted from the doorway with a grin on his face. "I need to talk to Bill."

Eleana glanced at Tiny, then at me, with raised eyebrows.

"It's nothing," I said. "Tiny has a new computer down at the station he wants to show me. I'll be back this afternoon."

She stared at me, not believing a word of it. "Take care."

"Davy," I said, "let me take you back to your room."

"Why don't you find a candy striper and send her in to wheel me back to my room?" Davy said, winking at me.

"Watch it, son. Women are trouble."

"You got any insurance?" Tiny asked as we got on the elevator.

"Why?" I asked.

"Your family sure is spending a lot of time here."

"Yeah, it's the good state government kind from Eleana's job. One hundred percent coverage. Your tax dollars at work."

Fred was putting his pants on when we barged in.

"You going somewhere?" I asked.

"Home," he said.

"We'll give you a lift," Tiny said.

"I can walk," Fred said.

"No, I insist," Tiny said firmly.

Fred glanced at Tiny, then at me. "Fine."

Tiny put Fred in the back seat of the patrol car, with the kiddy locks on the doors so Fred couldn't let himself out.

"Bill and I thought we'd take a little ride," Tiny said, "thought you'd want to come along so we could keep you out of trouble."

"I want to go home," Fred said.

Tiny drove up to Promontory Point and parked at one of the overlooks that now clutter that section of road, courtesy of the state tourist bureau. We watched the scenery for a few minutes, not talking.

"You got a point?" Fred asked, apparently not having as good a view through the wire cage between the front and back seats as we were having. "I have to get back so I can open the restaurant."

"I thought we might talk," Tiny said.

"Talk away," Fred said.

"No," Tiny said, "I thought you might talk."

"There's nothing to tell," Fred said.

"So why were you messing with Sally's computer in the middle of the night?" Tiny asked.

"I've got nothing to say," Fred said.

"Who hit you on the head?" I asked.

"I've got nothing to say," Fred repeated.

"Well, let's take a walk," Tiny said.

"Why?" Fred asked

"Just want to look around," Tiny said, "and check out the scenery. It's a nice day. You need the exercise."

"Speak for yourself," Fred said.

It went on like this as we got out of the car and walked awhile, following the road around Stan Cramer's place until we were on the backside of his property. Tiny pointed out the limo crash site on a cliffside in the distance, then pointed out a path leading up from the shoreline estates below. The Thortons' estate was one of them, occupying the prime spot on the bay. Chester's boat was out in the bay, heading in to his dock. We stood a moment, admiring the boat.

"I thought I remembered that path," Tiny said. "It wouldn't take much to hike up here from down there, would it?"

Fred shrugged.

"A man could do it in fifteen, maybe twenty minutes," Tiny continued.

I looked down, finding the path we Cub Scouts used to earn our hiking badges. As boys, we'd spend a whole day coming up and going down that path with a stop every few hundred feet for cookies and juice. Of course, back then, there hadn't been a road up to Promontory Point or any multimillion dollar homes down on the beach or up on Promontory Point, just nature and us boys and Bruce or Oma McPeters leading a pack of youngsters in search of wild game like jack rabbits and field mice. The scary parts of the hike were the rare encounters with low-soaring birds, big as eagles and condors, and the rarer encounters with snakes. Might even have been eagles and condors back then before humans wiped out their habitats.

I turned and look up to the crest of the ridge occupied by the late Stan Cramer's hacienda. "Goes right up to the quarters in the rear," I noted, pointing out the path.

"So it does," Tiny said and started up the bank to Cramer's place. "Come on, guys."

Fred glanced at me.

"Humor him," I said.

Fred gave us his I-can-take-both-of-you Rottweiler stare, then heeled and fell into line.

An eight-foot-tall chain-link fence ran along the back of the house at the edge of a stand of woods, mostly obscured by shrubbery in front of the fence. We followed Tiny through the woods along the outside of the fence. No need to breach it, just walk around it. Minutes later we were standing at the rear of the servants' quarters for Stan Cramer's house.

"You think that with all these woods and shrubs, somebody could have sneaked in here in the dark of night?" Tiny asked, looking at Fred.

"Sure," Fred said. "If they knew about the path."

"Who do you think knows about the path?" Tiny asked.

"Lots of folks," Fred said, "Just about anybody who grew up in Splendor Bay."

"That would include you and Bill and a few others wouldn't it?" Tiny said.

"And *you,*" Fred said. "Plus maybe whoever lives down at the bottom of the cliff, like Chester. And everybody's hired help. You talk to Cramer's hired help?"

Score one for my client. Maybe the FBI guys didn't know about it, maybe the yardman-agent had been watching the house and not the yard. I hadn't remembered it, but lots of other people could know about it.

Tiny looked at the hacienda. "You guys want to go inside?"

"I haven't lost anything in there," Fred said.

"Thought you might want to see where we found them, the crime scene," Tiny said. "I already showed Bill."

"I've never liked looking at gore as much as Bill," Fred said.

"It'll be worth your trouble," Tiny said. "Besides, the blood has probably dried by now."

Fred looked at me, questioning. Neither of us had any idea where Tiny was headed. Fred's eyes sought assurance I wouldn't sell him out. I nodded. My client, thick or thin. Unless you're the bastard who hurt my wife and son.

If I were Fred and I'd shot the late Mr. and Mrs. Cramer, I might be getting a little nervous. Probably more nervous than Fred was getting. But you never know when you play a game of bluff exactly how things are going to turn out.

Fred glanced at Tiny and shrugged. "Let's get it over."

Tiny led us around the front and dipped under the yellow crime scene tape strung between the trees. He turned around when we got to the front door. "After you," he said to Fred as he turned the knob and gave the door a shove to full open. Fred lead the way into the house while I wondered why nobody bothered to lock up houses where people had been murdered.

Fred stopped in the entrance foyer like he didn't know where to go next. At least he should know where Stan took delivery of his payola checks, I thought.

"This way," Tiny said, moving past Fred, leading us back to the master bedroom suite.

Fred paused at the bed. The now bare mattress was stained with Mrs. Cramer's blood.

"That's where he shot the wife," Tiny said.

Fred flinched and turned away. Tiny glanced at me as if that was significant, then led us into the master bath. The shower walls were still caked with Stan's dried blood and gray matter.

"This is where he was found," Tiny said. "A .38 in his right hand. Put the revolver in his mouth and blew his brains out the back of his head. At least the FBI thinks he shot himself."

"I've had enough," Fred said, looking sick as he turned away. "I have to open the restaurant. You guys can play ghost stories if you want, but I'm getting out of here."

"Just a minute," Tiny said. "Something else to show you."

"What?" Fred stopped in the doorway.

Tiny moved past Fred and led the way into Stan's media room and over to the wall beside the wide-screen TV. "There."

"What?" Fred said, then, "Oh."

Obviously Tiny hadn't been as unobservant as I had thought the other night. He'd seen the same photo I'd seen—Stan and Fred smiling at each other as Fred handed Stan the trophy.

"So?" Fred asked.

Tiny answered, "Thought you might tell me how come you and Stan were so close?"

"We weren't close," Fred said. "His team won. I shook his hand. What's the big deal?

"No big deal," Tiny said, "just wanted you to confirm something for me."

"What's that?" Fred asked.

"That Stan was a southpaw," Tiny said.

"Yeah, pure."

"Something else."

"What?"

"What were you doing at Sally's place?" Tiny asked.

"I have a right to remain silent. Talk to my lawyer."

"Who's that?" Tiny asked.

"Bill," Fred said, "would you tell Tiny I'm tired of playing cop games? Take me back to the restaurant."

Tiny glanced at me.

I shrugged. My client was right. Tiny had no reason to hold Fred, and obviously if Fred had anything to do with the Cramer murders he wasn't showing any sign of confessing when confronted with his victims' blood. He wasn't even very nervous. That didn't prove anything. Killers seldom are.

"By the way," Fred said, pointing to a wall that had been behind me when I'd sat on the sofa gazing at Stan's trophy photos and big TV. "Did you guys see this one?"

"No." Tiny peered at the collection of snapshots of Stan on a boat, Chester's boat.

I examined the photos. Damn. Some guys have all the talent. Not only was Stan a champion softball player, he was a champion fisherman. Chester Thorton, wearing a captain's hat, stood next to Stan and seemed pleased with Stan's success. Chester and Wallie and the butcher-baker-candlestickmaker-banker-builder crowd were all helping Stan hold his nice-sized shark for the photo, all wearing happy-to-be-here grins.

Perhaps one of the guys in the photo was the head hitter. Perhaps they all were. Perhaps none of them were.

THIRTY-TWO

Wednesday, May 30, 2:00 PM

We took Fred back to the restaurant. Fred left us with his I-can-hold-a-grudge-longer-than-anybody look.

"You ready to go after bigger game?" Tiny asked

I eyed Tiny. He was surprising me. I hadn't realized he had this much gumption in him.

"I've had enough," he said. "There's only so many murders you can take and not do something about it."

"What are you going to do, beat a confession out of him?"

"No," Tiny said. "I thought I'd just stand watch while you did. I saw the look on your face this morning."

"You think he's the one?"

"Who else is left?" Tiny said.

"You don't really think this is going to work, do you?"

"You never know," he said. "Let's give it a try."

Tiny aimed the cruiser toward the ritzy section of the beach where the Thorton estate took up a few acres of prime waterfront real estate. Chester answered the door.

"What happened to your butler?" I asked.

"He didn't like the weather," Chester said in his cowboy voice, then switched to an English accent. "Prefers the cold, damp rain of dear old England." Then back to cowboy, "Can I buy you boys a drink? What brings you down here this afternoon anyway? Just got in a while ago myself. I have a pretty good catch of fish if you guys want to take some home with you."

"Drinks would be good," I said. "Tiny's on duty, so all we're having is beer."

"Suit yourself," Chester said. "Come on back to the kitchen."

We followed Chester on the stroll through the bayside mansion, winding up in a kitchen the size of Rhode Island annexed to a media room the size of New Jersey. A glass wall offered a fantastic view of the water. A real wall held a wide-screen television set bigger than Stan's. Something else they had in common besides fishing. If any of Freud's successors wanted to look into modern-day penis envy, they should start their investigations with the owners of wide-screen TVs.

"Beers are in the refrigerator," Chester said, taking his seat in a black leather recliner in front of the television. "Mind if I finish watching this show?" He pushed the button to raise the footrest, then the button on the remote to raise the volume.

Chester was a big fan of the nature channel. That probably said it all. Kill or be killed. Big fish eat little fish.

Tiny and I grabbed beers from the refrigerator and settled into two of the several other recliners in the media area, watching the grand finale of an alligator eating a dog. It took the 'gator three bites to get the dog. Interesting how they do that. First the head. Then the upper torso. They save the legs for dessert. Unless they're not very hungry. Then, according to the narrator, they stick the leftovers in a hole in the mud under water until they're hungry again. Cold storage, alligator style.

"Lizabeth here?" I asked as the blood spread across the water in the swamp.

"In Center City, at one of her charity doings," said Chester as he flipped the channel to the weather station. "Slow day in Splendor Bay?" he asked, looking at Tiny.

"Yeah," Tiny said, "guess you could say that. We were up at Sally's place last night. She's had another intruder."

"You catch 'em?" Chester asked.

"No, 'fraid not," Tiny said. "But we carted Fred out of there. He must have been playing video games."

"Well, you know Fred," Chester said.

"Yeah," Tiny said. "'Course somebody hit him on the head while he was doing it."

"Don't say," Chester said.

"Hit Bill here on the head, too," Tiny said.

"That's too bad."

"And his boy."

"Is Davy okay?" Chester asked, concerned.

"I found him in the nick of time," I said. "Somebody hit him before he could take his shot and he was in diabetic shock when I found him."

Chester's eyes widened and he sucked in a breath. "I'm really sorry to hear that," said Chester sincerely, meeting my eyes.

"I know you are," I said, holding his eyes.

He blinked first. "Well, it was nice of you boys to drop by. Stop in again when you're in the neighborhood."

"It's this way, Chester," Tiny said and took a deep breath. "We think you're our head-hitter?"

"What makes you think that?" Chester asked.

"Just a feeling," Tiny said.

"Well, you shouldn't go around accusing people with just a feeling," Chester said. "Ask Bill about that, he's a criminal lawyer, or is that redundant?"

"An oxymoron," I said.

"See," Chester said. "Bill agrees with me."

"We found the files, Chester," Tiny said.

"What files are those?" Chester asked.

Damn. I wish I'd had more clients like Chester and Fred. Nobody had to warn them they had a right to remain silent. The old rooster was cool and cagey. No wonder Lizabeth was fond of him.

"The files on Sally's computers," Tiny said, trying to act cagey himself. "That's what we need to talk about."

"Talk away." Chester wasn't impressed with Tiny's cagey act.

"They show corruption, with you involved," Tiny said.

"How's that?" Chester asked.

"Explain it to him, Bill," Tiny said. "You're the one who figured it out."

"It's this way," I said. "When you tried to burn Moreno's campaign contribution records, you didn't get them all."

"What makes you think I tried to burn them?"

"Oh, we don't think you tried to do it personally," Tiny said. "Andrew Block and Mike Sartin did it for you."

"I see," Chester said. "How does that lead you to think I was involved? Last I heard, both them boys were dead. Best I recall, you or your boy shot one of them, didn't you, Bill?"

Good point, Chester, I thought. How do we prove Block and Sartin did the arson and then tie them to you? "We'll get to that," I said. "Back to what the FBI found in the microfiche copies of the paper records."

"Microfiche copies?" Chester said in a tone of voice that indicated he might be giving himself a mental kick in the rear.

"Yeah, microfiche. Among other things, we found photos from campaign gatherings and a list of campaign contributions. We were amazed when we found you thought enough of Moreno to give him nice big checks on a regular basis."

"I contribute to a lot of campaigns, Bill. Both parties. Three if the Libertarians run somebody. Good for business."

Another good point. He probably made contributions to anybody likely to win just so things would go smoothly for the Solana estate when it came to little government matters like building and environmental permits, roads, infrastructure to and from and on the properties, little things, big things, palm greasing things that made a business run smoother.

"Before that we didn't know you had any affection for Wallie," I continued. "There were five other guys in those Smiling Wallie pictures. The butcher, whose face is on half the packs of bacon and baloney in supermarkets everywhere; the baker who supplies bread to supermarkets throughout the state; the candlestick maker. And the banker. The last guy on the list is the largest construction contractor in the state."

"That's an impressive list of citizens," Chester said. "You really think they were up to no good together?"

"Yeah, I think so," I said, "but my problem was I couldn't figure out exactly what you guys had in common that would get you united behind Wallie. That's what was on Sally's computer. She's been looking for some way to get Moreno for years, and you know how those Solana women are. When they want something, nothing stops them."

"Yes," Chester said, "I've had a bit of experience with that. So what was on Sally's computer that has you boys so excited?"

"Well, it seems you guys were the principal beneficiaries of the prison reform legislation that Wallie pushed through. They mentioned it on the news the other night. We're talking billion-zillion-dollar beneficiaries when you piece it all together. You sold off some of the Solana lands for the new prisons at greatly inflated prices. Some of the money went back to the Solana Estate Trust. Some didn't."

Chester just stared at me and shrugged. "So? We sold some land, and they wanted it bad enough to pay our asking price. What makes you think those weren't legitimate contracts?"

"State purchasing agents have given the AG's office affidavits to the effect that Moreno ordered them to make the awards," I bluffed, "and that they also received extraordinary compensation from the recipients of the awards."

"Guess some of those guys might have problems, if what you say is true," said Chester. "I'll have to check into the Solana Trust and see what those trustees have been up to. There's at least a hundred head of lawyers and accountants keeping track of Lizabeth's and Sally's money. Not to mention the ones that look after Eleana's money. They just send me summary reports. If something's not making money, I tell them to buy something that is. Guess you have to watch people every minute to keep them from skimming, don't you?"

I studied Chester's face. He was sharp, he was smooth. There was probably no way to tie any shady dealings in the Solana Trust back to him.

"How does any of that make me a head-hitter?"

"I'll get to that," I said, wondering how I would.

"I heard the FBI decided Stan Cramer was the killer. Maybe one of his men is still up to no good."

"His people use guns," Tiny said.

Score one for Tiny, I thought. "Stan collected Moreno's kickbacks. Stan, as the head of the state police, served as chairman of the prison reform committee, so he could influence who got which contracts. And Stan was a very good enforcer. He put a little pressure on purchasing agents to make sure they awarded the right contracts. Any of their little sins would do. A DUI, a night with a whore, maybe even a threat of filing an ethics violation claiming a shakedown by the purchasing agent. You know how picky government agencies are about their employees' morals, how those civil servant guys will cave when someone threatens them with the loss of their job and pension. It didn't take much. And, of course, Wallie was putting a little pressure on Stan to keep him in line. Sent him little reminders."

"Bill," Chester said, "this is a terrific story. It might even make all the newspapers in the state real happy for months. And a few little people might get some jail time. If Moreno were still governor, it would topple him like a chain saw going after pine trees in East Texas, but he's dead and buried. Sally can get his job without dragging half the business people in the state through the mud. Sure, she thought about doing it the dirty-laundry way before, but I'm willing to bet she's had second thoughts by now. She's smart enough to know that what goes around comes around."

"Yeah, but Sally's running for governor. She wants to prove she'll make a war-on-crime governor, make the people happy."

"Not that happy. Her name is Solana. She starts this and some reporter will bring up the land sales and blacken her name. Sure, you could blab it, rake the muck, and it might embarrass some of these guys, but you have the problem of connecting the dots to link them to Stan Cramer's little strong-arm tactics."

I shrugged.

"I bet a case could be made that most of these fellows are honest, God-fearing citizens," Chester continued. "They never would have done anything if our late governor and his gestapo hadn't put the screws to them. Which gives all of them motives for killing Moreno and his henchmen. A good defense attorney like you used to be could punch holes in all of it. Besides, you start opening that can of beans and everybody in the state who does business with the government will become a target of the investigation. A few law firms could make a lot of money doing special investigations for the taxpayers. Who benefits from that? Lot's of people will get scared and do foolish things. A lot of innocent people could get hurt, might even hurt themselves."

"That could happen," I said.

Chester frowned. "Sure it could. I don't think you want to cause suffering or misery. Especially considering the character of the people murdered. I'd say somebody did the world a favor."

"What about the murder of Mrs. Cramer?" I asked.

"A strong argument could be made she wasn't an innocent victim. She knew where her new-found wealth came from. What kind of contribution did she ever make?"

"Chester," I said, "six people have been killed."

"Six people the world can do without," Chester responded. "And it's over if you let it be. You think Sally is going to use that information now? Not for a minute. She wants to be governor. She can get there without all that fuss and bother. You don't antagonize the haves and get to be governor. Even if you do, you never make it to the Senate or the White House. She knows that. She's a smart girl. Hell, Bill, all you're talking about here is the killing of a skunk who would've been roadkill a long time ago if people weren't afraid of the stink."

"He's got a point," Tiny said, perhaps reflecting on the fact that his own job security depended on political patronage.

"Yeah, what's a little corruption among friends? It's all the same, give a little of your money, get a lot of everyone else's money back, eliminate problem employees when necessary."

"Right, Bill," Chester said, "business."

"I was being facetious," I said.

"You do it so well," said Chester. "Do you know that's one of the few words in the English language with an a, e, i, o, and u in order?"

"You know," I said, "one of the things I like about you is your command of trivia."

"Your tendency to facetiousness, or to be linguistically correct, your sarcastic or acerbic wit, is one of the things I like about you," Chester said. "That and your taste in women."

"Why don't we skip to the chase, Chester?" Tiny said. Tiny didn't like word games, he didn't understand business, and he was embarrassed by talk about women.

"Certainly," Chester said. "Skip away."

"This is what we think happened," Tiny said. "You had lunch at Oma's on Friday. While Oma was busy, you borrowed her .38 and the diabetic kit she keeps under the cash register. And we know that Moreno came out to Stan Cramer's place for a poker party Friday night and you were there as well."

"How do you know that?' asked Chester.

"Never mind how we know it," said Tiny. "You and Moreno left the party, went out to his limo for a private conversation. The driver gave you a little privacy for whatever business you indicated you needed to conduct. While in the limo, you gave Moreno an insulin injection which caused his death. You called the driver over to see about Moreno and shot him."

"Tiny," Chester interrupted. "You think, you think, you think. You can't prove any of this."

"Let me finish," said Tiny. "Block and Sartin, who were on your payroll, moved Moreno to a state police vehicle and the driver back into the limo. One of them drove the limo and sent it over the cliff, one drove the sedan and picked the other guy up after he sent the limo over the cliff. Then they carted Moreno down to the beach and dumped his body in the water."

"Wow, this is just incredible," said Chester.

"While they were engaged in disposing of Moreno's body," Tiny continued, "they encountered Sally coming out of her driveway and gave chase. She managed to evade them, or they called you for instructions and you told them to back off. They then went on with the business of dumping Moreno's body. Afterwards they destroyed the campaign records at the Archives. Saturday morning you went to Oma's Kitchen during breakfast and returned the gun. Then it occurred to you to have Moreno's phone records checked. That's when you discovered Moreno had talked to Eleana just before leaving for Cramer's poker party, so you tried to eliminate Eleana in case she knew too much."

"Unbelievable," Chester said when Tiny finally paused for a breath. "This story is starting to make my head spin. I did all that? Not me. I'm an old man. Heck, you're years younger than me, and you're out of breath just talking about it. And I would never hurt Eleana."

"I'm about done," Tiny said and inhaled. "We think that during the time Sally was hiding from the state police, she told Lizabeth about her investigation into Cramer and Moreno and Lizabeth told you. That's when you killed Sartin and dumped him at Sally's beach house, either to eliminate your connection to Sartin and Block or as a threat to Sally of the possible consequences if she continued her investigation, or maybe both.

You killed Cramer to make sure Moreno's and the state police murders weren't traced back to you."

"Tiny, Tiny, Tiny," Chester said. "You'll never be able to prove any of this. Not in a million years."

"Maybe not," Tiny said.

"So, why're you bothering me?" Chester asked. "I'd think that before you come barging into a citizen's home and make accusations, you'd talk to the DA to see if he'd like to take this to a grand jury for an indictment. Nothing you've told me so far would make me want to do that if I were the DA."

Chester was right. No DA in his right mind would touch this. Probably not even if they'd caught Chester standing over one of the bodies with a smoking gun in his hand. There would be serious political consequences if you charged a man like Chester Thorton and didn't make your case.

"You sneaked into Cramer's house, shot his wife in the bed and shot Cramer in the shower," Tiny continued undaunted.

"The FBI said Cramer killed his wife and himself," Chester countered. "And they're convinced he killed the others."

"Yeah, but Cramer was a southpaw," said Tiny. "Funny, he shot himself with his right hand."

"Damn, Tiny," Chester said, "exactly how do you expect to convince a jury that an old man managed to do all that right under the collective noses of the state police, the FBI, and the Splendor Bay police. FBI agents were watching Cramer's home, weren't they? Lawmen of that caliber wouldn't let a murderer sneak past them, or admit they did. You ever think that maybe Stan Cramer was ambidextrous? That makes more sense than any of this. No way you can prove any of this guesswork."

"Well," Tiny said, "we thought you might confess."

"Why would I do that?" Chester asked. "To what? You just said you have no evidence that I committed any crime."

"We thought you might want to avoid the public embarrassment," I said, "perhaps a plea bargain to keep certain information from reaching the press."

"What embarrassment?" Chester asked. "If there's no indictment, there's no prosecution. Everything else is slander.

Besides, Bill, how do we know you and Tiny didn't cook up this little story to save your hide? Everyone knows what tight friends you are. And you have more motive than anybody else. Moreno was messing around with your wife."

"I'd say we have the same motive," I said, playing our trump card. "But in your case, there are photos of your wife with Moreno. I think you know the ones I mean. Sally probably had copies on the computer you nipped from her townhouse which is why you went after the one at the cliff house last night. And you probably surmised she might have sent me copies which is why you took my computer."

"Assuming I knew what you were talking about," Chester said, "what makes you think they were photos of Lizabeth and Moreno? Sally had a fling with Moreno. Maybe they were photos of Sally and Moreno, which would make your motive even stronger than mine. He got two of your women."

"The sister in the photographs had a little mole on her lip. Sally doesn't have a mole."

"I see," Chester said. "And these computer records you say you have, you guys found all that on Sally's computer?"

"Most of it," I said.

"And you rushed over here to tell me about it," Chester said. "I hope you secured your evidence."

"Well, Chester," I said, suddenly realizing our precarious position. Money could buy happiness and peace of mind. While we were out playing Cub Scout, Chester could have been helping himself to the computer in Tiny's store room.

I glanced at Tiny. He was having the same thoughts.

"Let me tell you what I did and you tell me whether you think it's enough," I proceeded to bluff again.

"Okay," Chester said, "tell me."

"I made four complete copies of all the files," I lied, remembering the lone CD now shelved between Lyle Lovett and Willie Nelson next to my garage-sale stereo equipment. "We carted the computer off to a secure location. I dropped one CD into the overnight mail to George Wertheim of the FBI, one to Johnny Miller of the Center County DA's office, one to our own Splendor Bay County DA, and another copy to my ex-law partners with a note asking them to turn it over to the news media if anything happens to Tiny or me."

Chester looked impressed. "No copy to Sally?"

"I think you're right about this not being the kind of thing our AG would try to use for a public inquisition. Otherwise she would have turned it over to the FBI already. Sally might tell your coconspirators privately what she knows and assure them that she'll be loyal to them if they'll be loyal to her, all the way to the White House. That's how it's done, isn't it?"

"That's probably the smart thing to do with this kind of information," Chester said.

"Yeah," I said. "Is that the deal she offered you?"

"You don't think I'd answer a question like that?"

"Just checking," I said.

"What do we do now?" Chester asked. "You fellows think I'm in a heap of trouble, yet you don't think the AG or the FBI will be interested in pursuing it."

"Why did you do it?" Tiny asked, meeting Chester's eyes.

"Bill," Chester said, shifting his gaze, "you're a criminal defense lawyer. Why don't you tell Tiny the facts of life."

"Oh," I said, "I covered all that in third grade. I don't think he needs a refresher course."

"What makes you think you can prove I did any of this? I'm an old man. Old men are harmless. Don't you know that? Harmless and impotent."

"I hope that's not true," I said.

"I'm sorry to tell you boys this," Chester said, "but that's true more often than not. Sooner than you might think."

"Assuming it wasn't true," I said, looking at Chester. *Assuming arguendo* was a game all lawyers liked to play.

"Assuming for the sake of argument that I wasn't a harmless old man," Chester said, rising to the bait, "I guess I might have had the same kind of motive a young man like you might have for killing a sumbitch like Wallie Moreno, especially if any of this story about Moreno and my wife were true. And I guess that once you kill one sumbitch, it starts to snowball, especially when certain greedy sumbitches get high-strung and you think maybe they might create other problems later on. But then, I'm just speculating."

"I can understand everything else," I said, "but why did you run Eleana off the road?"

"You're barking up the wrong tree on that score. I would never hurt Eleana."

"Who did?" I asked.

"How would I know that?" Chester asked.

It sounded like the truth. I studied his eyes.

Tiny said, "I think I ought to read you your rights. You have the right to remain silent, the right to an attorney—"

"I know my rights, Tiny," Chester said with a sigh. "Bill isn't the only lawyer here. I would ask you to defend me, Bill, but that would be too much of a conflict of interest for you. You will excuse me while I call my attorney, won't you?"

Tiny nodded.

Chester got out of his recliner and walked slowly into the kitchen to use the phone on the wall by the serving counter. He dialed the number, his eyes on mine as he waited for the other party to answer. Sadness filled his eyes and he sighed.

I saw him open the drawer, but I wasn't quick enough to stop him. I saw the anguish in his eyes as he pulled the gun out, stuck it in his mouth, and pulled the trigger. He was dead before I could get out of my recliner to stop him.

THIRTY-THREE

Wednesday, May 30, 5:00 PM

The afternoon passed quickly with the FBI and Tiny and the Chief buzzing around Chester's bayside premises. They found Sally's missing townhouse computer and my computer, and they found other evidence sufficient to indicate Tiny and I had accused the right man of murder.

That didn't make me feel any better. A man was dead. In my book, a man whose worst sin was stepping on some cockroaches that needed exterminating. In my book, his only sin against me had been harming Davy. My mission had been to stop more harm, not cause another death. Mission unaccomplished.

We had nothing more than circumstantial evidence to link Chester to the murders. But what we had was pretty graphic. Stored on Sally's townhouse computer were sexually explicit photos of Lizabeth and Moreno and an email from Lizabeth to Sally telling her Wallie had sent them to her, warning her that he would tell Chester about their relationship if she were to break it off. Unfortunately, while trying to copy files, George Wertheim accidentally deleted them. That's easy to do. It happened to me when I copied files from Sally's other computer.

I wondered why Chester hadn't already made a similar mistake. Perhaps he hadn't gotten around to it. Perhaps he didn't know how. Perhaps he wanted to confront Lizabeth. Perhaps he hadn't thought we would come after him.

But he had already seen the photos, or been told about them. Of that fact I felt certain. Because he believed me when I told him what I had found. He also believed my lie about copying Sally's files and sending them to law enforcement.

I was wrong about one thing. Chester hadn't borrowed Oma's insulin kit. He didn't need to. Chester was a diabetic, which an inspection of his medicine cabinet revealed. Diagnosed a couple of years ago, he had never told us. But then, Chester never was one to talk about his troubles.

Thinking about it, I eventually came to this scenario: Moreno's murder was a rash act. They were alone, perhaps in the limo taking a break from the poker party to discuss some sort of shady business. Maybe Chester was taking time out to give himself an insulin injection. Wallie may have said something about Lizabeth, may have mentioned the photos. Or Chester may have already known. Whatever. It was enough to trigger a murder. The insulin was handy.

But why had Chester taken Oma's gun and used insulin to kill Wallie? Maybe he intended to shoot Wallie, had gotten him alone in the limo for that purpose, but the insulin was handy. Perhaps Chester threaten Wallie with the gun and force him to give himself an injection. If the driver wasn't in the car, firing the gun would bring the driver. Afterwards, he had called the driver over to see about Moreno and shot him.

Who knew when Chester formed the intent to murder Wallie Moreno? Who would ever know? *Mens Rhea* is not my strong suit. And his choice to dump Moreno at the beach and the driver off the cliff was a problem for me, but then, murderers are seldom logical in the heat of the moment. Except Chester was the most logical man I have ever met. And he had Block and Sartin to help with such details.

Regardless of how the other deaths had happened, the bottom line was that Chester had killed himself because of my lies to him that very day.

After promising Tiny and George I would make the death calls to the family, I left the cops to destroy the Thorton home in their search for evidence and went to the hospital.

First I stopped by Davy's room. There, I learned they were keeping him an additional day, and that he had decided to study medicine. I suspected it had something to do with the pretty redhead in the red-striped uniform who was reading to him while he played the part of the suffering warrior better than I had ever seen. I remembered to ask him about the missing circuit breaker from the security alarm power panel.

"Oh, that," he said, "I borrowed it for a science fair project."

I left him to his education and went up to see Eleana. Gomez was still on duty. I told him about all he had missed, thanked him for his attention to my wife's safety and told him to go home. Then I ran into Eleana's doctor coming out of her room.

"How is she?" I asked.

"Better than we expected. She'll be able to go home by the weekend if you can arrange for a homecare nurse."

"And the baby?" I asked.

He touched my shoulder in an act of encouragement. "So far, the baby seems healthy. Keep your wife focused on that."

"Thank you, doctor. I will."

I went into the room and greeted Eleana with a kiss. "I love you," I said. "Please be my wife again."

"I'll think about it," she said.

"Thank you," I said and kissed her again.

"The doctor said the baby is okay," she said, looking into my eyes, probing my true feelings.

"I know, he just told me in the hall. Has he told you about the problems she might have?"

"Yes."

"And?"

"It doesn't matter. I'll love her whatever happens."

"That's what I told them, too."

"I need to tell you everything," Eleana said.

"I don't want to know," I said. "It's in the past."

"It's not about Wallie and me," she said. "There never was a Wallie and me. Not like you and me."

"I saw you together, Eleana. I heard your sobs when you learned he was dead. That sounded like grief to me. Grief means there were feelings between you."

"You're wrong. It wasn't grief. It was fear."

"Fear?"

"Yes," she said, looking into my eyes. "I was afraid you had killed him, that Davy and I would lose you forever."

It felt like the truth. But I had believed her, trusted her before. "It doesn't matter," I said. "About you and Wallie."

"It doesn't?"

"No. Not any more. There was a baby girl in the nursery. She opened her eyes and looked at me with that all-knowing gaze babies have. I realized then I could love a stranger's child if they sent her home with us. I knew I could love your child as my own."

"Are you sure?"

"I'm sure. I want you to put my name on her birth certificate."

"I had always intended to do that," Eleana said, holding my eyes with her sky-clear gaze, "from the moment I knew I was pregnant."

I stared at her, wondering why she was telling me this now that she had me committed to her and her child.

"Because you are her father. She's one of our IVF embryos."

I felt that feeling again. That feeling of wonder and amazement and fear. Wonder and amazement that we could create a child together. The same feeling with Davy, the same with Angela, and now with this child. And the fear. But the fear was different. Not the fear of being too young and too inexperienced to be a father that I had felt with Davy. Or the fear of being able to love another child as much as I loved Davy that I felt with Angela. There was always room enough in a heart to love another child. But now it was the fear of being too old, too damaged in my heart and mind to delight in this child's exploration of the world the way I had with Davy. A child needs parents who can still feel joy.

"I'm afraid, too," Eleana said, reading my thoughts. "I'll be sixty when she's eighteen."

"And I'll be sixty-four," I said. "My God, how did we get to be so old? We should be having grandchildren."

"We'll have them, too," Eleana said. "In case you haven't noticed, your son likes girls, and they like him. His father's son."

THIRTY-FOUR

Wednesday, May 30, 7:00 PM

I left the happiness in Eleana's room to call Sally. Like the coward I was, after promising Tiny and George I would make the death call to the Solana sisters, I had put it off as long as I could. As I dialed the number for Sally's townhouse, I felt dread and obligation, and great sadness. It rang ten times and no one picked up, not even the answering machine. I thought about driving over to Center City to Lizabeth's house, but I didn't have the guts to face her. I tried Sally's office number instead.

Sally took the news calmly, said she would go to the Thorton home and tell Lizabeth. She thanked me and hung up.

Easy enough. I had said something to the effect, "I've just forced your brother-in-law to kill himself." She said something like, "Thank you for telling me." Oh, the politeness death brings out in us all.

So what should I do now, with my duty as bearer of bad tidings discharged? I didn't want to go home. I thought briefly of going to Fred's, but decided Fred wouldn't be happy to see me after our little game of ghost hunt, and I intended to stay on the wagon, not an easy thing to do while sitting on a bar stool. So that left my other best friend, Baby, to hang out with.

I walked to the drug store to pick up the Wallie-in-death-on-the-beach shots. I glanced through them, thinking briefly about keeping a trophy, then tossed them all back to the photo clerk. "Nothing here I can use," I said. Then I walked the couple of blocks to the auto parts place that stayed open until nine, laid my VISA card on the counter, and said, "Fill her up."

"With what?" the counter clerk asked.

"'57 Corvette brakes, pads, liners, all four wheels, the works."

"You drive a '57 'Vette?" the kid asked, impressed.

"Yep, she's a beauty," I answered with pride. "Red convertible, white coves, classic, with the original engine."

"You're the guy! Man, I've seen that car around town. She's a beauty all right. You wouldn't let me take a close look at her sometime, would you?"

"I might, Roy," I said, reading his name off his shirt pocket. He wasn't much older that Davy, just a kid, in love with the greatest invention in America, the personal-size automobile.

"I'm not sure we've got the parts for a car that old," Roy said, "but we can order them. They're not cheap, you know?"

"I know," I said. "I talked with someone named Raymond about them on Saturday. He'd said he'd order them. Could you check in the back to see if they're here yet? Name is Glasscock."

Roy hunted a few minutes and came back with arms loaded with boxes. I noticed the piece of paper he tore off one of the boxes had 'Fragile Dick' scribbled across it.

"Guess these are them," he said.

"Would you have a set of instructions?"

"That's easy," he said, then launched into a combination auto lingo and hand signs form of instruction, finally deciding it would be easier to give a class. "Hey man, I can lock up in ten minutes. Why don't I show you how?"

"I thought you were open 'till nine, Roy."

"No problem. This is my uncle's place. My pleasure really."

I signed the charge slip and Roy carried the parts out to his truck. Ten minutes later he had locked up and we were driving up Cliff Road in a 1973 Toyota pickup with 300,000 miles on its engine that Roy was lovingly rebuilding from the ground up, starting with a hole in the floorboard big enough to see roadkill. He shared all the details of the remodeling.

Along the way I determined that Roy was Roy Burns, son of Johnny Burns, a guy I'd gone to high school with. The uncle and store owner, Raymond Burns, was two years ahead of us in school. Roy said his dad had died recently, reminding me again of my precarious mortality, of all our precarious mortalities.

I told him what a great guy I remembered his father being even though I couldn't put a face with the name other than I felt sure that both Johnny and Raymond were a couple of the little pricks who had called me Fragile Dick. Apparently Raymond still did.

We arrived at Sally's. Roy and I put the sad thoughts out of mind and went to work on Baby-the-Beautiful.

We finished the job, put the wheels on, and lowered the jack to the glow of security lights. I went in and brought out a couple of beers in furtherance of male-bonding while Roy inspected Baby's engine compartment. I bragged on her performance and all the scrapes we'd been through together over the years. Then Sally drove up in her Jaguar.

Roy's face was sadness personified when the Jaguar turned into the driveway and parked beside Baby. "I guess I'd better go. Your wife will want you in the house for dinner."

Somehow I didn't think so, but I shook Roy's greasy hand with my own dirty paw, thanked him for his help, promised to bring Baby around for him to test drive, and sent him on his way. He was almost teary-eyed when he waved good-bye. Men of all ages can feel that way about a car as beautiful as Baby.

Sally got out of the Jaguar and looked me over, taking inventory of the grease-stained shirt, pants, hands, and face as I rested on the safety of Baby's trunk.

"You need a shower," she said.

I extended my arms to examine them. "Guess I do."

"You can shower here," she said.

I met her eyes and saw the sadness. "I'd better not." She needed someone to hold her. I didn't think I would be able to resist if she said "please."

She sighed. "Lizabeth and I are meeting with the funeral director in the morning at ten, to discuss Chester's arrangements. Would you come with us?"

I nodded.

She started for the front door, then turned to look at me. "See you there," she said sadly.

I climbed into Baby and drove home, stopping briefly at Fred's to leave the keys to his Mercedes with the gal at the cash register.

I entered my shack and glanced around. Tomorrow I would set goals for getting Eleana and Davy and our coming baby daughter a proper home. But tonight I would repent my sin against Chester.

I was soon in my garage-sale recliner, feet up, television on. Around one in the morning, I turned off the talk show on homosexuality in the military or the lack thereof being debated in rude, loud voices. With no tears left, I showered and went to bed, snuggling into Eleana's pillow.

THIRTY-FIVE

Thursday, May 31, 6:30 AM

I woke early, took the board out for a couple of quick waves, dressed, and went by the hospital to watch Eleana struggle with her first round of physical therapy. Then I saw to Davy's discharge.

On the way back to the beach shack he asked me if he could borrow the Corvette Friday night. He had a date, his first, with the little redhead. Remembering the first time my own dad had trusted me with the keys to Baby, and my encounter with a tree that had battered her, I told him I would think about it. Maybe he ought to rent a limo instead. That would impress her more.

I changed into a suit while he settled down in front of the television. Then I left to attend to my ten o'clock duties to Sally and Lizabeth.

The last time I had been in Brewer's Funeral Home was thirty years ago, when I went with my father's law partner to pick out a casket for my father. Then, I pointed and ran, leaving the adults to finish the transaction. My father's law partner brought me back the next day for my father's service. It was brief and sparsely attended. More people hated him than loved him. The coffin was closed. The embalmer couldn't repair the damage to his head sufficiently for a public viewing.

He was forty-eight years old when he pulled the trigger. I was sixteen and I never forgave him, at least not until last year when I finally realized he couldn't live any longer without my mother's love. He had done his duty to me, made arrangements for my financial survival, then what his heart commanded. He was buried next to my mother, her grave then still raw after her death from cancer the year before.

Oma and Bruce took me home with them that night. I slept in the lower bunk in Fred's room as I had many times since childhood. I finished high school, went East to college, and from there into my life.

Last year, when I came back to Splendor Bay, I arranged to have a proper monument placed over my parents' graves. I've been there twice since, once to cry on my mother's side of the stone about my hurt over losing Eleana, and once to cry on my father's side when I stopped blaming him for abandoning me.

I have driven by our house many times over the years. It's the biggest Victorian mansion in Splendor Bay, a house that has stood empty all these years of my forced adulthood. I've arranged for repairs, paint, yearly inspections to make sure it stayed pest free and mechanically sound, and have otherwise done my part to keep it up to the standards prior generations expected. But I had never stepped foot inside our house since that day when I found my father in his chair in his study, the gun in his hand, his brains on the wall.

The twins were dressed in black. The widow wore a hat with a veil. They waited on a silk damask loveseat in the outer reception room of the funeral home, what might have been the parlor in the converted Victorian-era mansion. I noted the carpet was a light green instead of the blood red of thirty years ago.

Sally rose to meet me as I came in the door.

I offered my condolences to Lizabeth. She looked into my eyes, questions in her own.

"I'm sorry, Lizabeth. I'm so sorry."

"We all are, Bill," she said. "Please forgive yourself."

The funeral director appeared and cleared his throat. "Ladies, sir, follow me."

He led us to the end of the hall to an elevator big enough for a gurney, or a casket. We rode to the basement in silence, Sally clinging to my right arm, Lizabeth on my left.

The casket room was as I remembered, but I was an adult now. I couldn't run. And my father's law partner, Chester Thorton, was now behind one of the doors off the dismal hallway that led us here, probably naked on a slab of cold steel, the undertaker waiting for the family's instructions on final attire.

The undertaker began his spiel on casket quality—the exotic woods, the metals, the linings. We would want the most luxurious for our loved one in the hereafter, he suggested.

Sally and I exchanged glances. Yes, we thought alike, with the cool lawyer detachment that comes with being told many lies by many honest-appearing people. Chester was dead. No amount of expensive burial suits and padded silk linings and polished rare woods and burnished silver could change that. He would never feel a thing again. And we would always feel lost without him.

Lizabeth was of a different opinion, seeing to his comfort, generous with Chester in death as in life. "We'll take your best."

"Do you wish to view the body?" the undertaker offered.

Lizabeth, Sally, and I locked eyes. We were of one mind. "No," we said together.

"In that case, I need you to sign this, Mrs. Thorton, and we'll make all the arrangements. The service will be at the Old Solana Mission Chapel as you requested, tomorrow at two, closed casket, burial to follow in Splendor Bay City Cemetery, donations to the Diabetes Foundation instead of flowers, hold the obituary until after the burial. Is that correct?"

"Yes," Lizabeth said. "And the tomb. Do you handle that?"

"We'll contact the cemetery for you. It can be handled on this same contract. Of course, it will be built over the grave site at a later time."

"Yes," Lizabeth said, "do that."

He scribbled a few more words and numbers on the contract and handed it to Lizabeth.

She handed it to me to review. "Do you mind, Bill? You know these things."

I read it quickly. Embalming, funeral, graveside service, priests, Bach, and casket—the deluxe, satin interior, polished rosewood, silver handles, the finest burial accompaniments—were itemized. Tomb would be a simple Greek temple style, gray granite stone, room for two, inscriptions on the door, located at the top of Cemetery Hill, best view in town, three plots over from my parents. Lizabeth would wire transfer funds to the funeral home by close of business today.

I handed the contract back to Lizabeth and nodded. She signed, the undertaker handed me a copy, and we were done. She and Sally moved quickly to the elevator, me on their heels, out of the chilled basement of doom as fast as we could move.

Once outside the funeral home, Lizabeth collapsed in Sally's arms. I put my arms around both of them until the sobs subsided. Then I led them to Sally's car, depositing Lizabeth in the passenger seat, walking Sally around to her door.

Before Sally stepped in she said, "Please, will you meet me at Fred's later on."

"When?"

"Five?"

I nodded.

"I'll see you there," she said.

"Oh, Sally."

"Yes?"

"The contract said Lizabeth would wire transfer funds to the funeral home by close of business today. Would you call her accountant and have him call me for the details?"

"Yes," she said. "Thank you, Bill. Lizabeth will be lost without Chester to look out for her. We appreciate your help."

We will all be lost, I thought. Chester had always looked out for me, too. He felt it was his duty to my father, his friend and law partner, to show this scared kid how to be a man. And I had repaid him for his sacrifice by forcing him to take his life. My soul hurt.

THIRTY-SIX

Thursday, May 31, 5:00 PM

I walked up to the bar. Fred took his time noticing me, acting the part of Mr. Grudges Are Us. Finally, curiosity got the best of him. He poured two glasses of Scotch and handed me one.

"I heard about Chester," Fred said. "Heard you and Tiny were there when he shot himself."

"Afraid so," I said, looking at the Scotch, willing myself not to drink it. "Can I have a soda?"

Fred glanced at the Scotch. "Suit yourself," he said, filled a glass with ice, pulled a can from beneath the counter, placing both in front of me, then he moved the Scotch next to his own. "Well?"

"Well, what?"

"Did he confess?" Fred asked.

"Not exactly," I said. "We found stuff in his house that would indicate he had his reasons."

"It's a shame," Fred said, "a crying shame for a man like Chester to take his life over snakes like Moreno and Cramer. Those other gestapo types couldn't have been any better. A shame. A crying shame."

"I know," I said, feeling his pain and my own, reconsidering my decision on the whiskey. Before I could slip off the wagon, Sally came through the door and walked over to my stool.

"Hello, Fred," she said.

"Hello, Sally," Fred answered. "I was just telling Bill what a shame it is about Chester. You tell your sister how bad we feel. We're all crushed. Mom and Dad want to know about the arrangements."

"Thank you, Fred," Sally said, "I'll tell Lizabeth. The funeral is tomorrow at two, Old Mission Chapel. We would like it if you and your parents could attend."

He nodded. "Get you something to drink?"

"A white wine will be fine," she said, looking at my glass. "Still on the wagon, I see. Can we sit at a table?"

I followed her to a table by the window. Fred brought her wine then left us alone. I waited for her to start.

"Tell me what happened," she said softly.

I did. The sum and the substance, leaving out little and slanting nothing. Her expression never changed throughout the telling. Sadness to begin with, sadness at the end. No tears, just achy eyes. Chester was her friend, too.

"Bill," she said, "I want to tell you something. Attorney-client privilege, both myself and Lizabeth as your clients. Your review of the funeral contract will be compensated, and Lizabeth would like to retain you to handle Chester's estate matters and to advise her on the selection of new attorneys to handle trust matters. Will you accept? I want your promise you will keep all matters disclosed to you in strict confidence."

I looked at her. No! God, no! Not me, I wanted to shout. Please don't tell me any more secrets. I can't take any more confessions. Tell your priest the sins in your heart. Don't tell me. For God's sake, don't tell me. I have sins enough of my own.

But I said nothing. Duty. I had a duty to Chester. For all he had done for me. The duty to act as he would have to protect the secrets of these women.

She waited for me to meet her eyes.

I finally did, and nodded. "Okay, attorney-client."

"Lizabeth killed Wallie," she said.

I felt as if I were going to be sick. I had forced Chester to kill himself, a man who had been like a father to me, and he wasn't the killer. I felt the bile rising, burning. I struggled to absolve myself. "Why?"

"Wallie called Lizabeth Friday evening around eleven," Sally continued. "He said he was at Cramer's poker party, that Chester had mentioned she was alone at the beach house, that he was going to take a break from the game and come see her. He told her if she didn't see him, he'd give copies of the photos to Chester. She agreed to meet him at the boat, hoping she could convince him to leave her alone. They took the boat out into the bay."

I closed my eyes and breathed deeply. If Eleana hadn't turned down Wallie's dinner invitation would any of this have happened? Wallie, the state cops, and Chester would be alive. Eleana would have been Wallie's trophy for the night. And she and I would still be apart. "How did it happen?"

"Lizabeth told Wallie that he had to accept it was over between them. He laughed at her, then he raped her. She decided to end it once and for all. The insulin was handy. Chester kept kits everywhere like he did with reading glasses. And Wallie was sleeping after he finished with her. She gave him a loaded syringe of insulin and he never woke up. When she returned to the dock, she discovered the limo waiting for Wallie. She didn't know what else to do, so she called Chester."

"The limo driver?"

"Chester came to protect her as he always had. He sneaked up on the dozing driver and shot him. Then he called Block and Sartin. Both of them worked for Chester as security guards and spies on Moreno and Cramer. Block took the boat back out and dumped Wallie overboard while Sartin sent the limo off the cliff. They assumed the crash would take care of the driver, and the fish would take care of Wallie."

"Was Chester behind the arson at the Archives and the break-in at Eleana's house?"

Sally nodded. "He wanted to make sure no one tied him to Moreno. The break-in at your house was to retrieve bugs planted months ago as part of his surveillance of Wallie. Block wasn't supposed to hurt anyone, but Eleana came downstairs unexpectedly. After Block was shot at your house, Sartin panicked. He had the tape with the photos. That's why Chester killed Sartin. He didn't think Sartin would stay paid off."

"Cramer and his wife?" I asked.

"Cramer pieced it together. He demanded money, too."

"And your story about seeing Wallie with Block and Sartin?"

"I'm sorry. That was a lie. Lizabeth beeped me and I left you sleeping to go see about her, not knowing any of this had happened. She told me about Moreno's murder."

"And that's why you disappeared?" I said.

"What else could I do?" Sally replied. "Let Lizabeth be arrested for Moreno's murder and Chester for the driver's death? Next to you, they're the two most important people in my life. I couldn't call the police, even if it made me an accessory."

I couldn't have either, I thought.

"Chester went into town to return Oma's gun and see if anyone had discovered the wreck. He came back with news that both Moreno and the driver had been found and the police were looking for me."

"And that's when you decided to develop an alibi?"

"Yes," Sally said, "I thought if I could keep the police looking for me, they wouldn't think to look for anyone else."

"So you drove up the Interstate with Lizabeth instead of calling her later."

"Not exactly," Sally said. "I left my car in their beach house garage. We drove to Center City in her Mercedes. Lizabeth took me to my townhouse where I stayed until you showed up. Lizabeth and I talked by email. By the time you found me, I'd decided maybe all of it could be blamed on Block and Sartin. That's why I told you that story about seeing them with Wallie."

"And the stuff about the Cramer investigation?"

"That's all true. I thought that if the cops got involved in looking into crimes committed by Moreno and Cramer, it would deflect their concerns about the murders. I didn't know Cramer would try to blackmail Chester, or that Chester would kill him and his wife. I thought it was over."

"So we jumped where you wanted us to jump, to the conclusion that Cramer's involvement with Moreno in an extortion scheme was the motive for the murders, all part of some grand conspiracy involving bribery and kickbacks."

Sally sighed. "Bill, money is not the root of *all* evil."

"But Chester killed Sartin and the Cramers to keep from paying blackmail."

"It wasn't about the money. It was about making sure they didn't hurt Lizabeth. Alive, they would always be a threat."

"But by killing the Cramers," I said, "Chester opened up the investigation again."

"No. The police bought the Cramers murder/suicide, even tied ribbons on the package," she said. "If only Chester had left the computers alone, it would have been over."

I closed my eyes and sighed. It was all just a physics problem, a chain reaction set into motion. "Why tell me now?"

"Because I know you. You'll think about it. It won't add up. You'll decide Chester wasn't the killer and blame yourself for Chester's death more than you're doing now. Neither Lizabeth nor I want you to carry the burden of Chester's death."

I sighed. How could I not carry that burden?

"And you'll start looking for answers. I don't want you pulling on threads again and unraveling it all, leading to Lizabeth being charged with murder and me charged as an accessory. Lizabeth killed Moreno to preserve her marriage. Davy killed Block to protect his mother. Chester killed to protect Lizabeth, to protect you and your family, and to protect himself. The police are satisfied. I'm asking you to let it be over."

There was still something that didn't add up. "Oma's gun?"

"Chester used it on the driver because he had it in his pocket. Bruce McPeters had given it to him, asked him to get it appraised. Apparently it's a classic with its silver inlay grip. Oma never knew it was missing. Chester slipped it back under the counter while she was busy with breakfast customers Saturday morning. He didn't think she would realize the gun had been in his possession or Bruce would remember he had given Chester the gun. He never thought anyone would ever connect Oma's gun to the killing. They wouldn't have if she hadn't given it to you."

"And the computer thefts and hitting people on the head?"

"Lizabeth told Chester about sending me a copy of Wallie's email with the photos attached while I was hiding in the townhouse. And she told him about my investigation into Cramer's new-found wealth, which I let slip in an email to her. That's why he ransacked my office, took my computer at the townhouse. Then he realized emails went to the computers at the bayview house, too. That's when he encountered Fred. He took yours to make sure I hadn't forwarded anything to you."

"The photos. Where did they come from?"

"Moreno liked to record his conquest," Sally said ruefully. "Sartin came across the camera and Wallie's stash of tapes during his routine snooping at the mansion. He turned them over to Chester. All except one, the one with the photos that Moreno sent Lizabeth when she tried to call it off. Sartin found it when he searched the mansion in the early hours of Saturday morning while Block took care of the Archives. Chester met with Sartin to buy the tape. That's when he killed him."

"How do you know all this?" I finally asked, my heart in my throat as I considered the possibility that there were tapes of Eleana and Moreno still out there.

Sally shook her head and sighed. "Chester called me when he heard about Davy. He was sorry, very sorry. He was going to confess, say he'd killed Moreno and the rest of them so there would be no suspicion that Lizabeth was involved. He wanted to protect her. He asked me to help him determine his options—a plea bargain or fleeing to a country without extradition to the United States. I was working on that when you phoned about his death, looking for a way he could avoid the death penalty if he gave himself up, looking for a place he could go if he didn't."

"Chester knew about the affair before the photos?" I asked.

"Yes. Block and Sartin trailed her. But he knew Lizabeth would end it. She always did."

"Lizabeth killed Moreno over a meaningless threat," I said, shaking my head.

"No. She killed him because he raped her. Because he wouldn't accept 'no'."

"So what happened to the tapes?"

"Chester burned them," Sally said. "All of them. Even the last one. But he never viewed any of them. He couldn't."

I sighed and silently thanked Chester for another act of kindness he had shown me and my family.

"And the bugs they planted at my house?"

"If you check the evidence log for the shooting at your house, you'll find they retrieved several bugs from Block's pocket."

So Block had been in our house while we were out by the pool. "Sally… Sally," I said, but nothing more. What could I say? I couldn't ask the next question. Who had hurt Eleana? I didn't need to. The answer was in her eyes.

"I have to go," she said. "Lizabeth is waiting for me. We'll be at her Center City home this evening. She can't bring herself to go back to the beach house. She's leaving for Europe after the funeral tomorrow. I hope you will let that happen."

I met her eyes. Sadness. In her eyes and in mine. For Chester and Lizabeth, for all of us who would miss him, for all the lies we would keep secret to our graves.

Was it just that easy? Let it be. Perhaps. "Tell her to have a good life," I said. "And have a good life yourself."

Sally stood to leave. At the door she came back. "May I kiss you good-bye?"

I nodded and stood to take her in my arms.

Tender lips. Loving woman. But not mine.

I released her but she held onto my eyes, searching.

"If this hadn't happened, we'd still be together," she whispered.

I said nothing.

"I've loved you since the first moment I saw you, when Eleana brought you to our house to ask Lizabeth and me to be bridesmaids in your wedding. I wish you a happy life together, as I did then."

Then she was gone.

It was over. For Chester, and for the rest of us.

THIRTY-SEVEN
Today

We couldn't have proven Chester was the murderer. I knew that. Tiny knew that. Chester knew that. There wasn't enough solid evidence to link him to any of the murders.

The information we had extracted from Sally's computer was much too politically sensitive for any DA or even the Justice Department to do more than negotiate a plea bargain that perhaps suspended the poker group from getting any more government contracts. A probated sentence or two might have come out of it, but that would have been all. Most of the perps were too rich to ever be poor again, too used to buying their way out of trouble to ever pay much of a debt to society.

And Chester wasn't the kind of guy who would have ever confessed to the police. After he had talked to Sally, he had probably calmed down and realized he still had options. He knew Sally would not betray him, that she would help him. He had gone fishing to clear his head. Then Tiny and I confronted him, pushed him over the edge.

No, Chester would not have confessed. Killers only do that in mystery novels and movies. And Sally never would have betrayed his secrets while he lived, even to me. That's the way she was. But when Tiny and I confronted him, there were two more people who knew or had guessed, two too many.

So why had Chester killed himself? Other than my lies to him that day? Speaking as a husband, I believe the one thing that caused him to fold his hand was the fear of public exposure of his wife and Moreno relationship, which was bound to come out if he admitted to all the killings, one of his options. My own moment of discovery, seeing Eleana and Wallie together not so long ago, was almost enough to make me put a gun to my head. Chester could live with the private knowledge, but not the public humiliation. A male ego thing? Yeah. A primitive instinct that no amount of logic can explain.

Am I sure Chester was the sole perpetrator of the subsequent murders? Yes, I answer truthfully. Not just because Sally told me. As we searched his beach house, we came across evidence in Chester's business records linking him to Block, Sartin, and Cramer. For a long time, Chester had rewarded both Block and Sartin handsomely for their information on Moreno's whereabouts and Cramer's activities.

Sartin was one of the guards on Chester's hunting trip the previous fall, and he was the cop in the suit outside Sally's townhouse when I went looking for her. There is no doubt in my mind that Chester killed Sartin. How do I know besides Sally told me so? Sartin's blood was found in Chester's car.

Chester's cell phone records revealed a call to Cramer's home the night he and his wife died. Chester had made the call the agents had been unable to trace, perhaps to make sure Cramer was home, then he walked the trail up the cliff, entered under the cover of darkness, and disappeared in the night the way he had come. Just as Tiny suspected.

How do I know? Mud on a pair of hiking boots in Chester's closet came from the trail and tracks from his boots were found on the trail.

Lastly, and most important to my soul's need to feel my confrontation with Chester was necessary, is the fact that Davy's blood was found on the handle of the .38 that Chester used to kill himself, the same gun that had killed Sartin.

Proof beyond any doubt? No. Proof beyond a reasonable doubt? Yes. Enough evidence for me to know a murderer died from Chester's last act, even though he hadn't killed Moreno.

Am I proud of my role in Chester's death, knowing to a moral certainty that he was the killer?

No, I am disgusted. I'm sickened. I am haunted by my role in this tragedy. I have always been disgusted when confronted with man's inhumanity to man, whether under the guise of upholding the law or morality or justice or God's will, or under the guise of criminal endeavor. Especially my own. I am burdened by Chester's death. I may always be. Because I, more than anyone, am the one who forced the man who had been like a father to me to take that last desperate measure.

And what about Eleana's accident? Do I know who ran her off the road? I think I do. It had to be a person with easy access to a white Crown Vic, such as an attorney general. It had to be a person with a strong motive, such as jealousy.

Why did I not ask the last question? Even if I had, I would have been bound by attorney-client privilege not to reveal the answer. But the real reason is I didn't want to know. I prefer a state of reasonable doubt when it comes to that act of violence. Jealousy is a powerful motive for murder, as are protection of home and family and country. And I am the probable cause of that act of misdirected retribution.

Sally? She ran for governor in the special election and won. She's now in her first term, and already planning her campaign for the US Senate. I have no doubt that one day she'll be President of the United States and that I missed my chance to be the First Gentleman. Sally just about always gets what she wants. I hope someday she will want someone who will make her happy. At least George Wertheim seems willing to try.

Lizabeth? The last I heard, Lizabeth was living in Rome with some Count or Prince Somebody. I doubt she'll ever remarry. The tomb she built for Chester has room for two, and both their names are on the door. Even though the feeling may have faded, I suspect Chester was the love of her life. I know she was the love of his, a woman he loved enough to kill to protect, a woman he loved enough to die to protect.

Fred? Well, Fred is my lifelong friend, although he won't carry a bar tab for me any longer, not that I drink anymore. And Oma is my substitute mother, unchanged, and Tiny is Fred's friend and mine, even if we now respect him more for daring to do what other cops would not. Lifelong friends accept imperfections, believe excuses, and don't ask a lot of questions of each other. After our little game of ghost hunt at Stan Cramer's house, Fred told his lawyer why he was at Sally's that night. As you probably guessed, he was trying to eliminate any reference to his own complicity in the corruption. He was successful, or no evidence existed. At least, there was no evidence against Fred in Sally's computer, and I doubt anyone who cares will ever find out he fibbed on his liquor license application.

How do I live with these secrets and mortal sins, major and minor, those of others and my own?

I try not to dwell on them. They are the past. The past can never be changed and the present is all too full of living. I watch my bright, beautiful, perfect-in-every-way, small daughter play in the sand just out of reach of the waves that frighten her, and I think of my son now away at college and how he used to do the same at that age. With our young child and our older one, we have so many adventures and so much joy for the taking, if we don't waste our time on this earth trying to be what others expect us to be or dwell on the mistakes in our past.

Eleana is near me, watchful, ever ready to welcome our small daughter into her arms when exploring her world becomes too frightening, ever ready to offer our son a retreat from his larger battles to enter a world of Twenty-First Century expectations. I count my blessings and give thanks that I come from a simpler place and time, where little boys in Cub Scout uniforms could climb cliffs to chase after jack rabbits, and big boys with surf boards could play hooky from school without going to jail, and neighbors were family and friends who would take up the burden of raising an orphaned, grieving man-child.

Eleana and I are now confirmed residents of Splendor Bay. The be-all-you-can-be life is behind us. The be-all-you-should-be life is before us. Our dilemma at the moment is whether we have another child while there is still time. Oma, Bruce, Fred, Tiny, Mary Louise, and Gomez are part of our everyday lives, our family. This is our home. The house in Center City where our son became a killer is gone. It's someone else's show-the-world-how-much-money-I-make house.

Only the rose garden was transplanted to Splendor Bay when we reclaimed the house my great-grandfather built, the house left for me in a trust on my father's passing. The perfect rose Angela blooms on. With hammers and saws and paint brushes in our own hands we evicted the family of ghosts who had been closed up inside. The mother and father and boy who kept me away for so many years because I couldn't live with their sorrow are gone now.

I work a little, when one of our friends or neighbors needs a lawyer to help them through one of life's conflicts, but mainly we live on the proceeds of the sale of the Center City house and the money Dad left for my education, money Chester invested wisely for me over the years. Eleana's Solana family money is where it has always been, earning more for our children and future grandchildren to spend.

Yeah, maybe it's easier not to chase the almighty dollar if you already have enough. But perhaps it's as simple as deciding to make do with things that give you pleasure—time with people you love, time to read a book, watch a movie or a sunset, make the perfect omelet. Let the folks who measure their lives by leather-bound day planners squabble over the crumbs of life money buys.

Now, when I am making breakfast for my family and Eleana and our baby are cuddled together in our bed in the cool breeze of the morning, I look out at Splendor Bay and think—Waves? Play with the baby? Waves? Play with the baby's mom? Waves? Play lawyer? Waves?

I must report I now make the same self-serving choices I did at sixteen. Playing lawyer seldom rises to number one on my list of daily priorities. I doubt it ever will again except in self-defense or defense of people I care about. I have too many other important things to do. But it's always a tough first choice between playing with the baby or playing with the baby's mom. Riding a wave is usually third choice. Some days, I manage to do it all and end the day gazing at a breathtakingly beautiful setting sun with the woman I love beside me. A man couldn't wish for more.

Unless he's a certifiable fool.

LB Cobb, an attorney, grew up in Tennessee, practiced geology then law, and now lives and writes in Houston, Texas. Visit www.lbcobb.com for a schedule of author appearances and to sample works in progress.

Splendor Bay, LB Cobb's debut novel, earned awards in the Tennessee Mountain Writers, Cumberland Writers, Faulkner Pirate's Alley, and SMP/Private Eye Writers of American unpublished novel competitions.

ADVANCEBOOKS is an imprint of the Advance Books Company, Houston, Texas. View sample chapters of other titles at www.advancebooks.com.

Thank you for taking *Splendor Bay* home. If you enjoyed it, please tell a friend and please tell us by email at staff@advancebooks.com.

Coming in 2002
Promises Town

Advance Praise

"Humorous, believable characters, and more bite than a Texas rattlesnake"—Chris Rogers, author of *Bitch Factor, Rage Factor*, and *Chill Factor.*

"LB Cobb has the recipe for a delicious Tex-Mex reading feast: mix the full-bodied flavors of today's Texans with a dash of humor, stir the mixture into a broth of real human emotions, then hardboil all into a spicy legal thriller"—Roger Paulding

The Story

Assistant District Attorney Virginia Rodriquez, Bayou City's star prosecutor, is looking forward to a vacation with her son Nick when she's called back on the job. Federal prosecutor Stuart Fullerton, the nemesis of Washington elite, and his assistant have been murdered at a local hotel. Fullerton's wife was found with the gun at the scene and she has all the motive any woman needs to kill her husband. He did her wrong, and she caught him in the act. The wife is arrested quickly. Perhaps too quickly.

Virginia is smart, she's sassy, and she can hold her own against high-profile defense attorney, Leo Zachmann, who has taken up the wife's cause. But can Virginia knowingly prosecute a person she believes is innocent? When evidence uncovered by Zachmann shows the wrong person has been charged, Virginia finds a dismissal isn't that simple. Powerful people want a conviction, and they've made it clear that more than Virginia's career is on the line. Calculating killers have added her name to their list.

In addition to a lively mystery, *Promises Town* delivers a rich blend of memorable characters, a fascinating view of the two-sided search for truth in criminal cases, and Virginia Rodriguez, a woman who has it all—a killer of a job, child and dog to feed, house to keep, promises to remember, and no Prince Charming in view. Those are a few of the reasons it earned awards in the Tennessee Mountain Writers, Fort Bend (Texas) Writers Guild, and Cookeville (TN) Creative Writers Association unpublished novel competitions and received the 2000 Fowler Award.

Printed in the United States
3317